### THEY RAN FO~

A clay pot crashed somewhere, and Ivanova whirled around, which spooked an assailant hiding up the hill. He leapt to his feet and cut loose with PPG fire that streaked over Ivanova's head and raked a house across the street. Ivanova dropped to one knee, rested her elbow, and took aim; she cooked the gunner with a short burst of her PPG. Everyone else fled, including Mi'Ra, who vanished into the house.

G'Kar drew his own weapon and hoped that would be the end of it, but Mi'Ra burst from the house toting a PPG bazooka. "Kill them!" she shrieked. Her voice was drowned out by the roar of her own weapon.

Behind G'Kar, an entire house blew into flaming cinders. When he tore his eyes away from that horrible sight, he saw an army of thugs pouring from the buildings up the street. They came charging down the hill, howling like drunken, bloodthirsty lunatics.

"Retreat!" screamed G'Kar.

# BABYLON 5:
# BLOOD OATH

## John Vornholt

### Based on the series by
### J. Michael Straczynski

A Dell Book

Published by
Dell Publishing
a division of
Bantam Doubleday Dell Publishing Group, Inc.
1540 Broadway
New York, New York 10036

Based on the Warner Bros. television series *Babylon 5* created by J. Michael Straczynski. Copyright © 1994 by Warner Bros. Television.

Copyright © 1995 by John Vornholt

ISBN: 0-440-22059-9

Printed in the United States of America

Published simultaneously in Canada

October 1995

10  9  8  7  6  5  4  3  2  1

OPM

For Nancy, who never loses her sense of humor

Historian's Note: This story takes place prior to the events in *The Coming Shadows*.

# CHAPTER 1

The data crystal was dark, like a smoky quartz, and Ambassador G'Kar twisted it between his thick fingers. He marveled at the way its subtle facets could absorb and access data at speeds that rivaled the Narn mind. The best data crystals were grown on Minbar, and this one had the look of top quality. Something caught G'Kar's eye, and he furrowed his spotted cranium and squinted at the crystal's metallic connector. That was odd. The date and microscopic identity patterns had been removed by a laser beam, making the crystal all but untraceable. Who would want to send him an untraceable data crystal in his regular mail pouch?

Intrigued, the ambassador stood up and slipped the crystal into the viewer on his wall. A female Narn appeared on the screen, and what a female Narn she was! Young and slender, she was wearing a flowing gown of bloodred material, and it was cinched with a belt and scabbard that accentuated her curves. Her red eyes gleamed with intensity and arrested G'Kar to the spot. He didn't know what the young Narn was going to say on this recorded message, but she certainly had caught his attention.

"Hello, G'Kar," said the woman imperiously. "Do you recognize me? I am Mi'Ra, daughter of Du'Rog. I speak for my mother, Ka'Het, and my brother, T'Kog. We are all that is left of the family you destroyed. Yes, G'Kar, we are beaten, and our titles and lands are gone. Our father is dead, his name disgraced, and his attempt to kill you from the grave was a failure. To our shame, every assassin has failed."

G'Kar swallowed hard and leaned closer. He dreaded what was coming next.

Mi'Ra's lovely face contorted into rage. "You think you are safe within the Third Circle and the Earth space station. You are wrong! The widow, the son, and the daughter of Du'Rog have sworn the *Shon'Kar* against you! No more will you face inept assassins—but the very family you destroyed! The Prophets willing, by my own hands you will die. From this day forward, the purpose of our *V'Tar* is to kill you. Let this mark show my will."

With that, Mi'Ra pulled a short but vicious-looking sword from her scabbard and pressed the blade to her head. At once, the blood streamed from the wound and flowed down her delicate cheekbone to her neck and shoulder, where it mingled with the identical color in her gown. Involuntarily, G'Kar reached up and touched his own scaly brow.

The viewer blinked off, and he snatched the data crystal from the viewer. He half expected his tormentor to leap out of the closet with her bloody knife. No, she was not here this moment, but she would be here—someday. If he didn't do something about Mi'Ra, daughter of Du'Rog, she would strike him down in the middle of dinner or smother him while he slept. Knowing that, he would never sleep again.

G'Kar dashed to his terminal with the impulse of ordering her arrest. He stopped himself, realizing that he couldn't bring the full weight of his position down upon the family of Du'Rog. The *Shon'Kar* was a tradition that was central to the heart of the Narn; if he squashed them, it would only win them sympathy. Even Narn law would prevail against him. Worse yet, an action against Mi'Ra, Ka'Het, and T'Kog would bring to light the whole unsavory business of his ascendancy to the Third Circle, his treachery, and Du'Rog's disgrace. He had let this wound

fester too long, and now the infection was about to spread
—unless he took his knife and cut it out.

G'Kar sighed and slumped back into his chair, the stiff
leather of his waistcoat squeaking against the pelt covering
the cushion. He would have to do something—already the
family of Du'Rog had made two serious attempts on his
life, and here was the daughter threatening more! He could
count on some protection from Garibaldi and his security
forces for as long as he remained on Babylon 5. But who
wanted to live like a hunted animal? Besides, the station
was a sieve, with aliens and strangers of all types filtering
through by the hundreds every day. If Mi'Ra was as determined as she sounded, she would find some way onto
Babylon 5 and would stalk him until her Blood Oath was
fulfilled. Only death would stop her.

Therefore, thought G'Kar rationally, Mi'Ra would have
to die. Ka'Het and T'Kog might listen to reason if that
firebrand in the red dress was gone. Whom could he ask to
help him? No self-respecting Narn would take his side
against such a well-deserved *Shon'Kar,* and he couldn't
share his secret with humans, Minbari, or other races. If
only he could kill Mi'Ra himself and make it appear as if
somebody else had done it. G'Kar glanced around his quarters, just to make certain that his foe wasn't hiding behind
the curtains. He remembered well the other attempts on his
life, and how both had nearly been successful.

The first order of business was to put the daughter of
Du'Rog off the scent, make sure she was not hunting him
faster than he could hunt her. When she was at ease, he
would strike.

The ambassador tapped the link on his desk. "Good
morning, Na'Toth."

"Good morning, Ambassador," his assistant answered
crisply.

G'Kar cleared his throat importantly. "A special dispatch has just come in, and I must return to Homeworld immediately. I will pilot myself in my personal transport.''

He could imagine her puzzled face as she said, "Ambassador, the cruiser *K'sha Na'vas* is arriving tomorrow for a courtesy call. They could take you home in half the time of your transport."

"The *K'sha Na'vas*," said G'Kar thoughtfully, "and my old friend, Vin'Tok. That is tempting, but I prefer to pilot myself. I need some time alone—to think. I will be leaving in four hours, and I will do my own packing. Cancel my appointments, make my apologies, and do whatever is necessary. If anybody asks, this is personal business."

"Yes, Ambassador," said Na'Toth, not letting her surprise affect her efficiency.

"G'Kar out." He tapped the link and sat back in his chair. He wished he could tell Na'Toth his plans, but he knew her feelings regarding the *Shon'Kar*. Perhaps he could tell her when it was all over, if he was victorious.

Commander Ivanova shifted on the balls of her feet as she surveyed her domain: Command and Control, an air-filled bubble on the tip of the station. The commander's hair was pulled back from her attractive face in a severe on-duty hairstyle, and she felt tense, although she didn't know why. The fifty thousand kilometers of space surrounding the station were peaceful, even though departing traffic had fallen somewhat behind schedule. The only one complaining was Ambassador G'Kar, which figured.

"Ten seconds to jump for the *Borelian*," said one of the techs behind her.

Ivanova gazed at her monitor in time to see the jump gate blossom into pulsating rays of golden light. Like a tunnel into infinity, the lights stretched along the length of the latticework and swallowed the Centauri transport like a whale swallowing a minnow. Then the tube of light faded into blackness, leaving nothing but the skeleton of the gleaming latticework.

"Captain in C-and-C," announced a voice.

"As you were," replied the cheerful voice of Captain John Sheridan. Ivanova turned around to see the captain as he strode along the crosswalk, nodding to subordinates. His hands were clasped behind his back, which she had come to recognize as his nonintrusive approach. There was no emergency or urgent business to discuss, but Sheridan still looked concerned about something.

She gave him a brief nod. "Hello, Captain."

"Commander." He smiled boyishly. "How's traffic tonight?"

"Moderate. Departures are slightly behind schedule, but only one ship is complaining."

Sheridan frowned. "That would be Ambassador G'Kar, wouldn't it?"

"Yes," she answered. "He's in his personal transport, and he seems to be in quite a hurry to get out of here."

Sheridan scratched his sandy-gray hair. "I just found out he was leaving. This is rather sudden, isn't it? G'Kar isn't noted for leaving like this, without any ceremony."

"No, sir, he isn't. He was recalled to Homeworld unexpectedly. None of us knows why."

The communications officer broke in. "Commander, the ambassador wants to know if he's been cleared for jump."

"Patch him into me for a moment," said the captain.

At once, the Narn's spotted cranium and jutting jaw appeared on the monitor in front of Sheridan. He looked agitated. "What is the delay?" demanded the ambassador. "Oh, hello, Captain Sheridan. Is there some difficulty?"

"That was going to be my question," said the captain. "It's not like you to leave as suddenly as this, and I wondered if there was a problem. Is there anything we can do to help?"

The Narn shook his head impatiently. "I left word that this is a personal matter, which I must handle by myself. I'll be checking in with Na'Toth, and you can consult her about my return. Am I cleared to leave?"

Sheridan hesitated. "Have a safe trip, Ambassador. You know, it's a long way for someone to be flying solo in a small craft."

G'Kar's eyes narrowed. "We all have responsibilities, and some of them we must face alone. Good-bye, Captain."

"Good-bye," said Sheridan.

Ivanova felt an odd apprehension as she went through the prelaunch checklist. "Good-bye" was such a simple phrase; yet depending on how it was said, it could mean a cheerful parting for a few minutes or the anguished parting of forever. There was something ominous in the way G'Kar and Sheridan had exchanged those simple words. She glanced at Captain Sheridan, who was trying so hard to understand the alien ambassadors and, at the same time, keep his distance from them. Sheridan had yet to learn how futile it was to try to think like them, or how difficult it was to keep from being drawn into their intrigues.

She wanted to tell G'Kar good luck, but all she said was, "Narn transport, you are cleared for departure."

As the small cigar-shaped vessel disengaged from the dock and glided into the starscape, Captain Sheridan shook his head. "Was he in any kind of trouble with his government?"

"I don't know," Ivanova said with a shrug. "Contrary to popular belief, I don't know everything that goes on here."

"Thirty seconds until jump," said a tech.

Captain Sheridan was just turning to leave when it happened. The instruments tracking G'Kar's one-man ship shot off their scales.

"Reactor breach! Narn transport!" shouted a tech.

A colleague added, "Radiation increase of four hundred percent!"

Ivanova pounded her communications panel. "Narn transport, come in! G'Kar!"

The small ship continued to drift for a second until it exploded into a searing cloud of subatomic particles. The explosion blossomed outward through space, until it vanished like a rainbow chased by the sun. In less than two seconds, there was nothing left of G'Kar's personal transport but ever-expanding space dust.

"Oh, my God!" said a tech behind Ivanova.

Captain Sheridan leaned on a panel, gaping with amazement at the glimmering starscape, where there had been a ship a few seconds earlier. He swallowed hard and yelled, "Scramble a Starfury. And a rescue team!"

"Starfury One," said Ivanova, "scramble for reconnaissance—code ten—grid alpha 136. Also, search and rescue, go to grid alpha 136."

"There's nothing left of it," said one stunned tech. "There's not enough left to fill a thimble."

Nobody was going to rescind the order to send a Starfury and a rescue team, but it certainly looked pointless. A few seconds later, a tech announced that the Starfury was away and circling the coordinates. The rescue team was getting suited up for a space walk.

Captain Sheridan tapped his link and spoke into the back of his hand. "Sheridan to Garibaldi, come in."

"Yes, sir," said the security chief, sounding a little groggy, as if he'd been taking a nap.

"There's been a terrible accident." Sheridan glanced at Ivanova. "At least we *think* it's an accident."

"A plasma charge on the main reactor would do that," she said.

Sheridan heaved his shoulders. "Anyway, Chief, G'Kar is dead."

"What!" blurted Garibaldi. "How?"

"Meet me in C-and-C," grumbled Sheridan. "Out."

"Starfury One reporting." Everyone's attention turned to the sleek, quad-winged fighter on the overhead screen. A moment later, that image was replaced by a young man in a helmet. Warren Keffer's face was obscured by the reflections on his faceplate, but Ivanova could still see the worry under the Plexiglas.

"Report," she said.

Keffer studied his instruments. "I'm picking up lots of trace elements, residual gases, and a pocket of radiation. I see exactly where the explosion took place, but if you're looking for survivors . . . forget it. We'll be lucky to find any debris at all."

Ivanova nodded grimly, having expected the worst. She glanced at Captain Sheridan, and his usually unruffled face looked shocked and gaunt. That confirmed it.

G'Kar of the Third Circle, the Narn Regime's first Ambassador to Babylon 5, was dead.

# CHAPTER 2

Since G'Kar often worked in his quarters, Na'Toth used her access to go in and organize his transparencies, data crystals, and documents. G'Kar could be messy and disorganized when left to his own devices, and she was looking for commitments he hadn't told her about, perhaps even a clue as to why he had left so suddenly.

Could he be in trouble with the Council? G'Kar's allies in the Kha'Ri were supposed to keep him out of the political fray, to leave him free to do his job, but they were not always successful. G'Kar was outspoken, short-tempered, and secretive—he could have enemies and battles she didn't even know about. Na'Toth sank into the chair at his desk and saw half-a-dozen data crystals strewn across the desktop. She scooped them up and shoved them into a corner, still wondering about his mysterious departure, going alone and piloting himself.

The door chimed, and Na'Toth lifted her formidable jaw. Temporarily she was the sole representative of the Narn Regime on Babylon 5, and she had to conduct herself in a certain manner. The visitor was probably a constituent having travel difficulties, or someone making a complaint about some incident of Narn brutality. She had a special data crystal with autoerase for those complaints.

"Enter!"

To her surprise, it wasn't a confused tourist but Captain John Sheridan, followed by Security Chief Garibaldi and Commander Ivanova. Na'Toth bristled in her chair, thinking that they were after information. But even if she knew anything, which she didn't, she wasn't about to discuss G'Kar's personal affairs with a bunch of Earthers.

"Can I help you?"

Captain Sheridan halted and straightened his shoulders. He looked back at his subordinates, but they both looked dazed and unable to offer him any help. Na'Toth turned slowly in her chair, realizing that they weren't after information—they had come to deliver it.

"The ambassador . . ." Sheridan said hoarsely. "Ambassador G'Kar is dead. His ship exploded just before reaching the jump gate."

*"What!"* shouted Na'Toth, leaping to her feet. She brought her fist down on the desk with a thud, and the data crystals bounced out of the corner and rolled around.

"We're conducting an investigation," Garibaldi said. "We're wondering if you can tell us anything."

Na'Toth shook her head like a maddened wildebeest and went stomping around the room. "Have you searched the area? Is there any sign of him?"

"None," said Sheridan. "We've sent reconnaissance, rescue crews, repair crews to check the air-locks, everything we can think of . . . but his craft was obliterated. He couldn't have survived it."

"The debris pattern is consistent with a bomb," Ivanova added.

Na'Toth finally straightened her back, lifted her chin, and said calmly, "You must tell me everything you know. If he has been murdered, I will swear *Shon'Kar* against his murderers!"

*"Shon'Kar?"* asked Sheridan puzzledly.

"The Blood Oath," said Garibaldi. "Look, Na'Toth, there won't be any vigilante justice—Earth has got plenty of laws against killing people. If you want justice, just tell us who might have wanted him dead. If they're still on the station, we'll get them."

"If I knew who did it," Na'Toth answered, "I would be there right now, with my fingers around his throat."

"Then tell us what you do know," said Sheridan. "Did anybody threaten G'Kar recently? What was this trip back to Homeworld all about?"

The Narn shook her fists in frustration. "I don't know why he was going home. It could have had something to do with the Kha'Ri, his wife, who knows? He said he received a dispatch and was leaving on personal business. As for having enemies, you know that G'Kar has his share. He has a few right here on the station, such as Londo Mollari. I would look first at that sniveling Centauri if I were you."

"He's on my list," Garibaldi assured her. "But Londo has had years to try to kill G'Kar, if that's what he wanted to do. That's really not his style. Maybe it was somebody G'Kar recently met. Did he have any new associates? Did he seem worried about anything?"

Na'Toth wasn't really listening. The true weight of what had happened was finally descending upon her. G'Kar was dead, and she would have to devote the rest of her life to his *Shon'Kar,* the finding and killing of his murderers. These pathetic Terrans with their outraged sense of justice were not important, not when G'Kar's death must be avenged.

"Perhaps," she said, "it was bound to come to this. On Babylon 5, G'Kar was too prominent and surrounded by too many enemies. He risked his life to promote Narn interests, and this is what he got in return."

Sheridan cleared his throat. "Who else had access to his private transport? Try to help us here."

"His private transport has been docked for months, unused. Dozens of maintenance people had access to it, and most of them were *your* people. He actually believed he was safe here." Na'Toth snorted a derisive laugh. "Foolish man. He actually thought he was safe here."

Ivanova moved toward G'Kar's desk and picked up a data crystal that was perilously close to falling off the edge. She picked up the other data crystals, too, and leafed through the pile of transparencies.

"Is this the way he left his desk?" asked the commander.

Na'Toth shrugged. "Unfortunately, yes. He left everything as you see it. Perhaps there is something useful here, but I worry that he was lured by this message into a hasty departure."

Garibaldi took an evidence bag from a pouch on his belt and opened it. "Commander, could you please drop those crystals in here. And the transparencies."

As Ivanova dropped the evidence into the bag, Garibaldi told Na'Toth, "We're going to have to remove all his documents and seal off his quarters. I'll give you a receipt for his property, and I'll give it back to you after I've had a look."

"It doesn't matter," answered Na'Toth. "What are the leavings of a dead man but twigs on a dead tree?"

"I feel terrible about this," said Captain Sheridan. "Allow me to contact the Kha'Ri for you."

"No," snapped Na'Toth. "I will do it. There are several matters I must attend to right away. I will be in my quarters."

Garibaldi watched the woman square her shoulders and march out of the room. Na'Toth's reaction had been about what he'd expected—no tears, no denial, no accusations, and not much help either—just pure anger. Some people might have considered Na'Toth a suspect, but not him. He knew how much she admired G'Kar.

"Does she mean it with this *Shon'Kar* thing?" asked Sheridan.

"Oh, she means it all right," said Garibaldi. "If you remember from reading the reports, she had her own

*Shon'Kar* against Deathwalker. Na'Toth nearly killed that
woman with her bare hands the moment she stepped off her
ship. They take the Blood Oath very seriously.''

The chief tapped his link and said, ''Garibaldi here. I
want a security detail and a forensic team at Ambassador
G'Kar's quarters. On the double.''

''Let's freeze departures,'' said Sheridan.

Ivanova started to the door. ''I'm on my way to
C-and-C.''

The two men watched Ivanova leave, and Garibaldi felt
as if he were in suspended animation. His shock and grief
had put him into a sort of lethargy. He knew they should be
taking action, but they could do nothing to bring G'Kar
back to life. That made every action seem pointless. Still,
justice had to be served, whether one called it *Shon'Kar* or
revenge. If the perpetrator was still on the station, they had
to open every hatch until they found him.

''I've got condolences and reports to send,'' said Sheridan. The captain winced. ''There will have to be a station
announcement, then a press conference. Don't worry, I'll
keep the media away from you. You just press your investigation.''

''Thanks,'' said Garibaldi.

The captain strode out, and the security chief dropped
the bag of documents and data crystals onto G'Kar's desk.
Looking for more clues, he glanced around G'Kar's quarters, which were almost Mediterranean in appearance, with
heavy furnishings of dark metal and leather. On the walls
hung embroidered tapestries of hunts and battle scenes,
with bloodstone standing in for the blood. Garibaldi turned
his attention to the desk drawers and added a few stationery
items to his evidence bag.

''Welch here, Chief.'' Garibaldi looked up to see the security detail he had called for.

''Ambassador G'Kar is dead,'' the chief reported simply. "His ship exploded, and he was the only casualty. I can't give you any more information than that." Garibaldi frowned. "I'm worried about his aide, Attaché Na'Toth. She's not a suspect, but she could be a victim. And I think she knows more than she's telling us. You and Baker go to Na'Toth's quarters and keep an eye on her. Tell her you're just checking in, to see if she needs anything. If she goes anywhere, follow her and advise me."

"Yes, sir," said Welch. He and a woman officer hurried down the corridor.

Garibaldi pointed to the other two officers. "You seal off these quarters and wait for the forensic team. Except for them, nobody is to go in or out. All Narns trying to leave the station should be held for questioning."

"Yes, sir." The officers took positions on either side of the door.

Garibaldi thought about taking his bag of evidence to the laboratory, but he wanted to view the data crystals first, and he had a viewer only a meter away. He reached into the bag and brought up a handful of data crystals, which varied in shape and color. Their connectors were exactly the same, although they had different serial numbers and notations etched upon them.

That is, all but one had serial numbers and notations. One data crystal was so dark that it looked as if it had been irradiated, and it had no identifying marks. Slowly, he placed it into G'Kar's viewer.

A female Narn appeared on the screen, and she was breathtaking. She had on a clinging red dress that hugged her slender body. This couldn't be G'Kar's wife, could it? Garibaldi dismissed that idea out of hand, because if this was G'Kar's wife, he wouldn't have left her for months at a time.

"Hello, G'Kar," sneered the woman. "Do you recognize me? I am Mi'Ra, daughter of Du'Rog. I speak for my mother, Ka'Het, and my brother, T'Kog. We are all that is left of the family you destroyed. Yes, G'Kar, we are beaten, and our titles and lands are gone. Our father is dead, his name disgraced, and his attempt to kill you from the grave was a failure. To our shame, every assassin has failed."

Garibaldi grumbled a curse under his breath, because he had never heard of any of these murder attempts. The delectable Narn got really angry at that point and went on to threaten G'Kar's life. She vowed a *Shon'Kar* against him, as if they didn't have enough of those. Well, thought Garibaldi, this certainly qualified as a personal problem.

When she pulled out a sword and sliced open her own forehead, Garibaldi's jaw flopped open. The viewer blinked off at the same time that his link chimed. Garibaldi yanked the data crystal from the viewer and put it in his pocket before he answered his link.

"Garibaldi here."

"Welch," came the reply. "We have a problem, sir. Attaché Na'Toth is not in her quarters."

The security chief headed for the door. "All right, *find* her. In fact, I'm sending out a security alert. Detain *all* Narns for questioning!"

Ambassador Londo Mollari preened in front of his vanity mirror, shaping thick strands of black hair into daggerlike spikes. They framed his rotund face like the rays of Proxima Centauri. He touched a manicured finger to his tongue and ran the saliva over an unruly eyebrow, then he adjusted his sash and the medals on his burgundy jacket. He had to look good tonight—it was a holiday on Babylon 5! Winter Solstice, they called it, and he had no idea that solar astronomy was so popular on Earth. At a holiday commemorating the sun, what could be better than having one's hair look like the rays of the sun?

Londo chuckled and took a sip of chardonnay wine,

which he was drinking in honor of Earth's fiesta. Then he checked his purse to make sure he had his casino tokens, his winnings from the night before. But he didn't plan to gamble too much, not when the ladies were in a holiday spirit and there were exotic refreshments to sample. His experience with Terran beverages had proven them to be sweetly innocent in taste yet quite intoxicating in effect. A perfect drink with which to woo the ladies, he thought with another chuckle.

Slapping his ample belly and thinking about his wonderful meal of woolly embryo and brain pudding, Londo strode to the door. He began to hum a waltz melody, thinking that he might do some dancing tonight, and he was still humming when he stepped into the corridor. He didn't know there was someone waiting for him until the hand cupped his mouth and the knife slipped under his double chin.

"Quiet," commanded Na'Toth. "Your life depends upon it."

Londo's first instinct was to fight back, but the strong female was thirty years younger than he, and she had the advantage. Still, he couldn't remain quiet. "You fool!" he sputtered through her fingers. "What's the matter with you?"

The knife point pricked his chin, and it felt as if he had cut himself shaving. "Open the door," she whispered.

The Centauri did as he was told, because he didn't wish to be slaughtered in the hallway, for all to see. If he was to die, at least let it be privately and with some dignity. He jabbed his identicard into the lock, and the door slid open.

Na'Toth guided him into his quarters, taking a glance down the hallway to make sure they weren't seen. As soon as the door shut behind them, she pressed the knife closer to his throat.

"What's the matter with you?" he asked again in his

peculiar accent. "If you need to go to this much trouble to kill me, just kill me and be done with it!"

She gripped his ornate collar and shook him. "You killed G'Kar, didn't you?"

He laughed at the absurdity of it. "Kill G'Kar? Many times in my dreams, but he's still alive, isn't he?" He stared at her wary eyes. "Do you mean G'Kar is dead?"

She glowered at him. "You don't know anything about it, I suppose."

"I swear I don't! How did it happen?"

"Much more quickly than your death." Na'Toth pressed the knife into his throat.

There came a door chime, followed by a banging on the door. "Londo!" called Garibaldi. "Are you in there?"

The Centauri grinned at his attacker, showing a pair of sharp canine teeth. "Do you wish to be a fugitive or not?" he whispered to Na'Toth.

She pulled back the knife and stuck it into her sheath. "I can't kill you without proof. But if I ever find any proof . . ."

"It will be false," claimed Londo. He straightened his jacket and wiped a few beads of blood off his chin. Then he went to his control panel and opened the door.

Garibaldi rushed in, followed by two more security officers clutching PPG rifles, and the chief didn't look surprised to find Na'Toth there.

"I thought you had things to do," he said to the Narn.

"This is one of them," she answered.

Londo cleared his throat and loosened his collar. "I told her, and I'll tell you, Garibaldi—I had nothing to do with G'Kar's murder. In fact, I just found out about it."

"Yes, he was gunned down while walking along the mall," said Garibaldi.

Londo shivered. "Oooh, disgusting. I hope it didn't spoil your Terran holiday." Then the Centauri thought about what he had just heard. "You mean, the Narn ambassador was shot down in plain view, like a dog, and you don't know who did it? You are slipping, Garibaldi."

The security chief looked sheepish. "That's not really how he died."

"Oh!" said Londo with disappointment. "Now you're playing games with me, hoping to trip me up. It won't work. In this matter, I am as dumb as you are!"

Na'Toth scowled. "If it wasn't you, if it wasn't one of our enemies, then who was it?"

Londo cocked his head, trying not to smile. The idea of never having to see G'Kar's smirking face again had its appeal, but there would be a price for such relief. First, there would be the inevitable suspicion cast upon him and all Centauri, and that would grow worse if no one was arrested. Second, there was bound to be much gnashing of teeth and rattling of swords from the Narn Regime. And finally there would be a *new* Narn ambassador to B5, one who might prove more unpleasant and pigheaded than G'Kar, if that was possible.

The ambassador lowered his head. "Of course, I will relay my condolences to the Narn Regime, but I ought to wait until there has been official confirmation."

Garibaldi pointed toward the Centauri's desk. "Check your terminal in a while, and there should be an announcement from Captain Sheridan. He scheduled a memorial service for G'Kar at 1800 hours tomorrow in the theater on Green-9. Don't expect a lot of details about this—we really don't know what happened. It may have been an accident."

Now Londo permitted himself a smile. "I don't think so. A man like G'Kar always dies badly."

Na'Toth glared at him, and her hand flew to the hilt of her knife. Londo laughed. "Did you really think G'Kar would die of old age, in a soft bed somewhere?"

"No," Na'Toth admitted, letting her hand drop from the hilt of her knife.

"I have sources of information," said Londo Mollari. "Permit me to ask around a bit, purely in the interest of aiding Mr. Garibaldi. Perhaps I can uncover some tidbit of knowledge that has gone unnoticed."

"Just watch yourself," Garibaldi cautioned him. "We don't want to lose any more ambassadors."

That wiped the smile off Londo's face. "Thank you for spoiling my evening."

"Think nothing of it." Garibaldi turned to the Narn attaché. "Na'Toth, I think you had better come with me. I have a few questions for you, based on some new information."

Na'Toth said nothing to apologize for the unprovoked attack on Londo; in fact, she glared at him for a moment before brushing past the security officers. Garibaldi and his officers followed her out, and the door clamped shut behind them.

Ambassador Mollari heaved a worried sigh and poured himself another glass of wine. The death of an ambassador, even a *Narn* ambassador, was bound to create wounds that might take years to heal. It could set back the peace negotiations that staggered forward in starts and stops, and scare away the League of Nonaligned Planets. The death of more than one ambassador could doom the entire mission of Babylon 5.

Londo set down his wine glass and hurried to his communications panel. He pressed the panel and snapped, "Vir! Come to my quarters immediately."

"But, sir," answered the voice of his portly aide, "I thought we had agreed to meet in the casino." Londo heard a shriek of laughter in the background.

"The fiesta is over for us. We have intelligence to gather. I take it you do not know that G'Kar is gone?"

"Is he here yet?" asked Vir, having a hard time coping with the noise in the casino. "No, I haven't seen him."

"Never mind," said Londo. "You'll hear about it soon enough. Come to my quarters, as I ordered. And look out for suspicious persons, especially suspicious *Narn* persons. Mollari out."

*Hmmm,* thought Londo Mollari with a wry smile, *they suspect another Narn.* But they hadn't made any arrests or even admitted that it was murder, so their case must be lacking. He would help them, if he could, because he didn't want to feel any more Narn blades at his throat. On the other hand, if this incident were to mushroom out of control and cause chaos on the Narn Council, that could lead to a weakened grip on some of the Narn colonies, which was not such a bad thing. It might be a good time to foment insurrection on those colonies stolen from the Centauri.

Londo Mollari sipped his wine thoughtfully.

# CHAPTER 3

"I have things to do!" said Na'Toth as she planted her feet firmly in the center of the corridor and refused to budge.

"Like roughing up the ambassador," said Garibaldi. "If you really want to find G'Kar's murderer, you'll make time to come with me."

She lowered her jaw slightly. "You know who did it?"

"Let's just say I have a pretty good guess. Come on, the captain is waiting."

When Garibaldi and Na'Toth reached the captain's office, Ivanova was just completing her report. Basically, the repair crew, the rescue crew, and the reconnaissance ship had uncovered a whole bunch of nothing. There was nothing wrong with the docking mechanism or the air-lock, and there was nothing left of the small craft and her pilot, except for a billion particles scattered through space. It would take days to gather enough of these particles to analyze them, and she had assigned crews to the task.

All eyes turned to Garibaldi, and he extracted the unmarked data crystal from his pocket. "This is one of the crystals G'Kar left on his desk. I popped it into his viewer because it didn't have any serial numbers or markings on it."

"I always clearly label our data crystals," said Na'Toth, bristling at the idea that she would be such an inefficient administrator.

"I'm sure you do," said Garibaldi, "but I don't think you've seen this crystal."

He activated the captain's viewer behind his desk and inserted the crystal. He heard several intakes of breath when the vibrant Narn woman in the red gown appeared on the screen.

"Hello, G'Kar," she began. "Do you recognize me? I am Mi'Ra, daughter of Du'Rog. I speak for my mother, Ka'Het, and my brother, T'Kog. We are all that is left of the family you destroyed."

Na'Toth slammed her fist on the back of Sheridan's chair and cursed colorfully. Garibaldi instantly paused the playback.

"I take it you know this woman?" asked Captain Sheridan.

Na'Toth's lips trembled, whether from anger or sorrow it was hard to tell. "I know what is coming next."

Garibaldi resumed the playback, and the Narn in the red dress swore the *Shon'Kar* against the dead man. She invoked the Prophets to allow her to kill him with her own hands. Garibaldi didn't warn them that she was about to cut a gash in her own forehead, and there were more abrupt intakes of breath. The playback ended, leaving the room in silence.

· "Charming," said Ivanova.

Na'Toth stalked to the door, and Garibaldi headed her off. "After what's happened, I don't want to make things hard for you, Na'Toth, but I want you to tell us everything you know."

The angry Narn stared from one human to another, and Garibaldi had a terrible fear that she would smash his head and bolt for the door.

Finally, Na'Toth growled deep in her throat and began to pace Sheridan's tasteful office. "I had just arrived on Babylon 5. I had never met G'Kar, but I was excited about my new position and eager to prove myself. At that time, Du'Rog, her father, was dying. As his dying wish, he hired an assassin from the Thenta Ma'Kur to come to the station to kill G'Kar. To make sure that G'Kar suffered and knew why he was to die, Du'Rog sent him a message like that one, on a data crystal.''

She laughed without humor. ''In fact, G'Kar thought *I* was the assassin! What a fool Du'Rog was, as his assassin would have succeeded without the advance warning.''

''Why didn't you tell us about this murder attempt?'' said Garibaldi.

''It was the time of the religious festival,'' answered the Narn, ''and you had your own problems. Besides, this was a private affair. G'Kar did cause grave wrong to the Du'Rog family, and their vengeance was justified. We managed to stop them the first time, but this time they apparently . . .'' Na'Toth bowed her majestic head, unable to finish the thought.

Captain Sheridan scowled. ''So this is another incident of *Shon'Kar?* I had heard the Narns were civilized, but vengeance killings and blood feuds went out with the Middle Ages! They won't be tolerated on this station.''

Na'Toth said, ''Why don't you tell that to Mi'Ra. She obviously doesn't know that rule.''

Sheridan came out from behind his desk, letting his anger subside. ''Listen, Na'Toth, we're all angry about this, and we all want to see the killers brought to justice. This message is almost a confession, but we still don't have any proof. But one thing I want to make clear—I won't have this Blood Oath business on my station.''

Na'Toth moved her head from side to side, as if forcing her thick neck muscles to relax. She was still enraged, thought Garibaldi, but now G'Kar's death made some kind of sense according to her view of the universe. It wasn't inexplicable or random anymore—there was a face to it.

''The Du'Rog family should be easy to find,'' declared Na'Toth, ''on Homeworld. And guess where I am going.''

''We're not letting any Narns leave the station,'' warned Garibaldi.

Na'Toth straightened. "I have diplomatic immunity. They can't stop me, can they, Captain?"

Sheridan shook his head. "No. You and G'Kar can leave the station anytime." The captain looked saddened for a moment when he realized that he had used G'Kar's name in the present tense.

"What exactly did G'Kar do to Du'Rog?" asked Ivanova.

Na'Toth's shoulders slumped. "It's not a pleasant story, and you won't think highly of my superior when you hear it. After the first murder attempt was foiled, G'Kar told me the truth as a reward for earning his trust. It began when he wanted to succeed to the Third Circle."

At Sheridan's puzzled expression, she explained, "You see, Narn society is highly regimented. We have circles— you might call them social classes. The Inner Circle is what you would call the royal family. The Second Circle is made up of our spiritual leaders and prophets, and the Third Circle is the highest to which a commoner can aspire. As you can see, to aspire to the Third Circle is very ambitious, and G'Kar was very ambitious."

Na'Toth gazed at the blank viewer as if remembering a school lesson from long ago. "There are a number of chairs in the Third Circle; the number is always constant. To be seated, a chair must be empty."

She glanced back at them. "Someone in the Third Circle died, and there was an opening. G'Kar and Du'Rog vied for it, lobbying their friends and allies. Du'Rog was the elder man, with more experience, but G'Kar was more ruthless.

"During this time, there was a famous war crimes trial against a revolutionary name General Balashar. The tribunal had been hammering at him to know where he had obtained certain weapons, and he knew he would be sentenced to death no matter what he said. One day out of nowhere, the general said Du'Rog had sold him the weapons. Although there was no evidence, a hue and cry went up and Du'Rog was ruined. He was removed from the Council.

"After General Balashar was executed, G'Kar laid a substantial sum upon the general's family and had them relocated for this little favor. Du'Rog was banished, and G'Kar succeeded to the Third Circle and had his choice of plum positions. He chose to become ambassador to Babylon 5."

"Okay," said Sheridan, "but it didn't end there. Is this woman, Mi'Ra, capable of carrying out her threat?"

Na'Toth lowered her head and looked at the captain through hooded eyes. "Captain, the *Shon'Kar* is not an idle threat—it is a life's ambition, a goal for which you would gladly sacrifice your life. I do not know Mi'Ra, but I saw her draw the blood. She had determined that the most important thing in her life was to fulfill her *Shon'Kar,* and she would do so or die."

Sheridan cleared his throat uneasily. "There were two more terms I didn't understand. You said Du'Rog hired the Thenta Ma'Kur. What is that?"

"A league of professional assassins," answered Na'Toth. "Expensive but extremely reliable, under most circumstances. We were lucky to foil them the first time."

"And what is the *V'Tar* she mentioned?"

"The purpose in life." Na'Toth lifted her chin. "Mi'Ra is saying there is no higher purpose in life than to fulfill the *Shon'Kar*. That is as it should be."

The captain shook his head. "If you wouldn't mind, can you explain a little more about how Narn society works? I'm trying hard to understand all of this."

Na'Toth said, "Narn social structure is very old, nearly as old as our race itself. When the Centauri conquered us, they made us all equal—slaves. They killed many in the

Inner Circle, as you can imagine, because a conqueror always kills the leaders first. We have learned that lesson well.''

Her jaw clenched tightly. ''I cannot tell you what it does to a people—to have a race from the stars enslave you. It was the defining moment in our history, because it made us strong and ruthless. Children were hidden from the Centauri, papers were forged, and the bloodlines continued. When we cast off the Centauri, we returned to our old class system with a vengeance. Only those in the Inner Circle can govern, with the help of the Kha'Ri.''

Softly, she added, ''Before the Centauri landed, we were farmers—simple people. If they hadn't invaded, we would probably still be living in sod houses and plowing fields.''

''Now you're the conquerors,'' said Garibaldi, ''and the Centauri are a fading power.''

Na'Toth smiled. ''That is by design.''

''But you don't have to continue this Blood Oath, do you?'' asked Sheridan. ''You're a civilized people now. Can't you let it end?''

She glared at the captain. ''You haven't understood a word I have said.'' With that, the Narn shouldered her way past Garibaldi and strode out the door.

The chief called after her, ''Let us handle it!'' She ignored him and marched down the corridor.

When Na'Toth started out, nobody could think of a reason to stop her.

''How soon can she leave?'' asked Garibaldi. ''Are there any Narn ships in dock?''

''No,'' said Sheridan, ''but there's one docking tomorrow. I didn't get a chance to tell you yet, but I talked to members of the Narn Council. They don't like our explanation for G'Kar's death, or rather our *lack* of an explanation. They haven't exactly accused us of negligence, but they

want to know how this could have happened. I offered to
send a delegation to answer questions and show them
vidlogs, maintenance reports, whatever pertains to the case.
That crystal should help—it makes it clear that this is probably a Narn internal matter.''

"They'll let her go," said Ivanova.

Sheridan stiffened. "If this Mi'Ra person is off the station and back on Homeworld, it's out of our hands. One
more thing—there's going to be a big memorial service for
G'Kar on Homeworld, and there's no way for dignitaries to
get there from Earth in time. So our delegation will also
have to attend that service. Make sure you take your dress
uniforms.''

Garibaldi gulped. "I beg your pardon, sir?"

"You mean *we're* going?" said Ivanova.

Captain Sheridan managed an encouraging smile.
"Commander, you're the best one to answer questions
about launch procedures and C-and-C. Chief, you're the
best one to answer questions about security, and you also
have that data crystal. You're part of my staff—on short
notice, you're the best I could do for dignitaries.''

"The murderer may not have left the station," said Garibaldi.

Sheridan glanced at his computer terminal. "The *K'sha
Na'vas* doesn't dock for almost twenty-four hours, so you
have some time. But get packed—you will be on that ship
when it leaves.''

"Bring your heavy coat and your speedo," said Ivanova.

"Why?" asked Garibaldi.

"The Narn Homeworld has thin atmosphere, low humidity, and very little air pressure. In one location, temperatures can vary sixty degrees in one day, between freezing
cold and broiling hot. Ever see a Narn sweat?"

Garibaldi shook his head. "No."

"Me neither," said Ivanova.

Garibaldi grabbed the data crystal and headed to the door. "But I'm going to make some Narns sweat right now."

The giant red sun glowed high in the sky, making it a warm afternoon in the Homeworld city of Ka'Pul. It was in the upper forties of the Celsius scale, G'Kar estimated. Odd how he kept thinking in Terran terms—he must really try to get away from that blasted Earth station more often.

"Good afternoon, Ambassador," said an acolyte, passing him on the catwalks stretching between the cliffside hotel on one side of the canyon and the university annex on the other side. It was a metal catwalk, enclosed against accidents, and it spanned a rugged depression of steaming pools and jungle growth about fifty meters below. This remote canyon was one of the few places on the planet where the vegetation hadn't been destroyed by the Centauri. Thanks to the red sun, the leaves had a copper glow to them.

G'Kar nodded curtly to the acolyte. Since he was one of the guest lecturers, it was rather impertinent of the acolyte to address him at all. He walked on, content that the young man had felt his displeasure. There were fewer people than he imagined would be out on a beautiful day like this, but then he remembered that it was Feastday. Many of the acolytes had returned to their homes and would not be coming back until the evening. He would give his first address that night at the faculty dinner.

Two more acolytes entered the catwalk near the annex, and they humbly lowered their heads as they walked toward him. Seeing the acolytes dressed in their crude, unadorned robes reminded him of when he had studied for the Eighth Circle. He remembered it as an austere time of life, full of discipline and study. Still, he had made valuable contacts in the university, contacts which served him well once he reached the Eighth Circle. After that, there was no formal training as one moved up the ranks, just hard work, self-discipline, and ambition. Always ambition. Perhaps a little luck was useful, but G'Kar had always felt that a person should create his own luck.

He took a deep breath that included the fragrance of the *tibo* blossoms wafting up from the steaming jungle below. Ah, it was good to be alive and back in a simple place with real air. Babylon 5 could be so claustrophobic at times. The pagoda that housed the annex was in sight, and it was gilded with gold and encrusted with gemstones. He quickened his step, because he was slightly late for an appointment with the regent.

The two acolytes were coming closer now, and the catwalk wasn't really intended for more than two people to walk abreast. To G'Kar's approval, the acolytes formed a single file and melted against the metal meshing, allowing the ambassador to pass. He gave them an approving smile as he walked by.

One of them moved a hair too abruptly, which caught his attention, and G'Kar's peripheral vision caught the other one lifting his arm. The reptile center of G'Kar's brain told him to duck, and he did so before the knife could strike his neck. It glanced harmlessly off his leather waistcoat. He whirled around to catch the arm of the second assailant, and a small hand weapon clattered to the walkway.

The two of them were frightened now, and their panic betrayed them. The unarmed man froze, and the one with the knife lunged for G'Kar's throat. The old self-defense training came back, and G'Kar gripped the man's knife hand and snapped the small bones of his wrist, eliciting a yelp of pain. The unarmed man finally dove for the gun on the walkway, but he was too late. G'Kar lashed out with his foot and sent the weapon sailing, then he threw the attacker with the broken wrist on top of the other. The would-be assassins sprawled on the walkway like helpless infants.

"Plebeians!" he spit at them.

He was looking forward to permanently crippling them when their accomplices reacted. From the jungle below came a familiar pop. The blast from the PPG cannon hit the catwalk and warped its molecular structure, and the floor literally melted beneath G'Kar. He dropped through a hole up to his waist, hanging desperately to singed metal, his legs dangling in space.

This gave his foes on the catwalk another opportunity. The one with the broken wrist was still howling in pain, but the other one snatched up the knife. Grinning with pleasure, he was about to carve G'Kar's head into a jack-o'-lantern, when the pop sounded again. The sniper had picked the wrong target, however, and a wavering beam ripped through the man with the broken wrist, turning him into smoldering pulp.

This indiscriminate killing spooked the man with the knife, and he leaped over G'Kar and ran toward the pagoda. Struggling frantically, G'Kar managed to extricate his legs from the hole. He had just regained his feet when another PPG blast severed the walkway behind him. The stressed metal groaned ominously, and G'Kar was pitched backward. He clawed for a handhold, but the dead man rolled on top of him. G'Kar screamed in horror as the lifeless form careened into space and dropped through the branches below with barely a sound.

G'Kar lost his grip and started to fall. The jungle swirled beneath him . . .

With a shriek, he bolted upright on a dirty cot. Confused and disoriented, the Narn gaped at his surroundings, which looked like a shack made of rusty sheet metal and old tablecloths. The smell was some atrocious mixture of curry and ground *aryx* horn. He nearly gagged, but at least he realized that he had only been dreaming.

An old Narn poked his head through the flap of the doorway. "Will you be quiet!" he commanded. "Even in Down Below, people can recognize your voice."

"Sorry," he whispered, rubbing his eyes. "I forgot where I was. Had a bad dream, too. What time is it?"

"Just after midnight," said the old Narn, whose name was Pa'Nar. He was one of G'Kar's operatives, stationed in Down Below to gather information. From nearby came the sound of drunken voices, and the old man slipped inside the shack. "You've only got about fourteen hours to go. Don't start panicking on me, or you'll get us both killed."

"I didn't panic." G'Kar looked down. "I was dreaming, that's all. I was reliving a terrible experience that actually happened to me."

"We don't have any control over dreams like that," admitted the old Narn. "The Prophets send those dreams, to keep us on our toes."

"Well, they did a good job," said G'Kar. "I'm as nervous as a *pitlok* on Feastday." He stood up and banged his head on the metal sheet that formed a sort of roof.

G'Kar groaned and slumped back onto the cot, then he checked his timepiece and found that it was night, or what passed for night on Babylon 5. "I don't know if I can stand this for fourteen more hours."

"It was your idea," said Pa'Nar. "Although I can't understand whatever gave you the idea to pretend to be dead. You must be in considerable trouble."

Even dressed in rags, the ambassador had a regal gaze. "I pay you to do my bidding, and my reasons are none of your concern. You just make sure I am safe."

Pa'Nar chuckled. "How much safer can you be? You are *dead*." The old man scooted out the door and tied the flap behind him.

G'Kar moaned and lay back on his cot. He might as well sleep, for there was nothing else to do in the dismal shack. But sleep didn't sound appetizing after that horrible dream, which was all the more horrifying because it had been real. He couldn't remember what had happened to him after he lost his grip on the catwalk and fell into the branches, but he had woken up in the infirmary, with only a concussion and superficial wounds to show for all the mayhem. To avoid having anyone pry into the past, he had hushed up the attack and returned to Babylon 5 without saying anything to anyone, including Na'Toth. The assassins had escaped, and the dead man had never been identified.

But G'Kar didn't need to be told who they were or who had hired them. It was the Du'Rog family. They had become unhinged! After engineering two attempts on his life with paid assassins, now they had sworn *Shon'Kar* and were coming after him themselves.

Had they no respect for his rank and position? He supposed not, since he had destroyed their father to get his rank. That desperate act had troubled him more than once over the years, but he had always thought it would fade from importance with the passage of time. His crime had not been ambition—Du'Rog was just as ambitious as he—his crime had been impatience. He could have let Du'Rog have that chair in the Third Circle while he bided his time. Another vacancy had recently come open, and he would have gotten it, with his wife's help. But then Du'Rog, or someone else, would have become ambassador to Babylon 5. The last few years of his life would have been radically different.

G'Kar snorted. Considering his present circumstances— hiding out in the slum of Down Below, pretending to be dead—changing the past didn't sound like a bad idea. It just couldn't be done. G'Kar's only choice was to change the future, to kill the remnants of the Du'Rog family before they killed him. He had taken a chance leaving the data crystal behind, but he wanted to leave some record—in the hands of the humans—in case genuine death was imminent.

He felt movement on his skin, and he opened his eyes to see a cockroach scuttling across his wrist. He caught it in his hand and studied the squirming insect for a moment.

"I am G'Kar, Third Circle," he told the bug. "Who are you to annoy me?"

When the roach didn't answer, he squashed it, pretending that it was Mi'Ra, daughter of Du'Rog.

# CHAPTER 4

The alarm went off, and Susan Ivanova rolled over and swatted the panel button like it was an annoying tarantula. A few seconds later, an overly cheerful computer voice informed her, "Downloading messages and schedule."

She stared bleary-eyed at the ceiling, wondering if it would be possible to grab an extra forty winks. Then she remembered—she had a full shift of work ahead of her, followed by the station's memorial service for G'Kar, and then a visit to the Narn Homeworld, which would probably take at least a week, counting travel time.

How much blame would Narn officials place on the personnel of Babylon 5 for this tragedy? Ivanova already felt considerable guilt, because the murder—or accident, in the unlikely event it turned out to be an accident—had happened on her watch. It had happened within her sphere of control, in the space between B5 and the jump gate. Was there anything she could have done to prevent it? In hindsight, it was easy to say that they should have prevented G'Kar from taking off on a long trip in a solo craft, but what could they have done to stop him?

G'Kar's transport had sat idle for months, and there was no way of knowing when it had been sabotaged. It was clear from the story about Du'Rog that G'Kar had been courting disaster. Even his most trusted subordinate had admitted that he deserved to be killed for what he had done to Du'Rog. Vengeance was a strong emotion, as Ivanova knew from firsthand experience. If she had been raised in a culture that honored revenge killing, she might have hunted down those responsible for her mother's death.

She dragged herself out of bed and made a small pot of coffee. It was important, she decided, to win back Na'Toth's trust. In all likelihood, the Narn attaché would be on the same ship with her and Garibaldi, and they would desperately need a guide on Homeworld, somebody they could trust. She glanced at her clock and saw that she had an hour and a half before the start of her shift. Much of her day would be spent scheduling senior techs to act as her replacement in C-and-C, which was work she hated to do. She didn't like to think the station could function without her, especially for an extended period of time.

Ivanova adhered her link to the back of her hand and touched it. "I would like Attaché Na'Toth's quarters."

To her surprise, the strong-willed Narn answered, "Na'Toth here."

"This is Susan Ivanova," she said quickly. "We had a stressful meeting yesterday, and I would like the opportunity to make it up to you. Could I buy you breakfast? I promise not to dissuade you from your *Shon'Kar*."

She held her breath during the long pause that followed. "I suppose," said Na'Toth warily.

"Shall we meet in the cafe on Red-3? Say, in twenty minutes?"

"Very well."

She found Na'Toth waiting for her in the busy cafe on Red-3, and the Narn attaché was drumming her fingers impatiently on the table as Ivanova approached.

"You are two minutes late," she said.

"Sorry." Ivanova slipped into her chair. "I didn't allow myself enough time to get dressed and check my messages. Have you ordered yet?"

Na'Toth nodded. "Yes, smoked eel. It was the most expensive item on the breakfast menu."

"I like smoked eel," said the commander without hesitation. "Perhaps I'll have the same." The waiter appeared, and she ordered smoked eel, a bagel, and some more coffee.

"What did you want to see me about?" asked Na'Toth. "It wasn't really to make up for yesterday."

"As a matter of fact, it was," said the commander. "You've got to understand that humans are a very guilt-ridden species. We feel guilty all the time, about everything. Since G'Kar died outside our station, we feel it's our responsibility. Garibaldi is turning the station upside-down looking for Mi'Ra."

Na'Toth lifted her spotted cranium and regarded the human with piercing red eyes. "He needn't bother. G'Kar was a Narn, and his murderers were Narn. He brought the *Shon'Kar* onto himself through his actions. You need feel no guilt, nor do you need to do anything, except to stay out of our affairs. Our society will not punish his murderers if they were fulfilling the *Shon'Kar*. You must know that if you expect to come with me to Homeworld."

Ivanova blinked at the Narn, marveling at how quickly she had gotten to the point of the meeting. "You don't mind that Garibaldi and I are going with you?"

"If your purpose is to honor the memory of G'Kar, how could I mind? If your purpose is to deprive me of my *Shon'Kar,* I mind a great deal. This will not be easy for me, because I will be accused of negligence in letting G'Kar die."

"That's hardly fair."

"Fair or not," said the Narn, "an attaché is also a bodyguard. That is one reason why my vow of *Shon'Kar* is so important to me. I am shamed by his murder."

"Now who's feeling guilty?" asked Ivanova.

"I am," admitted Na'Toth. The waiter brought their plates of eel, and the two women ate in silence.

\* \* \*

In a dilapidated shack in the depths of Down Below, the dead man washed his face in a shallow pan of grimy water. He had never realized what Pa'Nar had to go through to live down here—he would have to give the man more money.

He took a ragged bit of cloth and dried his prominent chin and brow. This banishment to Down Below would be over mercifully soon, he told himself, and he would be safely aboard the *K'sha Na'vas*, headed back to Homeworld. He would arrive in disguise and attend to his business with the Du'Rog family, ending it once and for all.

There was another commotion outside in the grimy corridor, but he had learned to ignore the petty thievery and drunken brawls that typified life in Down Below. He had occasionally ventured down here for amusement, but he would never come here again, if he could help it. The shouts grew louder outside the shack, and he nearly threw open the flap to order them to be quiet. No, he cautioned himself, this was not the time to be assertive.

Suddenly, the flap flew open, and Pa'Nar crawled in, looking distraught. "You must hide!" he hissed.

"Hide?" growled G'Kar. He glanced around at the dismal shack. "I *am* hiding!"

"It's Garibaldi!" warned the older man, glancing over his shoulder. "His officers are making another sweep, looking for your killers. We caused a disturbance to delay them, but they are searching everywhere!"

G'Kar grabbed his PPG pistol and looked around. There was no rear door to the pathetic shack, and no place to run even if he got out. He climbed back onto the cot and clutched the weapon to his chest.

"Throw the blanket over me," he ordered. "Tell them I am sick."

They both jumped when a fist pounded on the corrugated

metal wall, nearly bringing the shack down. "Excuse me," barked a voice, "is this a Narn household?"

"I am coming!" called Pa'Nar. He threw the blanket over G'Kar, who turned his back to the door. Trembling with fear, the older Narn scurried out.

G'Kar could hear their conversation. "Sorry to bother you," began the officer, "but we're looking for undocumented Narns in connection with Ambassador G'Kar's death. Are you listed on the station roster?"

"I should be," said the Narn. "My name is Pa'Nar. I came here on the *Hala'Tar* about a year ago. Lost all my money gambling, and now I'm stuck here. You couldn't help me get off, could you?"

" 'Fraid not. Can I see your identicard, please."

G'Kar suffered a few tense moments while the security officer presumably checked Pa'Nar's identicard on his handheld terminal. "Yes, I have you listed," he agreed. "Any other Narns in your household?"

*Careful,* G'Kar thought in panic. The wrong answer could be disastrous. But what was the right answer?

"Only my brother is here," said Pa'Nar loudly. "He is very sick."

"I'll have to see him," insisted the officer. "I'll just take a look inside and check his identicard. Excuse me."

G'Kar kept his back to the doorway, wondering if he could possibly be lucky enough to encounter a security officer who didn't know him on sight. Probably not. As one of the four alien ambassadors on the station, he wasn't exactly an unknown quantity. He could feel his heart pounding as the security officer shuffled through the flap.

"Excuse me," he said, "we're looking for undocumented Narns in connection with Ambassador G'Kar's death. Are you on the station roster?"

G'Kar coughed and wheezed and tried to sound very sick. He pulled the blanket tighter around his broad shoulders with one hand and gripped his PPG weapon with the other.

"Did you hear what I said?" insisted the officer. "I need your name, and your identicard."

"Ha'Mok," wheezed G'Kar. From his waistcoat he pulled out his fake identicard and tossed it onto the floor behind him.

"Thank you," said the officer sarcastically. G'Kar could envision him bending down to retrieve the card, then running it through his machine. G'Kar had no problem feigning labored breathing during the moments that followed.

"You are listed on the roster," said the officer. "But I have to see you to make positive identification. Turn over, please."

That, decided G'Kar, he could not do. He cursed himself —why hadn't he donned his disguise earlier? It was too late now, and this young man had put himself squarely in the way.

"I don't wish to vomit all over you!" croaked G'Kar. "I have virus . . . a potent one! It is liquefying my intestines."

The security officer rose up and banged his head on the low roof. G'Kar wheezed, "It would kill a human in a day or two!"

Now the officer was lifting his hand to his link to call for instructions, just as Pa'Nar crept up behind him and smashed a crowbar on the back of his skull. The officer crumpled to the grimy floor in a gray heap.

"I hope you didn't kill him," said G'Kar, rolling to his feet. He bent down and retrieved his fake identicard from under the officer's nose. Warm moisture on the card revealed that the officer was still breathing.

"We'll have to kill him, won't we?" asked Pa'Nar.

"No," snapped the ambassador. "This matter is not his concern. His death would dishonor my actions even further.

Besides, I have to come back to B5 someday, after I step forward and admit to this deception.''

G'Kar brought the heel of his boot down upon the officer's handheld terminal, smashing the case and grinding the chips into silicon. Then he bent down and ripped the link off the back of the man's hand and thrust it into the trembling hands of the old Narn.

"Take his link far away from here, so they can't trace him by it," ordered G'Kar. "While you're at it, you had better keep going, Pa'Nar. Clean yourself up and get off this station on the first public transport."

"We're just going to leave him here?" gasped Pa'Nar.

G'Kar scowled. "If you want to carry him out, be my guest."

The old Narn gulped, stuck the link in his pocket, and scurried out. G'Kar turned his attention to the unfortunate Earthforce officer sprawled on the floor and said, "Your boss, Mr. Garibaldi, is very thorough. I must remember that."

The Narn began to undress, replacing the disgusting rags Pa'Nar had provided with the humble robe of an acolyte. The choice of the acolyte had been his, in memory of the deceit employed against him by the assassins at Ka'Pul.

From the pocket of his robe G'Kar produced a mirror and the most important piece of his disguise—the skullcap. The thin layer of artificial skin covered his entire cranium and matched his skin color perfectly except for one thing— the spots were completely different. Where pools of dark pigment had blossomed on his head, the skullcap had seas of bronze, and vice versa. It was surprising how much the appliance changed a Narn's appearance, and he supposed it was like a human exchanging ebony hair for golden hair.

Then he applied another piece of his disguise, the contact lenses that turned his eyes from their usual vibrant red to a dull brown. A Narn who met him would think that his eyes were quite unusual, but tests had shown that the effect of brown eyes on humans was just the opposite. They perceived a face that was bland and friendly, a forgettable face, much like one of their own. The final part of his disguise was an attitude adjustment—instead of his usual arrogance and bluster there would be a subservient timidity that required his head be lowered most of the time.

G'Kar jumped when a groan issued from the floor. Without a moment's hesitation, he scooped his old clothes off the floor and threw them into a cloth bag. He checked to make sure he had the proper identicard and the proper attitude as he lowered his head and ducked through the flap hanging in the doorway.

# CHAPTER 5

"Officer does not respond," came Lou Welch's report from the Brown sector of Down Below.

"What?" answered Garibaldi into his link. Some crazy derelict in an access duct overhead was hollering just to hear the echo, a phenomenon that was typical when a person consumed too much dust. Everyone had shouted at the guy to be quiet, to no avail, and now two of his security officers were on their way to grab him and take him to medlab. This interruption had slowed down Garibaldi's search through the Green sector of Down Below, putting him in an even worse mood. He was dreading all the diplomatic schmoozing he would have to be doing in a couple of hours, and he could barely hear himself worry.

"I said, 'Leffler doesn't respond!' " shouted Welch. "He was working a corridor alone, and now he's just disappeared. We're trying to trace his link, but it's not where it should be. I'd like permission to give up the search for Narns to search for Leffler. We may need to do a house-to-house."

"Permission granted," answered Garibaldi. He winced at the howling that reverberated over his head. "We're stalled here, too, so I'm coming over there. Garibaldi out!"

He turned to his subordinates in Green sector and yelled, "As soon as you get him quiet, keep checking Narns until you're relieved, or you hear from me. I'll be in Brown sector."

The chief jogged to get away from the din, but he didn't find it any quieter in the connecting corridor. The explosion of G'Kar's ship and the rousting of the Narn derelicts had unleashed a kind of sullen resentment in the bowels of Down Below. There was some incidental ranting about heavy-handed Earthforce, and a few Drazis glared at him. No one looked as if they particularly wanted to see him.

With a start, Garibaldi realized that this might not be the best time to be wandering alone through Down Below. Leffler was missing and not responding, and he had been working alone, too. The chief didn't make a big deal about it, but he slowed down his pace long enough to give every doorway, corridor, and alien a thorough inspection before he drew close. His hand dangled near the PPG weapon on his belt.

He was beginning to get the feeling that somebody in this collection of interstellar misfits knew something about G'Kar's death. Something was hidden down here, as it usually was. Garibaldi tried to concentrate on Mi'Ra, the Narn in the blood-soaked dress. She was the key. Could she be brazen enough to sneak onto the station and use Down Below as her base of operations? To kill an ambassador, you would need a place like this to wait, to bide your time. Hell, *everybody* in Down Below was biding their time, and the cost of living was low. The cost of dying was also low, and she could hire accomplices if she needed them.

There was just one thing wrong with this theory. Mi'Ra was a rather striking-looking woman, and Narns were comparatively rare in Down Below. She wouldn't blend in easily, not like a Drazi or a human.

Garibaldi's attention was snagged by a Narn male skirting the other side of the corridor; he was wearing a cloak that looked as if it were made out of burlap. The man's head was lowered respectfully, and he moved slowly, as with age. Garibaldi got the distinct impression that he knew the Narn, so he permitted himself a closer look and wondered whether he should take the time to identify the man and check his identicard. The Narn glanced briefly at him then lowered his head, and Garibaldi realized that he didn't know him. In fact, he seemed a harmless sort, probably some kind of monk. Well, Garibaldi mused, Down Below was a good place to live out a vow of poverty. He let the Narn go without hassling.

His link buzzed, and he lifted his hand. "Garibaldi here."

"This is Welch," came the familiar voice. "We found Leffler's link in a really foul latrine, but he's not in there. We're breaking up to go house-to-house now. There are a lot of boiler rooms and shanties around here."

"Buddy system," said Garibaldi, glancing around at sullen stares. "No more singles. I'll be there in five minutes."

Garibaldi signed off and continued his wary stroll through the byways of Down Below. The security chief knew these mean corridors as well as anyone, and he kept to the best-lit routes, the ones closest to the exits and lifts. He couldn't help but feel that time was getting away from him in this investigation. His instincts told him to clamp down, but he had to dash off to the Narn Homeworld—to turn the case over to them, knowing they wouldn't do a damn thing with it. He looked around at the squalor and knew that it wasn't doing his mood any good. It was time to turn the grunge work over to his subordinates and start doing his packing.

He veered toward an exit when his link buzzed. "This is Garibaldi."

"We've found Leffler," said Welch with relief. "He's out cold, and he may have a cracked skull—but he's breathing. A medteam is on its way. We got lucky with a tip from some kids, and we found him knocked cold in a shanty."

"Question those kids," ordered Garibaldi. "What exactly did they see? Who went into the shack with him?"

"We can't find them," said Welch apologetically. "They

yelled down from the top of a catwalk, pointed out the shack, then ran off. We've been looking everywhere for them, but they're gone. At least we have Leffler. Want us to break off and look for those kids?"

Garibaldi stopped, thinking that he was just spinning his wheels no matter what direction he ran in. "No, just concentrate on the Narns. Ask them if they've seen an attractive female Narn."

"With pleasure," said Welch a little too cheerfully. "But we'll keep looking for the kids, or anyone else who might've seen what happened to Leffler. Welch out."

Garibaldi rubbed his eyes, wondering what the hell he could've been thinking. If the secret was in Down Below, they would never find it, anyway. This place was a black hole. People, information, stolen goods—they just sank into the muck and were never seen again. Better admit it, thought Garibaldi, if anybody was going to find the murderer, it wouldn't be he; he was going to leave B5 for a few days and be out of the loop.

He pushed the exit door open and headed up a ramp. As he walked, he tapped his link again. "Could I have Talia Winters's quarters?"

Luck was with him, and he caught the telepath on the first try. "This is Talia Winters."

"Hi, this is Garibaldi. I've got a favor to ask."

"Ask away," she said. "With G'Kar dead, nobody's in much of a mood to conduct business. What happened to him?"

"That's what we're trying to find out. Could I call you later to do a scan on one of my men? A fellow named Leffler. Something happened to him in Down Below, and he may need help remembering."

"I plan to stay close to home," promised Talia. "The only place I'm going is to G'Kar's memorial service."

"Can't forget about that," said Garibaldi, snapping his

fingers. "I'll call you as soon as I get a report on Leffler. The medteam is just getting to him—he isn't even conscious yet."

"I'll be waiting," said the telepath.

Garibaldi signed off and headed to his quarters to start packing.

Commander Ivanova checked her uniform in a shop window on the mall, content that it was as straight as it was going to be. She couldn't guess how the Narn delegation from the *K'sha Na'vas* would react to the news that G'Kar had been murdered, complete with self-incriminating suspects but no one in custody. Would they shrug? Would they declare war? She had to be prepared to be diplomatic whatever their reaction.

A shadow fell over her, and she turned to see Ambassador Londo Mollari strolling to her side. He was smiling, although his black uniform was rather reserved and funereal, even if it did look like a braided tuxedo. "Good afternoon," he said. "Mind if I accompany you, Commander?"

"No, Ambassador, although I don't know if I'll be great company. I'm not looking forward to this memorial service, or the next one."

"I should say not." Londo's smile dimmed only slightly. "I heard you were going to the Narn Homeworld. Good luck in your travels. It's such a dismal place."

"Yes, well, it'll only be for a few days," she answered. A few *pointless* days, she almost added.

"But you *do* have a suspect," Londo said matter-of-factly.

Ivanova glanced at the Centauri and his thick crown of ebony hair. Was he fishing for information, or was this common knowledge by now? Maybe she would fish back.

"Who do you think killed him?" she asked.

Londo shrugged. "It wasn't us. More than likely, it was

one of his own kind. You know, they have this ghastly tradition called the *Shon'Kar,* where they kill each other for
the slightest offense. You will learn, under that cultured
exterior, the Narn are beasts.''

She wasn't about to reply to that slur. A Narn would
have argued that the Centauri were a hundred times more
brutal, especially to other species. It did seem as if Londo
had found out or guessed at the motive behind G'Kar's
murder. But on this day, hearing him dump on G'Kar and
his race was more than she could handle.

''Why are you bothering to come?'' she asked.

''Why, my dear commander,'' he said, feigning shock,
''I am *speaking* at the memorial service. Both myself and
Ambassador Delenn have volunteered to speak about our
colleague, and Captain Sheridan has agreed. You needn't
worry—during this somber occasion, I won't sully his reputation with the truth.''

Ivanova turned away from the ambassador, annoyed at
his jovial good humor. It seemed that at every funeral she
had ever attended, there was always somebody in a good
mood. She darted ahead of him into the monorail car that
ran along the spine of the station. Glancing at her timepiece, Ivanova realized that they would arrive at the dock in
plenty of time to meet the *K'sha Na'vas,* so she contented
herself to watch the girders and reflective panels whiz by.
Londo respected her silence and said nothing during the
high-speed ride through the core of the station.

To her relief, he was frowning gravely as they stepped
off the car and made their way through a throng of people
clustered around the docking bay. Wordlessly, Ivanova and
Londo took their positions among the other dignitaries,
which included Delenn and Lennier, Na'Toth, Dr. Franklin,
and representatives from the Nonaligned Worlds. Ambassador Kosh was conspicuously absent, and so was Garibaldi.
Captain Sheridan gave her a brief nod and a pained smile.

It was a full day after the tragic event, and the captain still looked stunned.

Life never seems so fragile, thought Ivanova, as when a vibrant person like G'Kar suddenly disappears from this plane of existence. *One moment he is here—an unpredictable, exasperating force in the universe—and the next moment he is gone.* Ivanova resolved to sit a short shivah for G'Kar, perhaps during the journey to his Homeworld, and to honor him by lighting a kaddish candle. She wiped her eye, unable to fathom how all this grief could bring any peace to the broken Du'Rog family.

She spied Garibaldi dashing down the corridor, fastening the buttons on his dress uniform. Before she could get his attention, she heard a whooshing sound, and she turned to see four Narns striding out of the air-lock and down the ramp. Their heavy boots tromped along the ramp like syncopated drums. The two men and two women were dressed in military finery, and their somber faces matched everyone else's.

They saluted Na'Toth with a fist to the chest, then they bowed stiffly to Captain Sheridan. Ivanova glided her way through the crowd to get closer to Sheridan. He was bound to want to introduce her early on in the proceedings.

"And here she is," said Sheridan with relief, "my first officer, Commander Susan Ivanova." She nodded and met their eyes. Narns, like humans, were one of the few races who liked eye-to-eye contact, especially upon introductions. Considering the circumstances, she didn't smile.

"Greetings," said the tallest Narn, who had a cadaverous hatchet-face profile. "I am Captain Vin'Tok of the Fourth Circle. This is my first officer, Liege Yal'Tar." A husky woman nodded curtly at them. "Our military attaché, Tza'Gur, and my chief engineer, Ni'Kol." He motioned to an older pair of Narns, female and male, respectively. There was a flurry of introductions as the four Narns met Londo, Dr. Franklin, Lennier, and Delenn.

The Narns blinked curiously at the diminutive Minbari ambassador. ''What I had heard about you is true,'' marveled Captain Vin'Tok, reaching out to touch Delenn's streaked hair. His fingers stopped and trembled.

Delenn nodded sympathetically. ''Every day we find we have more in common with other races. Today we share your grief.''

''Yes,'' said Vin'Tok. ''Captain Sheridan, we haven't received many details about this incident. Could we go somewhere to talk?''

''That was going to be my suggestion.'' Sheridan mustered a polite smile. ''Before the memorial service, we're having a reception in the cafe on Green-3. Ambassador Delenn will be happy to show your party to the reception, and you can come with me, Captain, for a briefing.''

''I insist upon going with you!'' said Attaché Tza'Gur. The older woman had seemed the grandmotherly type until her sharp voice cut through the murmur.

Sheridan smiled uneasily. ''Very well. My office is this way.'' He pointed into the crowd and it magically parted, helped by Garibaldi's security. While the smaller party of two humans and three Narns headed for the monorail, Delenn rustled through the crowd in her silken robe, and the larger contingent followed her to the free food.

No one noticed a hunched Narn in a simple cloak who walked up the ramp and mingled with the crew of the *K'sha Na'vas.*

In Sheridan's office, they stood in silence as they watched the visual replay of the wrenching explosion that blasted G'Kar's transport into space dust. There was very little to say, thought Ivanova, except that if it wasn't a bomb, it was a very faulty reactor that should have been discovered during routine checks. Captain Vin'Tok's face never betrayed the slightest emotion, but Tza'Gur could be heard muttering under her breath.

When the vidlog ended, Captain Sheridan held up his hand to quiet the murmurs. "Before we jump to any conclusions, I have one more thing to show you. This is taken from a data crystal that was discovered on Ambassador G'Kar's desk after his death."

With that insufficient warning, the captain played the visual of Mi'Ra, daughter of Du'Rog, vowing the *Shon'Kar* against the dead man. Both Vin'Tok and Tza'Gur watched intently as the young Narn woman slit her scalp and let the blood flow down her face. When it was over, Tza'Gur was breathing so heavily that she had to find a chair to sit in.

"So that is it," said Vin'Tok with bitter acceptance. "Naturally, when we heard of the ambassador's death, we feared the worst. We feared that his murder was politically motivated, which would bring terrible repercussions. Now we know it was a personal matter."

"Under our law," said Garibaldi, "if we catch the murderer on Babylon 5, we're going to bring him to trial."

Vin'Tok sighed and looked at Na'Toth for help. "Have you explained the *Shon'Kar* to them?"

"I have," Na'Toth said dryly. "They are stubborn in their beliefs."

"I have studied Terran law," a cracked voice broke in. All eyes turned to the older woman, Tza'Gur, as she rose from her chair. "Under Terran law, the *Shon'Kar* would be called 'justifiable homicide.'"

"I hate to correct you," said Sheridan, "but that's something entirely different. Justifiable homicide is when a person is attacked and is fighting for his life. This is a revenge killing, pure and simple. We call it premeditated murder."

"Come, now," said Tza'Gur. "You Earthers are not

pacifists. You have many instances where murder is permitted—justifiable homicide, warfare, capital punishment. What is the difference between the *Shon'Kar* and your justice, where you catch a murderer, try him, and space him?''

Sheridan shook his head and tried not to look exasperated. ''In one case, there's been a fair trial that removes all doubt that the accused could be innocent. In the other case, it's vigilante justice, which we don't condone.''

''There is no doubt in a *Shon'Kar*,'' said the old woman. ''It is never sworn unless there is certainty, and the end result is the same.''

Sheridan sighed. ''Then it's true, even if the Du'Rog family is guilty, nothing will happen to them?''

Vin'Tok glanced at the captain and smiled. ''I wouldn't say that exactly. The ambassador had many friends. The Du'Rog family knew they could be sacrificing their lives to fulfill the *Shon'Kar*. We appreciate your diligence and concern in this matter, and after seeing this crystal, I am sorry that you must send a delegation to Homeworld.''

''We wish to go—to honor G'Kar,'' said Ivanova.

Vin'Tok nodded in a courtly manner. ''Understood. It will be our honor to transport you. Now if you'll excuse us, I think we should join the others at the reception.''

''Come,'' said Na'Toth, motioning toward the door, ''I'll show you the way to the reception.'' With that, the three Narns filed out of the captain's office.

Sheridan's lips thinned. ''I wish we could catch the murderer on the station.''

''I sent you a report about one of my officers,'' said Garibaldi. ''I don't know if it's related to this, but Leffler had his head bashed in while we were sweeping for Narns in Down Below. He's in a coma, but the doc thinks he'll be all right. Somebody didn't want to be carded.''

''I read your report,'' answered the captain. ''Don't

worry, Garibaldi. I'll follow through while you're gone, and we'll catch them, if they're here.''

Ivanova said, ''Big 'if.' ''

''Oh, one more thing.'' Sheridan bowed his head apologetically. ''You can't take any weapons to Homeworld or aboard their ship. In exchange for that concession, I got you diplomatic immunity.''

''Great,'' said Garibaldi, brushing back his short-cropped hair. ''We'll be unarmed and unable to do anything if we meet the murderer face-to-face. In fact, she can *brag* about killing G'Kar if she feels like it!''

Sheridan straightened. ''Let's do the only thing we can for G'Kar—show how much we miss him.''

The small amphitheater in the Green sector had seen a number of plays and concerts, recalled Ivanova, but it was doubtful whether it had seen any greater drama than the memorial service for G'Kar. Mourners and the curious were packed in, clogging the aisles, hanging from the rafters. She could see Garibaldi and his officers trying to keep the aisles clear and the riffraff out, but it was a losing battle. At least they managed to keep a row of seats roped off in the front, and that was where Ivanova was sitting with Captain Sheridan, the ambassadors, and the visiting Narns.

The doors to the theater slammed shut, and the unruly crowd began to quiet. From the seat beside her, Captain Sheridan rose to his feet and scanned the audience. When he was content that they were finally settling in, he strode to the stage and stepped behind the podium. His commanding presence brought the audience to a gradual hush.

''Thank you for coming,'' he began, ''to the memorial service for Ambassador G'Kar of the Narn Regime. I know the shocking and sudden nature of his death has left all of us feeling stunned. We wish we could do something to turn back the clock, to prevent it from happening. But we can't.

And we can't become obsessed with the tragedy—we must move on to our real purpose in gathering here today. We have come here to remember G'Kar as one of the founders of Babylon 5, a driving force in its creation and success.''

Sheridan cleared his throat and let his gaze fall on Londo Mollari. ''G'Kar used to say that serving on Babylon 5 was a great honor because he was facing his enemies. But I don't think even his enemies considered *him* the enemy. Underneath his warrior exterior, he was a peacemaker, a person who was helping us search for reasons to have peace instead of war. I won't claim that G'Kar and I were old friends or knew each other well, but I always felt that G'Kar was trying to make things better.''

The captain bowed his head. ''Humans often say a prayer in a situation like this, which is a way of talking to our creator, so you'll excuse me if I indulge. Dear God, we wish G'Kar a swift journey to the afterlife, in whatever form he believed. We wish a minimum of grief to those he leaves behind, and we hope You can heal the call of revenge in our hearts. Finally, we pray that G'Kar's search for peace will have an everlasting effect on Babylon 5 and the governments which support her. Amen.''

''Amen,'' Ivanova repeated with the Jewish intonation.

Sheridan looked momentarily nervous as he realized what was coming next. ''Being an ambassador on B5 means being on the point for your entire culture, and it takes a special person to do that. G'Kar had few peers on this station, but we are fortunate to have two of them with us today. Before Ambassador Delenn speaks, Ambassador Mollari has a few words.''

There were shocked murmurs throughout the hall, and the Narn delegation glared at Londo as he ambled importantly toward the podium. He smiled knowingly, which came out looking like a sneer.

''You do not know my race,'' he began, ''if you think we

have no respect for our enemies. We have enormous respect for the Narn Regime, even though they keep stealing our ancestral holdings, but that is a discussion for another day. In fact, that is a discussion I often had with my departed enemy, G'Kar. There was *nothing* we agreed upon, yet we understood each other as few friends do. We knew the difficulties of our position on this station—the way our governments expected us to be wise and brilliant, when we were only mortal. Both of us felt our allegiance to home mixed with a strange sense of belonging to something bigger, something we found here, on Babylon 5. As few others can say, he was my equal—this G'Kar of the Third Circle—and I will miss him.''

Londo shrugged fatalistically. ''They will send another, but he will not be G'Kar. I will miss seeing the veins pop out of his neck when he is yelling at me, or the way he sputtered when he did not get his way. The next ambassador will certainly not yell or sputter as zestfully as G'Kar.'' The Centauri touched his fist to his chest in the Narn salute. ''Good-bye, my enemy.''

Like several people in the audience, Ivanova was sniffling, and she had to fish a handkerchief out of her pocket. This memorial service was turning out to be just what she feared most, a heartfelt tribute to a person who had gone before his time. G'Kar had died just when he was making his greatest contributions—all to satisfy a primitive urge for revenge. She wanted to scream, but she couldn't. So instead she cried.

Ivanova looked up to see Delenn sweep across the stage and stand next to the podium, which would have dwarfed her had she stood behind it. Her shocks of auburn hair gave her a softer appearance than she'd had before her transformation; it added to her beatific presence. Today, however, her fragile face looked angry and determined.

''The death of G'Kar is an outrage!'' said Delenn, drawing hushed breaths from the crowd. "I came here to remember my colleague, but I don't truly want to do that. Instead, I want my colleague to be *alive,* as he always was. I do not feel like forgiving his murderers and moving on, although I know that is the prudent thing to do. You must excuse me while I vent my outrage first, because my friend, G'Kar, is not here to do it for himself."

The Narns squirmed in their chairs, and Delenn apparently took some comfort in that. "When I came here, Babylon 5 was just a collection of people from different worlds. It had no personality, no identity, not much chance to survive. Then I met Ambassadors G'Kar, Kosh, Mollari, and I renewed my acquaintance with Ambassador Sinclair —and my mission became real to me. It is not an easy thing to willfully submit oneself to an experiment, but that is what we have done here on Babylon 5. G'Kar firmly believed in our mission, and he accepted Babylon 5 as his home. This was a great inspiration to me and many of us who had strong ties to our homeworlds. I took strength from G'Kar, and I am weakened now that he is gone."

Delenn's anger gave way to a nostalgic smile. "G'Kar could be belligerent and difficult, but I remember him for his moments of kindness, openness, and generosity. For him not to be here anymore—in the Council meetings or at official receptions—is unthinkable. I have a sense of overwhelming loss, when I know that I should be feeling acceptance. So let us acknowledge the fact that G'Kar has transformed, while we have remained the same."

Delenn folded her hands and looked at the Narns. "The candle is a universal symbol of the light that even one small soul can cast in this lifetime. Would you permit a small procession of candles?"

Captain Vin'Tok nodded, and the lights were dimmed. Lennier stepped forward, accompanied by six Minbari priests, each bearing a long, tapered candle. Lennier waved a spark over each candle, and they seemed to burst into flame simultaneously. The lights were dimmed further, and the candlebearers moved in a circle around the stage while a melancholy flute sounded from somewhere in the balcony. The procession was simple and unhurried, six white lights floating through the darkness while the flute mourned aloud for everyone.

After what seemed like a brief but healing time, the houselights were brought back up, and the six Minbari priests and their candles formed a line leading out the door. Despite the pandemonium that ensued when everyone was entering the theater, the somber audience filed out in respectful silence, gazing at the candles as they passed them. Ivanova swallowed back a lump in her throat, thinking that B5 was probably strong enough to survive the passing of G'Kar, but it was still a tremendous blow.

"Are you up on your Mark Twain?" she heard a voice ask.

She turned to see Londo Mollari looking expectantly at her, a half-smile on his face.

"I've heard of him, but I'm no expert on Early American writers," she admitted.

"Too bad," said Londo. "You could enjoy this more."

Before she could question him further about the odd literary allusion, Captain Vin'Tok stepped between them. "We leave in forty-six minutes," he told her. "We expect punctuality."

"You'll get it," said the commander, "as long as you have some coffee on board."

"We recently added coffee to our stores," replied the Narn with a slight smile. He started to follow Na'Toth out the rear exit, then stopped. "I suggest you bring both warm and cool clothing."

"I've done my research," she assured him. "I'm prepared for anything."

Vin'Tok gave her a curt bow. Several security guards stepped in and escorted the Narn delegation through the backstage area. Ivanova turned to look for Londo, and she saw his spiked hair cutting through the sea of alien heads like the dorsal fin of a shark. She was too far away to catch up with him, so she let her eyes wander. Finally she spied Garibaldi, leaning over the railing of the balcony and looking down on the mourners like a vengeful angel.

She tapped her link. "Ivanova to Garibaldi."

"I see you," said the chief with a wave. "What's up?"

"I just wanted to tell you that we leave for Homeworld in forty-five minutes."

"Do you have any idea what we're getting ourselves into?" he asked with concern.

"Nope," she admitted. "But I did hear one bit of good news."

"What's that?"

"They have coffee on board."

"But at night I expect hot chocolate," said the chief. "I've got a million things to do before we leave, but I'll be there. Garibaldi out."

A dust devil swirled through the copper-colored sand, across pockmarked walls, up a cement post, and finally found a street sign to play with. The sign twisted and squeaked on its corroded metal rings, tossing rust confetti to the playful dust devil. Mi'Ra, daughter of Du'Rog, paused under the sign, which read simply "V'Tar." She had to laugh that such a poverty-stricken street, squeezed dry of all life and hope, could be named after the spark of life.

Street V'Tar consisted of two rows of three-story buildings, each one more weary and forlorn than the one before. Even in this wind, she could smell the burning rubber. The only light came from clay pots that swung in the wind, casting shadow races on the dilapidated buildings. With frightening sameness, Street V'Tar stretched down a hill until it was mercifully swallowed in darkness. Mi'Ra shivered, knowing this drained section of the border zone was her home, worse than a plebeian's.

"Hurry!" she called into the wind, wondering where her lazy brother, T'Kog, was hiding now. T'Kog was a grave disappointment to her, and she found she was wasting too much energy keeping him focused on the *Shon'Kar*. He still acted as if life was going to change, get better of its own accord, and she knew it was not.

"Mi'Ra! Mi'Ra!" he screamed, stumbling out of the darkness.

She drew her compact PPG, thinking T'Kog was being chased. When the Narn saw that her younger brother was laughing and waving some bits of newspad, her sharp features bent into a scowl. "Stop using my name!"

"Do you see what this is!" he said, shoving the newspad in her face. "G'Kar is dead! G'Kar died in an explosion launching from Babylon 5!"

Mi'Ra grasped the sheets out of his hands and stared at them, each symbol registering on her smooth reptilian face. Her spotted cranium throbbed, and her lips twisted back. *G'Kar the destroyer was dead!* Their hated foe, killer of their father, defiler of their name, and object of their *Shon'Kar*—he was dead. Killed in a suspicious explosion. Clearly, somebody had gotten to him, but who?

She shouted at the night sky, "Why wasn't it *me*?"

"Hush, sister. Let the fates have some play here," T'Kog cautioned her.

"Who gave you these?" she demanded, flashing the newspads in his face.

T'Kog pointed innocently behind them. "A man down there, he was giving them away. Several people seemed to know about it already."

Mi'Ra had already leveled her PPG and was scanning the shadows when she heard a voice spring from inside a dust devil. "Don't be afraid, my dear," it crooned.

She knew this disembodied voice was a trick—some said the Thenta Ma'Kur had learned it from the technomages— but the assassins had made it their own. The young Narn woman moved in a crouch with her pistol drawn, trying to find the source of the voice. She had reason to hate the league, and they her—but she knew that if they wanted her dead, they would strike without issuing a warning.

"You haven't come to kill us, have you?" she asked.

"Not at this time, my lady," said the voice. "Come to the nearest archway in the wall."

T'Kog was slinking away from the confrontation, but Mi'Ra grabbed him by his shabby collar and thrust him against the wall. He hit the pockmarked cement head-on and moaned as he massaged a knot on his dotted cranium.

"You picked up the message," she told him. "So you go with me."

Mi'Ra dragged him the rest of the way and threw him against one side of the archway, while she leaned against the other. She holstered her weapon and watched the light in the clay pot sway back and forth. "We're here!" she shouted into the wind.

A slim man wrapped in black shawls eased out of the shadows and slumped against the wall beside her brother, who gasped. Slinking back, T'Kog managed to get control of himself and face up to this apparition. The black shawls covered every part of him, including his face, and they flapped leisurely in the wind that groaned around them.

"You've been making trouble for us," said the man in a cultured bass voice. "Telling people that we don't fulfill our contracts."

"Well, you don't!" Mi'Ra spit at the ground. "The Thenta Ma'Kur is a sham, and that's all I tell them."

The man swaddled in black flinched for a moment but settled into the archway. "You cannot say that anymore. We have fulfilled our contract with your father. G'Kar is dead."

Mi'Ra narrowed her blazing red eyes at the assassin, knowing that he and death were familiar friends. "Is this true? G'Kar is truly dead?"

"Go to Jasba," said the man. "Find any public viewer. You will see, G'Kar is dead. The newspads are real."

Mi'Ra breathed deeply and sank against the ancient archway. "Then it is over?" she asked in disbelief.

"Not for you," said the assassin. "Many suspect you because of your brave but indiscreet *Shon'Kar*. Next time, leave this work to professionals."

Mi'Ra glared at him. As much as she despised the cold-blooded scavengers of the Thenta Ma'Kur, she was ready to accept the fact that they had fulfilled their contract.

Still, the Narn woman straightened her shoulders and declared, "I am proud of my *Shon'Kar*."

"Of course you are, my dear, but the humans of Babylon 5 do not appreciate the *Shon'Kar* as much as we do. G'Kar also has many friends, important ones. Our advice to you is this—neither admit nor deny your hand in his murder, and do not mention us. Your Blood Oath is well known, and all will come to accept it."

Mi'Ra bowed. "I will do as you wish. From now on, I will speak highly of your fellowship."

The black-shrouded figure bowed in return. "Earthforce personnel are coming to Homeworld to answer the Council's questions. We will stay close to them and watch them, in case they interfere too much. As of now, our business with you is concluded."

With that, the black-shrouded man stepped from the light of the archway and strode into the darkness, which accepted him without hesitation.

# CHAPTER 6

Michael Garibaldi stayed behind in the theater balcony, watching the mourners depart after the memorial service for G'Kar. He wasn't the sentimental type, except when it came to old friends and young ladies, but the memorial service had been oddly touching. Even Londo had risen to the occasion. As Delenn had said in her address, it was easy to be angry and deny what had happened, and it was much harder to accept the fact that G'Kar was gone. It was like a whole section of the station was suddenly missing.

He leaned over the balcony again, wondering if there was a murderer in the well-behaved crowd. The security chief had no idea anybody was watching him.

"Hi, my name is Al Vernon!" crowed a loud voice directly behind him. The security chief whirled around to see a human male approaching him from the back of the balcony. He was a portly fellow dressed in a checkered sport coat, and sweat glistened on his florid face. He held out a pudgy hand as if it was the most important thing in the world that he shake Garibaldi's hand.

"Do I know you?" asked Garibaldi.

"No, sir, you do not," answered the man cheerfully, but that didn't prevent him from grabbing Garibaldi's hand and yanking for all he was worth. "My name is Al Vernon, but I already said that. You're Garibaldi, the security chief of this fine station, am I right?"

"That's no secret," growled the chief. "Listen, I've got to leave the station soon, and I'm busy." He glanced down and saw Talia Winters filing out of the amphitheater with the others, which reminded him of another matter still up in the air—officer Leffler. He demanded of his chubby acquaintance, "Do you think you could get to the point?"

"It's quite simple, sir." He stood on his tiptoes to whisper to the taller man. "Rumor has it that you're going to the Narn Homeworld aboard the *K'sha Na'vas*. I'd like to tag along, if I could. I've been trying to get there for six months, and I was hoping you would prevail upon the Narns or Captain Sheridan to get me aboard."

Garibaldi gaped at the man. "You've got a lot of nerve. If you know all of that, then you also know that we're an official delegation. The *K'sha Na'vas* is not a transport— you can't just buy a ticket on her."

Al Vernon laughed nervously. "That is one reason why I must appeal to you, sir. I've managed to come this far—I only just arrived—but I find myself short of funds for the journey to Homeworld. However, I've got excellent lines of credit there, plus many business associates who will vouch for me."

"You've been to Homeworld?" asked Garibaldi, sounding doubtful.

"Been there, sir? Why, I lived there for ten years! Have a wife there, I do. Well, she's an ex-wife by now, I should imagine. Darling little thing, except for when she used to get mad at me." He whispered again, "Don't marry a Narn unless you can stand a woman with a temper."

Now Garibaldi was intrigued. "Do they often marry humans?"

"No, not often," admitted Al. "The number of humans living on Homeworld is very small, but a family with too many daughters might see fit to marry one off to a human who was prosperous. Children are out of the question, of course, but sexual relations are not. No, indeedy."

Garibaldi scowled at the man's sly grin, but he was still intrigued. "What kind of business did you do there?"

"Importer of alien technologies," answered Al. "The Narns are crazy for anything from outside the Regime. Toys, kitchen goods, communications . . ."

"Weapons," suggested Garibaldi.

The man bristled. "Nothing illegal, I can assure you. In fact, had I not been so scrupulous, I would have avoided the business reversals that have kept me away from Narn for so long."

Garibaldi rubbed his chin. "You know, it might not be a bad idea to have a guide along, somebody who knows the territory. We've been summoned to answer questions about G'Kar's death, but we don't want to be held up in a bureaucratic nightmare for days on end."

"I still have some friends in high places," Al assured him. "I could save you considerable time and help you to avoid many pitfalls."

"You would be part of the official delegation—no weapons, no funny business—and you would have to attend a memorial service for G'Kar."

Al Vernon rubbed his chubby hands together. "I would be honored to attend a service for Ambassador G'Kar, whom I met many years ago. What a tragic loss."

"Yeah." The chief tapped his link and spoke into the device. "This is Garibaldi to C-and-C."

"Lieutenant Mitchell on duty," came a sprightly female voice. "Go ahead, Chief."

"I would like the complete records on a human male who's here on the station. He goes by the name of Al Vernon. I also want to know how long he's been on B5, and what his financial status is. And I want to know if there is any record of him ever living on the Narn Homeworld."

Garibaldi smiled at his new friend, who seemed to be sweating just a little bit more. "You only have half an hour on this, so get back to me as soon as you can."

"Yes, sir. C-and-C out."

Al Vernon chuckled and tugged at his collar. "You're a thorough man, aren't you, Mr. Garibaldi?"

"I just want to make sure you are who you say you are. I'll talk to the captain and do the best I can. Meet me in forty-three minutes in dock six, and be ready to go."

"Yes, sir!" said Al, snapping to attention and thrusting his stomach out.

Garibaldi winced at the man's eagerness and strode to the steps leading down from the balcony. He didn't feel as if he had made much of a commitment, because if Al Vernon's story didn't check out, he wasn't going anywhere. If by some miracle Al did check out, he could be a valuable ally, a human who knew his way around the Narn Homeworld. Garibaldi wanted to trust Na'Toth to be their guide, but he was afraid that the attaché had her own agenda.

Maybe if he was lucky, thought the chief, there would be a break in the investigation before he had to board the *K'sha Na'vas*. Maybe they'd find Mi'Ra in Down Below, or Leffler would jump up in bed and identify both his assailant and the murderer. *Get real,* thought Garibaldi, knowing that he would never have a lucky streak like that.

He stopped in the corridor and watched the last of the mourners, who were breaking up into small groups and going about their business. After a moment, the chief tapped his link and said, "Garibaldi to medlab."

"Franklin here," came the response. "Are you checking up on your officer?"

"Yeah, Doc. Has Leffler regained consciousness?"

"I just got back from the service. Let me check." A minute later, Franklin reported back, "Leffler gained consciousness briefly, but he became agitated and we sedated him. His vital signs and EKG look good, but you can't be too careful with head trauma."

"Can we wake him up to be questioned?" asked Garibaldi.

The doctor's tone was cool. "I think he's several hours away from that. Perhaps tomorrow."

"Thanks," said Garibaldi. "I'll be off-station by then, so could you contact Captain Sheridan as soon as Leffler is well enough to be questioned about his attack?"

"I'll make sure. Anything else?"

"Nope. Garibaldi out." He tapped his link again. "Garibaldi to Welch."

"I read you, Chief."

"Any luck down there?" he asked, expecting the worst.

"Afraid not. We've checked every Narn in sight, and we've found a handful with expired identicards. But we've made positive ID on all of them, and none of them are recent arrivals to the station. No one seems to have any connection to the Du'Rog family."

"What about the attack on Leffler? Anyone see anything?"

"No, sir. But then, nobody ever sees anything down here."

Garibaldi frowned at the back of his hand. "All right, Lou, call it off for now. I'm off the station in about forty minutes, but there is one thing I want you to follow up on."

"Sure, Chief."

"When Leffler comes to, question him. If he can't remember who hit him—and people often lose their memory after a head injury—contact Talia Winters. She can do a scan on him and help us fill in the blanks. She's already agreed to do this, so all you have to do is call her."

"Gotcha. Have a good trip."

"Yeah," said Garibaldi. "Out."

After stopping at his quarters to pick up his duffel bag and rescue his heavy coat from mothballs, Garibaldi headed toward Captain Sheridan's office. He was about ten meters from the captain's door when his link buzzed.

"Garibaldi here!" he snapped at the back of his hand.

"This is Lieutenant Mitchell in C-and-C, and I have that data for you on Al Vernon. Want me to upload to your link?"

Garibaldi checked the time and saw that he was running out of it. "Send it to Captain Sheridan's terminal. I'm just outside his office. Garibaldi out."

*Be there, Captain Sheridan,* he muttered to himself as he pressed the chime. To his relief, a voice called, "Enter!"

Garibaldi ducked through the door and was relieved to see that Sheridan was alone in his office. He was peering at his flat-screen terminal, a bemused expression on his face.

The captain barely looked up. "Hello, Garibaldi. Ready for your trip?"

"Not really, sir," admitted the security chief. "I hope I haven't caught you at a bad time, but this will only take a moment."

Sheridan frowned at his screen. "Would you believe I'm looking at Narn legal texts? Most of them are centuries old and predate the Centauri invasion. It seems as if they prefer debating the meaning of these old laws, most of which are irrelevant to a spacefaring society, to writing any new laws. Their beliefs are mired in the past. This *Shon'Kar* business reminds me of Earth a few centuries back, when it was legal to fight duels to the death."

Garibaldi stepped to the side of Sheridan's desk. "Sir, I was expecting a download from C-and-C, and I had them send it directly to you. Could I take a look?"

Sheridan pushed his chair back and motioned toward the screen. "Go ahead."

Garibaldi angled the screen and punched in some commands. As information and a photograph blossomed on the screen, he began to read aloud, "Full name is Albert Curtis Vernon, aka Al Vernon, and he hails from Mansfield, Ohio." He stopped and pointed to a window of text. "This is interesting, sir—he's done a lot of traveling around, but you can see that the Narn Homeworld was his legal residence for almost ten years. He was registered with both the embassy and the trade commission. Yeah, he seems legit.''

''Is this man a suspect in G'Kar's murder?'' asked Sheridan.

''No, sir. This may sound crazy, but I would like to take Al Vernon with us to Homeworld, to be sort of a guide.''

Sheridan blinked at him. ''How well do you know this man?''

''I just met him. He came up to me after the service and said he wanted to get back to Homeworld. He agreed to be my guide if I arranged passage on the *K'sha Na'vas*.''

''That's not our ship, Garibaldi. I can't order them to take a stranger on board a military vessel.''

The chief cleared his throat. ''Begging your pardon, sir, but it's your prerogative to pick the people for the official delegation. I don't remember volunteering, yet here I am. You could put Al Vernon on the list. Since he's married to a Narn, he is sort of a pioneer in Narn-Terran relationships.''

''How long has Al Vernon been on the station?'' In answer to his own question, the captain glanced at his screen and said, ''He just arrived here two hours ago, so he couldn't have been involved in G'Kar's death. He didn't waste any time getting to you, did he?''

''No, sir. I don't intend to trust him with my life—all I know is that he fell into my lap, and I'd feel like a fool if I didn't take him. He said he was broke—how many credits does he have?''

Sheridan gazed at his screen. ''He hasn't used a creditchit on the station, so we have no record of his financial status. Look at all the places this guy has been—Centauri Prime, Mars, Antareus, Betelguese Four, not to mention ten years on the Narn Homeworld. Look here and here

—there are a lot of gaps where we don't know where he's been. If you take this man with you, he'll have to be your responsibility. I'll hold you personally accountable for his actions."

"Yes, sir," Garibaldi answered gravely, wondering if he was taking leave of his senses. He had absolutely no reason to trust Al Vernon, just a hunch that providence had dealt him a trump card in a plaid sport coat.

Captain Sheridan pressed his console, and the main viewer on the wall blinked on, showing a communications graphic. "This is Captain Sheridan to the Narn cruiser *K'sha Na'vas.* I would like to speak to Captain Vin'Tok, if he is available."

The graphic was replaced by a view of the bridge of the Narn heavy cruiser, *K'sha Na'vas.* The lights were dimmed drowsily, as if takeoff were hours away instead of ten minutes. Vin'Tok sat down in front of the screen, and his face was half-bathed in shadows.

"Hello, Captain," he said. "May I be of help?"

"Captain, I wish to include one more dignitary on the list of delegates from Earth. His name is Al Vernon, and he's a civilian."

Now Vin'Tok sat up abruptly in his chair and scowled at Sheridan. "This is highly irregular, adding a passenger only ten minutes before we depart."

Sheridan smiled pleasantly. "We are only trying to show our respect to Ambassador G'Kar by sending a worthy delegation. I can upload to you the records of Mr. Vernon, so you can see for yourself that he's a fitting symbol of the cooperation between our worlds."

"Very well," muttered the Narn captain. "I trust this will not delay our departure. Out." He punched a button, and the screen went blank.

On the dimly lit bridge of the warship *K'sha Na'vas,*

G'Kar's sharp chin jutted out of the shadows. "You fool! Bringing a complete stranger on board!"

"What was I to do?" asked Vin'Tok. "A three-person delegation is still small. How was I to refuse the humans? Believe me, they have been quite genuine in their grief over your demise. The memorial service was heartwarming. When this is all over, my friend, you will have to tell me why you have taken such a desperate action."

G'Kar sat stiffly in his chair, his lips tight. Dead men have little influence, he was beginning to find out.

"Data download from Captain Sheridan is now complete," announced a Narn tech.

"You'd better get below," Vin'Tok told G'Kar, a note of dismissal in his voice.

G'Kar wanted to protest, but his power and prestige were evaporating before his eyes. No longer was he G'Kar of the Third Circle. He was a dead man—a nonentity. His lot was to be hidden away, hunted, and now ignored. When he had hastily devised this scheme, he had never realized the jeopardy in which he was placing himself. He had assumed that his associates would treat him as they always had, realizing that he was still G'Kar. But G'Kar was officially dead; he had no strings to pull and no teeth to his bite. He was dependent upon the kindness of friends, and they seemed more curious than helpful.

He would try to arrange being discovered floating in space, and still alive, as soon as his mission to Homeworld was over. And he would conclude that business as quickly as possible.

With armed guards at his back, G'Kar marched toward the ladder that would take him down into the hold. There his furnished cell waited.

Garibaldi was ambushed just as he was coming off the lift on the docking level. Ivanova stopped him with a palm to the chest and peered at him with eyes that were darker and more intense than usual.

"What is this about a stranger coming with us?" she demanded.

"You mean Al Vernon," Garibaldi said sheepishly. "He's a stranger to *us,* but he's no stranger to Homeworld. We'll need someone who knows their way around."

"What about Na'Toth? I took her out to breakfast this morning—bought her smoked eel! She's agreed to help us."

Garibaldi scowled. "Until she catches sight of Mi'Ra and goes for her throat. I want to get in and get out with the least amount of trouble, and I think Al will be a big help."

He struggled with his duffel bag and his heavy coat while trying to check the time. Damn it, he didn't want to go someplace where he had to wear a coat, where the temperature shot up and down the thermometer like a yo-yo. He liked it on B5, where the temperature was regulated for optimum comfort.

Ivanova hefted her own luggage and bulky jacket. "We'd better keep moving."

"Mr. Garibaldi!" bellowed a voice. They turned to see a squat man in a loud sport coat waddling toward them, dragging a huge suitcase in each hand.

Ivanova gave Garibaldi a raised eyebrow. "Don't tell me that's him?"

"I'm sure he'll tell you himself." Garibaldi managed a smile.

His round face beaming, Al Vernon dropped his suitcases in front of Ivanova. "I'm Al Vernon," he said proudly, "and you must be Commander Ivanova. This is a real pleasure, yes, indeedy!"

The commander frowned darkly. "I wasn't consulted about you coming with us, and I'm not sure I agree with it. This is a delicate mission, and we may need to be tactful."

She glanced at Garibaldi. "On the other hand, neither one of us knows how to be tactful. How about you?"

Al dabbed a handkerchief at his moist forehead. "I don't know how tactful I am, but I do know Narns. With them, you have to deal from a position of strength. If they sense weakness, they'll eat you alive. Have you got anything to bargain with?"

Garibaldi looked at Ivanova and shook his head. "No, all we've got is a data crystal, some vidlogs, and a desire to get home. If we're sticking to the truth, why should we have to bargain?"

"One hand washes the other. That's a human phrase, but the Narns could have invented it." Al picked up his suitcases and grinned. "I hate to be late! Shall we be going?"

With Mr. Vernon plunging ahead in the lead, the Terran delegation made their way to bay six, where the *K'sha Na'vas* was docked. Waiting for them was Na'Toth, who gave the three humans a disdainful look.

"I hope you aren't turning this into a circus," she said.

Nonplussed, Al Vernon looked at her and smiled. "The flower of Narn womanhood is the thorn."

Na'Toth blinked at him in surprise. "Where did you learn that?"

"From my lovely wife, Hannah. Well, that's what I called her; her real name is Ho'Na. She was a great student of the *Vopa Cha'Kur*. I have always been attracted to powerful women, Narn women." He shrugged. "It is a terrible weakness. I cannot wait to return to the land of thorny women."

Na'Toth laughed, a rich, ribald sound. "Under the thorn is the softest fruit," she added.

"How well I know," agreed Al Vernon.

Garibaldi and Ivanova looked blankly at one another, neither one of them being an expert on Narn double entendres. On the plus side, Al Vernon seemed to have made his first conquest among their hosts.

He bowed formally to Na'Toth. "May I have the pleasure of serving you dinner tonight?"

Na'Toth frowned at the invitation. "I'm sure we'll all eat together. If you'll excuse me, I'll tell the captain that the Terran delegation is here." The lanky Narn strode through the air-lock.

"I'm afraid to ask," said Garibaldi, "but what is this *Vopa Cha'Kur*?"

Al smiled. "It's equivalent to Earth's *Kama Sutra*. Required reading on Narn, old boy."

With that, the portly man gripped his bags and rumbled up the ramp. Ivanova and Garibaldi struggled along in his wake. The air-lock door whooshed open, and they walked down another ramp into the receiving compartment, where Captain Vin'Tok, his first officer, Yal'Tar, and Na'Toth stood waiting. A crewman bolted the hatch behind them and made ready for departure.

With importance, Captain Vin'Tok proclaimed, "On behalf of the Narn Regime, welcome aboard the cruiser *K'sha Na'vas* of the Second Fleet of the Golden Order."

"It is our pleasure," said Commander Ivanova. "I just wish it were under happier circumstances."

A communications panel on the wall made a chirping sound, and the first officer rushed to answer it. "This is Yal'Tar."

"Our escort has arrived," came the reply. "We have completed the checklist, and we are cleared for departure."

"Escort?" muttered Garibaldi.

Vin'Tok shrugged. "Two smaller cruisers. It is nothing —just three ships with the same destination. We Narns like to travel in packs."

"Ah, yes"—Al Vernon beamed—"I always feel safe on a Narn vessel. They take the extra precaution."

Vin'Tok narrowed his eyes at the colorfully dressed human. "I did some checking. You disappeared from Narn two years ago—listed as missing, presumed dead."

Al laughed nervously. "Well, as the great Mark Twain said, the reports of my death were greatly exaggerated! I will tell you of my adventure over dinner tonight, Captain. Suffice to say, I am happy to be returning to the land that cries in bloodstone."

Vin'Tok cocked his head and smiled, apparently taken off guard by another Narn homily. He issued some orders to his crew, and Garibaldi looked at Ivanova only to find that her brow was deeply furrowed in thought. "Are you trying to make sense of this?" he whispered.

"No, he mentioned Mark Twain." She frowned in thought. "That's twice I've heard that name today."

Garibaldi looked around. "I'm more worried about why we need three warships to get to Homeworld."

A hatch opened, and two crew members came in to pick up the passengers' luggage and coats. Captain Vin'Tok led his guests through the hatch and down a short walkway that was surrounded by ducts and access panels. They went through another hatch and entered a chamber that contained about sixty seats arranged in a semicircle, facing center. To Garibaldi, the room looked like a combination troop transport and briefing room. With no troops present, the chamber seemed oddly hollow, like the inside of a tomb.

Vin'Tok motioned to the empty seats. "You will be comfortable here. Please strap yourselves in with the restraining bars, as there will be an increase in g's and weightlessness for a few minutes. After we have entered hyperspace, I will escort you to your quarters."

Na'Toth immediately took a seat, as if showing that she was a passenger who knew her place. Al Vernon hustled to the seat beside her and unnecessarily helped her pull down her restraining bar. With fifty-some empty seats, Garibaldi had a wide range of choices. He always liked to sit at the back of a vessel, where he could keep an eye on everybody else, so he wandered in that direction. Still embedded in her own thoughts, Ivanova trailed after him.

Garibaldi pulled the molded bar down over his head and lifted his eyebrows at Ivanova. The Narns kept watch on their four passengers until each one was safely strapped into his or her seat. Only then did they leave them alone in the transport section.

A few aisles away, Na'Toth and Al were chatting like old friends, although it sounded as if they were now talking about restaurants instead of sex.

"What do you know about Mark Twain?" Ivanova asked.

"Plenty," said Garibaldi. "I love Mark Twain."

Suddenly Garibaldi heard a hollow clanging sound that reverberated around the empty chamber. *We're pulling away from the station,* he thought. The skin on his face stretched back, his hair follicles tingled, and he could feel a flurry of butterflies in his stomach. They were on their way to the Narn Homeworld.

As the three Narn cruisers approached the jump gate, they looked like a school of stingrays with twin tails. In formation, the sleek ships darted into the jump gate and were swallowed in a blaze of light.

# CHAPTER 7

Dr. Stephen Franklin bent over his prized patient, Dan Leffler, and smiled at the man. "Just relax. Don't try to move. It's especially important to keep your head still."

"Okay," muttered Leffler, gazing around at medlab. The blinking lights and instruments blinded him, and he twisted his head from side to side. That gave him a terrific headache, so he stopped doing it and just screwed his eyes shut.

"Lower the lights, please," said Dr. Franklin very calmly. He placed his dark hands on Leffler's chest, and the disoriented man felt a wave of comfort. "Don't move around, please. Just try to stay calm."

"Chief Garibaldi," croaked Leffler. "I . . . uh . . . the Narns . . ."

"Chief Garibaldi has left the station, but Captain Sheridan is on his way here, and so is your friend, Lou Welch." He smiled pleasantly. "You're a popular fellow, Leffler. I hear that our resident telepath, Talia Winters, wants to see you, too. You just try to collect your thoughts, and don't move around too much. Okay?"

The doctor stood up, looking confident, calm, and authoritative all at the same time. "Be sure to tell me if you have any serious pain anywhere. We can sedate you again."

"All right," said the officer, taking a deep breath and starting to feel more like a human being than a blob of confusion. He tried to collect his thoughts, but they seemed to be rather nebulous—just a few scattered images floating weightlessly beyond his grasp.

Leffler didn't know how long he lay there, getting reacquainted with his various appendages and assuring himself he wasn't seriously hurt, except for the foamcore bandage around his head and the dull throbbing that would not go away. Somebody had sure dinged his rocker panel, but he couldn't remember who, only that it had something to do with Narns. Well, his brother, Taylor, always told him he had a hard head. He guessed that was better than the alternative.

When he heard voices speaking softly nearby, he opened his eyes and saw the good doctor conferring with Lou Welch, Captain Sheridan, and Talia Winters, who looked like an angel with a halo of blond hair around her head. "Lou!" he croaked.

His fellow officer rushed to the bedside, his sardonic face creasing into a smile. "Yeah, Leffler, we send you to do a simple job, and you get your head busted open."

"Lou, I don't know who did it. I can't tell you anything."

"Relax," Dr. Franklin cautioned. "You won't remember it all at once. Your memory will come back in bits and pieces—it may take days." He looked pointedly at Captain Sheridan. "Your health is the primary concern."

"Of course," said Sheridan. He smiled at Leffler with his ruggedly handsome face. "Soldier, do you think you're up to answering a few questions?"

"Yes, sir." Leffler tried to relax. "I'll do the best I can."

Sheridan glanced at Welch, who consulted a handheld device. "Let me tell you the details that we have so far, and maybe they will jar your memory. You were in Down Below, corridor 112 of Brown sector, checking for undocumented Narns among the lurkers. This was in connection with the death of Ambassador G'Kar."

"Yes," said Leffler slowly, the assignment coming back to him. "I remember all of that. We were looking for some family . . ."

"Du'Rog," answered Welch. "That's right, Dan. You're doing good. That stretch of corridor has a lot of small shacks made out of all kinds of discarded stuff. You were checking around, running ID on Narns. Some kids told us that you went inside one of those shacks. Do you know what happened next?"

"I went inside one of them," Leffler repeated to himself, squinting into their faces. Then he grew frustrated. "I went inside several of them, running lots of identicards. I don't remember one in particular—I don't remember what was so special about it."

"Let me ask you this," said Captain Sheridan, "do you remember anything odd happening to you? Anything unusual?"

Leffler shut his eyes, hoping it would improve his memory. His mind did possess one odd image—an old Narn, lying in bed with his back to him. "There was a Narn who was sick," he said. "I never saw his face."

Sheridan leaned forward. "You never saw his face. So you never verified his ID?"

"I guess not," admitted Leffler. "Or I did, but I just don't remember it."

"May I try?" Talia Winters asked softly. Sheridan nodded and motioned toward the patient. The telepath, dressed elegantly in a gray suit with leather trim, stepped to the edge of the bed and smiled sympathetically at Leffler.

"I'm reluctant to scan you in your condition," she said, "but if we can find out what happened to Ambassador G'Kar . . ."

"I understand. It's okay," said Leffler, trying to appear brave in the presence of the beautiful telepath. "What have I got to hide?"

"I won't find that out," said the telepath. "This scan is going to be very specific, concentrating on what happened to you in Down Below. But if the pain becomes too great, for either one of us, I'm going to break it off."

"Okay," agreed Leffler, taking a deep breath.

Slowly, Talia Winters pulled the black leather glove off her right hand, revealing a delicate appendage that was even whiter than her porcelain face. She explained, "I want you to concentrate on an image in your mind from earlier today, when you were in Down Below. It could be a person, like that sick Narn, or a place, or a number on a bulkhead. Just think of something that you clearly remember from earlier today."

Leffler tried to remember the sick Narn who was lying on the cot, his back toward him. He seemed important for some reason. Then he felt Ms. Winters's cool fingers on his wrist, and the image became crystal clear, populated by a mob of people and impressions vying for his attention. All kinds of memories came cascading into his consciousness, including some from years ago, but Ms. Winters's cool, white hand was there to push most of them away. With her calm assistance, he suddenly knew where he was—in the corridor, outside the row of dilapidated shacks in Down Below.

He heard words, but they were hollow, slurred, and badly amplified—as if he were hearing them over a blown speaker. Then he realized they were his own words, saying to someone in Down Below, "Sorry to bother you, but we're looking for undocumented Narns in connection with Ambassador G'Kar's death. Are you listed on the station roster?"

An old Narn looked queerly at him, his face fading in and out of memory. Suddenly, Ms. Winters's hand reached forward, grabbed the Narn by his patchwork collar, and pulled him into sharp focus. "I should be," answered the Narn. "The name is Pa'Nar. I came here on the *Hala'Tar* about a year ago. Lost all my money gambling, and now

I'm stuck here. You couldn't help me get off the station, could you?''

'' 'Fraid not. Can I see your identicard, please.''

In indelible slow motion, every movement magnified, Leffler saw himself checking the Narn's identicard. He saw the readouts in blazing letters on his handheld terminal. ''Yes, I have you listed,'' warbled the hollow voice. ''Any other Narns in your household?''

''Only my brother is here,'' echoed words as loud as a scream. ''He is very sick.''

Leffler felt himself backing away, as if he didn't want to pursue matters further. He knew he should insist upon seeing the sick Narn, but he also knew there was danger lurking inside the dilapidated shack. The white hand pushed him in the back and urged him to do his duty.

''I have to see him,'' came his own hollow voice. ''I'll just take a look inside and check his identicard. Excuse me.''

Pushing back a dirty canvas flap, Leffler plunged into the darkness of the shack. He cringed at the certain danger, and he wanted to run—but the white hand again pushed him firmly ahead.

''It's all right,'' said a soothing female voice. ''We're only going to look.''

Then the vivid image of the sick Narn lying in the cot returned to his mind, and Leffler felt as if he had arrived somewhere, at some kind of understanding. ''Excuse me,'' he said, ''we're looking for undocumented Narns in connection with Ambassador G'Kar's death. Are you on the station roster?''

The Narn coughed and wheezed and sounded very sick, as he pulled his blanket tighter.

''Did you hear what I said?'' insisted the officer. ''I need your name, and your identicard.''

''Ha'Mok,'' wheezed the sick Narn. *Ha'Mok, Ha'Mok,*

*Ha'Mok,* echoed the voice in Leffler's mind, replayed at various speeds and pitches. What was there about that voice? he wondered.

An identicard clattered to the grimy floor, and Leffler bent down to pick it up. Every motion continued to be magnified in importance, scrutinized down to the last detail. ''Thank you,'' moaned the voice, sounding like it came from inside a cave. He saw the identicard sliding through his terminal like a sailboat slicing across the waves. The little letters danced for a moment, then spelled out the message ''ID confirmed.''

One last step, Leffler knew. What was it? *Oh, yes, his face. His face!* But there was no record of his face, even though the white hand swirled around the dingy shack trying to find it. There were only voices.

''You are listed on the roster,'' a voice roared in his ears. ''But I have to see you to make positive identification. Turn over, please.'' *Turn over please. Turn over please.* But the figure was as motionless as a stone.

Like a slap to the face, the Narn's words struck him: ''I don't wish to vomit all over you! I have a virus . . . a potent one! It is liquefying my intestines. It would kill a human in a day or two!''

Leffler tried to stagger away, to escape from the faceless danger and the inhuman voice, but the white hand jerked his head around and made him listen again. *It would kill a human in a day or two! It would kill a human in a day or two!*

Leffler's own intestines didn't feel so good. He lifted his hand to speak into his link, but the confounded slow motion of the dreamworld betrayed him. He felt a horrible darkness descending, and he was unable to move quickly enough to avoid it. His head felt as if it were caught in a vise, and he screamed with terror.

Instantly, the contact on his wrist vanished, and the

strange voices floated away on a gentle breeze. As his eyes fluttered open, images became indistinct and blended into the quiltwork of lights in medlab. The first thing he saw distinctly was Talia Winters; her angelic face was troubled as she hurriedly pulled her glove over her naked right hand.

"It'll be okay," he assured her. "I won't feel a thing."

She gave him a friendly smile. "You can rest now."

"Excellent idea," agreed Dr. Franklin, pushing Captain Sheridan, Ms. Winters, and Lou Welch away from the bed. Franklin motioned to a nurse, and the patient felt a sting in his shoulder where she gave him a hypo. A friendly darkness descended, and Leffler was snoring within seconds.

"First, I have some names," Talia Winters told Sheridan and Welch. "Two Narns named Pa'Nar and Ha'Mok. I'm certain they're the ones who hit him. At least, I'm sure the attack occurred in the shack where these two were living."

Welch entered the data on his handheld terminal, and the three of them waited for the results. "Hey," said Welch, "this Pa'Nar guy is listed as a passenger on a transport that's boarding right now! Headed for Earth."

"Go get him," ordered Sheridan. "I'll hold the transport."

As Welch rushed out the door and Sheridan contacted C-and-C, Talia Winters tried to collect her thoughts. Memory wiped clean by a trauma to the head was often the most difficult to probe. It was like trying to resurrect computer files that had been disrupted by a strong magnetic field. There was just no way to fully trust what you found.

"Do Narns sound the same to you, Captain?" she asked.

He gave her a puzzled look. "Sound the same as what?"

"Their speaking voices. Does one Narn sound a lot like another?"

Sheridan shook his head in frustration. "I'm not a good one to ask. Why? Did you recognize one of their voices?"

"I thought so," she answered with a shrug. "That is, a voice reminded me of someone I knew, and it reminded Leffler, too. But I don't think it could be him."

"How do you know? Who are you talking about?"

Talia Winters smiled sheepishly at the captain. "Ambassador G'Kar. But he's dead, isn't he?"

Captain Sheridan stared at her, and she went on, "Officer Leffler remembers talking to a Narn, whose face he didn't see but whose voice sounded like G'Kar. But two Narn voices might sound the same, especially to a human."

"Yes," Sheridan answered thoughtfully. "That is, we saw his personal transport blow up, but we never saw a body. How certain are you of this?"

Talia laughed, shaking her blond hair. "I'm not certain at all. I'm telling you this based on a scan of memory that has been damaged by trauma to the head. I wouldn't give it much credence—it's just an impression I had. But I would ask one thing, Captain—if you find these two Narns, I'd like to be there when you question them."

"Certainly," answered Sheridan. "Thank you for your help."

Talia Winters sighed. "I hope it helps."

In the transport section of the *K'sha Na'vas,* Michael Garibaldi stared at the hatch, expecting it to open, but the door refused to budge. It must have been ten minutes since they entered hyperspace—he could feel the return of gravity caused by the rapid acceleration—yet their hosts hadn't returned. Normally he would enjoy passing the time chatting with Ivanova, but she kept babbling on about Mark Twain.

"I remember hearing about Tom Sawyer and Huckleberry Finn," said Ivanova, "but I don't remember the details. I knew I should have read more Mark Twain and less Dostoyevsky.''

Garibaldi frowned. ''Are you trying to recall a book by Twain, a short story, or one of his essays?''

''I wasn't thinking about Mark Twain at all,'' admitted Ivanova, ''until Londo mentioned it at the memorial service. And now this man quoted Mark Twain.''

''The quote Al gave, about reports of his death being greatly exaggerated, is famous. Anybody from North America would be likely to say that, if they were mistakenly accused of being dead. I hate to ask, but what exactly did Londo say about Mark Twain?''

''Only that I would enjoy the service more if I was up on my Mark Twain.'' She gave Garibaldi a quizzical frown.

''Okay,'' said the chief, ''let's think about that. What could he mean? The most famous scene from Twain is probably the scene where Tom Sawyer gets his friends to whitewash the picket fence. Then you've got Injun Joe chasing them around the cave, and the scenes with Polly, but I don't know how they relate to any of this. In Huck Finn, there are the scenes along the river, but that doesn't have anything to do with a funeral.''

Garibaldi caught his breath. ''There is a funeral scene—the one where Tom and Huck watch their own funeral.''

''What did you say?'' asked Ivanova.

''There's a scene where Tom and Huck watch their own funeral,'' repeated Garibaldi. He stared at Ivanova. ''Was Londo trying to tell you that G'Kar is still alive?''

''I thought I saw him die,'' the commander whispered. ''But the sudden way he left, piloting solo—I've been thinking about how weird that was. You know, if G'Kar was willing to risk a space walk and had an accomplice to open an air-lock for him, he could've put the ship on autopilot and gotten off before it left. But why would G'Kar stage his own death? The data crystal was real, wasn't it?''

"This is too crazy," muttered Garibaldi, rubbing his eyes. "But a man who fears for his life will do crazy things. You know, it seemed awfully easy the way I found that crystal, like he wanted me to find it."

Before Garibaldi could say more, the hatch opened and Captain Vin'Tok strode into the transport section. He was smiling like a cultured host, but the chief wondered what secrets he was hiding in that oversized, spotted cranium. *Calm down,* Garibaldi told himself; he already knew not to base suppositions on anything Londo said. Just because a couple of people quoted a famous North American author didn't mean anything—it was probably a coincidence. Al Vernon's use of that quote was reasonable considering somebody had just accused him of being dead when he was clearly alive.

That brought up even more questions, such as, could they really trust Al Vernon? What were the mysterious conditions under which *he* left Homeworld and was reported dead? For that matter, what the hell were they doing on this Narn ship? Garibaldi looked down at Al Vernon and Na'Toth, still chatting as if they were old friends at a cocktail party.

"We have a flight of forty-four hours until reaching Homeworld," explained Captain Vin'Tok. "With our full complement of thirty, we don't have a lot of spare cabins on the *K'sha Na'vas,* but we have done our best to make your stay comfortable. If you will come with me, please."

The captain tapped a panel button, and a whoosh of hydraulics sounded as their restraints lifted automatically. Garibaldi helped Ivanova to her feet, and the commander still looked stunned by her suspicions.

"Don't say anything about it for now," he whispered.

Al Vernon waved to them. "Didn't I tell you that Narn ships were the best? How did you like that entry into hyperspace? Smooth, eh?"

"Very impressive," said Garibaldi, striding down the aisle with a big smile on his face. "In fact, I'd love to have a tour of the ship."

"Me, too!" seconded Al.

Na'Toth cast a disgusted look at the two humans. "This isn't a pleasure craft. The next thing you'll be wanting is a swimming pool."

Garibaldi glanced back at Ivanova. "On good advice, I did bring my speedo."

Vin'Tok cleared his throat. "A tour is not out of the question. We only have three decks, and we have to pass through all of them to get to the quarters. As you can see, we put a troop transport here on the top deck by the outer hatch, allowing armed troops to exit first. Outside this hatch is an access tube, and you'll have to use the ladder. The gravity effect can be tricky on a ladder, so watch your step."

They followed the captain into the access tube, only to see him grasp the handrail of the ladder and leap down through a hatch in the deck, landing smartly on the top rung. Al Vernon rushed to take the position behind the captain, bombarding him with questions. Ivanova climbed down after them, her lithe body moving gracefully in the lighter than normal gravity. Garibaldi hung back, hoping to grab the rear position, but Na'Toth stood firm.

"You go first," the Narn insisted.

"Whatever you say," said Garibaldi, grabbing the handrail and dropping through the hole in the deck. He wondered if he dared to trust the Narn attaché with their suspicions about G'Kar. They had no proof, just a literary allusion from a Centauri troublemaker. But they had no body either. No, he decided, Na'Toth wouldn't give much credence to anything Londo said, and neither should he. He had to convince himself that G'Kar was still alive before he could try to convince anyone else.

If such a thing could be true, did the Narns on the *K'sha Na'vas* know about it? And where *was* G'Kar?

They climbed down the ladder and stepped off onto a cramped and darkened bridge, illuminated only by lights from monitors and instrument panels. A reddish glow permeated everything, including the six stoic crew members at their various stations. Their reddish eyes gleamed at the passengers for a split second, then turned back to their monitors. Garibaldi could see Ivanova peering over the shoulder of the helmsman, trying to make sense of the orange figures that danced across his screen.

"The bridge," said Vin'Tok simply. He motioned to a set of interlocking, plated doors behind them. "Through those doors are weaponry and engineering. For efficiency, all command stations are on one deck."

"Wouldn't that make them easy to take out?" asked Ivanova.

"No," answered Vin'Tok. "We are shielded by upper and lower decks. The bridge, weaponry, and engineering are in separate modules, each with its own power and life support. The bridge can be totally sealed off from the rest of the ship."

"Great design!" said Al Vernon. "I have always admired Narn workmanship and planning."

Vin'Tok nodded at the compliment. "We have learned much in a short time." He motioned back down the ladder. "Right this way, please, to the crew quarters, mess hall, and latrines."

This time, Garibaldi accepted his place in line, descending after Ivanova, with Na'Toth above him. He was beginning to feel trapped in the confines of the small craft, as if there were no place to go. In truth, there was no place to go. He realized why he preferred cities in space to tin cans in space.

The ladder came to an end on a bare deck in the intersection of two corridors, leaving them with a choice of four directions to travel. In one direction, the smell of meaty food and the presence of large metallic doors made it clear which corridor led to the mess hall. Another walkway was marked with the universal symbols for sanitary facilities, and there were Narn crew members loitering farther down. The other two corridors were lined with small hatchways, apparently leading to the cabins.

The captain explained, "Our cabins are designed for two crew members, so we hope you won't mind sharing. We have divided you according to sex, with women in one cabin and men in another, but we can change that arrangement to suit your needs."

"It is acceptable," said Na'Toth at the same time that Ivanova answered, "That's fine."

Garibaldi looked glumly at Al and said, "Hi, roomie."

"Don't worry, I'm a heavy sleeper," grinned Al. "Once my head hits the pillow, I'm out."

Garibaldi pretended to listen as the captain described the mess schedule, but he was really trying to figure out how he could avoid going directly to his cabin. He wanted to take a look around first—on his own.

"Excuse me, I have to use the facilities," said Garibaldi, striding down the corridor that led to the latrines. No one came after him, he noticed with relief, and he slipped inside the automatic doors. Garibaldi leaned against the bulkhead for a moment, thinking that he would simply walk out and make a wrong turn. That might buy him a few minutes of unimpeded exploration.

He got a whiff of a strong antiseptic odor that almost made him gag. He glanced at the facilities, which were encased in a gleaming, copperlike metal; salmon-colored lighting added to the rosy effect. The commodes were recessed into the wall to form a suction with the air system and allow use during weightlessness. To Garibaldi, they looked like medieval torture devices.

Thinking that he had given himself enough time, the chief walked out the door and turned left instead of right, strolling along the corridor like an absentminded tourist. Although Captain Vin'Tok didn't come after him, he quickly realized that this would be a short walk, because the two Narns he had spotted at the end of the corridor were not loiterers but armed guards. As he walked toward them, they hefted their PPG rifles in a manner that could not be called friendly.

Beyond them there was a small hatchway. Garibaldi could only conclude they were guarding it. Why? Since there was no one on the ship but the regular crew and the four passengers, he had to assume they were guarding it from the passengers. Blithely, he stuck his hands in his pockets and ambled toward the guards.

"Halt!" one of them shouted, pointing the business end of his PPG at Garibaldi's chest.

"Whoa there!" said the human with a friendly smile. "I just took a wrong turn. Where is Captain Vin'Tok?"

The Narn guard used his rifle to point the other way down the short corridor.

"Gotcha." Then Garibaldi asked innocently, "Where does that door go?"

"The hold. It does not concern you."

"Garibaldi!" called a disapproving voice from the other end of the corridor. The human turned to see Na'Toth glaring at him.

He waved to the dour guards and rejoined his fellow passengers at the intersection of the corridors. "What were you doing?" asked Na'Toth with suspicion.

"Going to the bathroom. Then I turned the wrong way, I guess." He smiled at Captain Vin'Tok. "Keeping something valuable in the hold, are you?"

The captain's eyes narrowed, and the veins on his naked cranium pulsed slightly. "We regret the need for guards, but we were on a delicate mission when we were rerouted. You understand, I'm sure."

"Oh, yeah," agreed Garibaldi. "I'm sorry, what did I miss?"

"I was explaining the mess schedule," said the captain. "I also apologized for not being able to offer you any recreational facilities."

"That's all right," said Garibaldi pleasantly. "I don't think we'll be bored."

"I can tell him the schedule," Al Vernon offered.

The captain continued, "Your cabins are the two at the end of the corridor, across from each other. Women are on the starboard side. The cabins are unlocked—just touch the panel. Your luggage has already been placed there. Now if you will excuse me, I must check our course."

Once again Na'Toth demonstrated how to be a good passenger as she set off at a brisk walk toward the women's cabin. Garibaldi fell into step alongside Ivanova but, unfortunately, so did Al Vernon.

"Dinner is in two hours," Al said cheerfully.

Garibaldi looked pointedly at Ivanova, making it clear that he had something he wanted to talk about. But how could he, without bringing Na'Toth, Al, or both of them into his confidence? Ivanova was sleeping in the same cabin as Na'Toth, and Al was sleeping in his cabin.

"After I change into my sweats, I'm going to do my isometric exercises here in the corridor," Ivanova said.

Garibaldi nodded. "See you later."

"We'll be seeing a lot of each other," said Al, making it sound like a threat.

Garibaldi glanced at his chubby companion, wondering if he had been wrong to bring the stranger on this trip. But Al seemed to know how to insinuate himself into the

Narns' good graces, and that was a useful thing to learn. Besides, they had a daunting task ahead of them—trying to negotiate a strange planet filled with stubborn Narns. How could they be any worse off with Al along?

The chubby human pressed the panel, and the door slid open. "After you!"

# CHAPTER 8

Captain Sheridan looked at the elderly Narn sitting before him in one of B5's detention cells. Pa'Nar managed to look defiant and guilty at the same time. Lou Welch stood nearby, slapping a billy club against his palm with loud whacks. Sheridan would never allow a prisoner to be beaten, but maybe the Narn didn't know that. At any rate, nothing else they had said or done had had any effect on the prisoner. He had adamantly refused to say anything, other than his name and his story about going broke.

"Listen," said Sheridan sternly, "you might as well make this easy on yourself. We know you were involved in an attack on one of our security officers. Why don't you tell us why? What were you trying to hide?"

The Narn glared at the humans. "Do your worst to me."

Lou Welch moved toward him threateningly. "He's asking for it, Captain. Let me treat him the same way he treated our guy."

Sheridan waved Welch back. "I'd rather not. I think Pa'Nar will realize that he could spend an awfully long time in an Earth prison if he doesn't cooperate."

The Narn smiled. "You mean, you have something worse than Down Below? I am well accustomed to hardship."

Welch glared at him. "Where is your accomplice?"

Pa'Nar shrugged. "I don't know who you're talking about."

"Ha'Mok," answered Welch. "What happened to him?"

The Narn crossed his arms defiantly. Captain Sheridan

was about to give up and stick the elderly Narn in a holding cell until Leffler was well enough to identify him, when a security officer appeared at the window.

"Ms. Winters is here," said his amplified voice.

"Show her in," ordered Sheridan.

Pa'Nar looked a bit ill at ease as the attractive telepath was escorted into the holding cell. She gazed thoughtfully at the Narn and said, "I don't suppose he's told you anything."

"Nothing," answered Sheridan. "Do you think you can scan him?"

"I could try," she answered, "but I haven't had much success with Narns in the past." She began to remove the glove from her right hand. "When I start, would you ask him questions to focus his mind?"

Welch grabbed the Narn's arm and pinned it to the armrest of his chair. He struggled a bit, but the burly security officer was much stronger than the elderly Narn. The telepath touched Pa'Nar's hand and instantly recoiled, as if receiving an electric shock. But she bravely resumed the contact, although she swayed uncertainly on her feet.

"Why did you attack the officer?" asked Sheridan.

The Narn flinched and tried to remove his hand, but Welch held it firmly. "Where is Ha'Mok?" demanded the captain.

"Leave me alone!" the Narn growled.

"Does this have anything to do with G'Kar?" asked Sheridan.

With that question, Talia's back stiffened, and a grimace distorted her lovely face. She yanked her hand away from the Narn's wrist.

"Are you all right?" asked Sheridan.

"Yes," she said, rubbing her forehead. "This definitely has something to do with G'Kar. In fact, he thought of G'Kar with every question you asked. I wouldn't want to swear to it, but I have a feeling that he thinks G'Kar is alive.''

"Bah!" scoffed the Narn. "This woman is crazy."

Sheridan studied Pa'Nar. In an hour of questioning, that was the only charge he had bothered to refute. "All right," said the captain, "it's time to contact the Narn Council, the Kha'Ri."

"No!" snapped Pa'Nar. "If you do that, you will put lives in danger."

"Whose lives?" Sheridan demanded.

The Narn crossed his arms and closed his eyes, apparently done talking.

Sheridan's lips thinned with anger. "Keep him locked up in here until we get Ivanova and Garibaldi back safely. No visitors, no legal counsel, no nothing."

"Yes, sir," answered Lou Welch, slapping the billy club into his palm.

In the corridor outside her cabin aboard the *K'sha Na'vas*, Ivanova did some stretching exercises to limber up. Then she put her hands against the bulkhead and pushed with both arms until she could feel the muscles stiffening along her back and shoulders. Under her sweat suit, she could feel the perspiration starting to flow.

The door across from her whooshed open, and Garibaldi stepped out. He whispered, "Al is asleep. He wasn't kidding about his head hitting the pillow." The security chief glanced down the corridor. "I'd like to see what's in that hold."

Ivanova put her right foot against the bulkhead and flexed her leg. "We don't want to start an incident. Let's just get through this ordeal and stop thinking that G'Kar is alive. Two quotes from Mark Twain don't make much difference against a *Shon'Kar* and a plasma explosion."

The door across the hall slid open, and Na'Toth stepped

out. Ivanova kept exercising, and Garibaldi did a few half-hearted jumping jacks.

The Narn glared at them. "You two have disappointed me. I thought I knew you, but since you came aboard you have acted like prisoners trying to escape from a jail. Have you no sense of decorum? You have undertaken this journey to honor G'Kar, not to indulge in petty suspicions and plots."

Garibaldi looked at Na'Toth for a moment, then turned back to Ivanova. "I'm going to tell her."

"Go ahead," said Ivanova, who stopped her exercises to watch the attaché's reaction.

Garibaldi lowered his voice to say, "We suspect that G'Kar isn't dead—that he faked his death."

Na'Toth recoiled as if she had seen the Narn equivalent of a ghost. "You are jesting."

"I don't jest about stuff like that," Garibaldi answered. "I'm not going to tell you that we have any proof, and I'm not going to tell you who tipped us off—but I am going to tell you that they're hiding something on this ship. And you know that as well as I do."

A Narn crew member entered the corridor at the intersection and glanced suspiciously at the gathering at the other end. Ivanova bent over and touched her toes, and Garibaldi laughed at nothing. The crew member found his cabin and ducked inside.

Na'Toth looked back at her human companions. "Why would G'Kar fake his death?"

"Maybe because people have been trying to kill him," said Ivanova. "You didn't tell us about the first attempt, and he didn't tell you about the second attempt. And now it's turned into a full-blooded *Shon'Kar*."

Na'Toth glanced down the deserted corridor. "Yes, the *Shon'Kar* is a serious threat. Do you think G'Kar is alive and aboard this ship?"

"Look at it this way," Garibaldi answered, "his personal transport explodes, leaving no body. Mi'Ra's data crystal is left conveniently on his desk. The *K'sha Na'vas* happens to be in the neighborhood, less than twenty-four hours away. And no one can explain why G'Kar returned to Homeworld, or why he chose to go alone."

Ivanova frowned and lowered her voice. "Everything happened so fast, we didn't have time to think about that on the station, but now we do. Would his mind work like that, faking his death to deal with the Blood Oath?"

Na'Toth narrowed her red, reptilian eyes. "Yes, I could see him reaching that conclusion . . ."

Garibaldi motioned toward the intersection of the corridors. "There are two guys down there, guarding the hold. Do you think you could find out what's in it? Maybe ask around."

"I believe in the direct approach." Na'Toth turned on her heel and strode down the corridor. Ivanova and Garibaldi ran to keep up with the muscular Narn as she turned the corner and strode toward the guards. Ivanova stopped at the intersection, motioned Garibaldi back, then peered around the corner to see what was happening.

The guards were apparently not threatened by Na'Toth's approach. Their PPG rifles remained pointed at the deck as they ambled forward to meet her. She waved pleasantly and stopped to engage them in conversation. It appeared as if she asked for something, because one of them rested his weapon on his forearm as he searched his pockets. The other one laughed loudly at something she said. While one guard was laughing and the other one was searching, she lashed out with a wicked jab that caught the guard's laughter in the throat. The rifle tumbled from his hands, and she grabbed it in midair, swinging the butt around to catch the other one in the mouth.

By the time Ivanova and Garibaldi ran down the corridor

to help, Na'Toth had knocked both guards to the deck. There wasn't anything left to do but grab them and hold them there before they could sound an alarm. While Ivanova and Garibaldi wrestled with the guards, Na'Toth secured both weapons and leveled them at her fellow Narns.

"You don't know what you're doing!" insisted a guard.

"I think I do," she replied calmly. "Commander, check the hold."

Ivanova leaped to her feet and pressed the outer panel to open the hatch. The door slid open, revealing a cramped access tube and a ladder descending into darkness. The commander had a feeling that she only had a few seconds, so she swung down onto the ladder and proceeded to jump from rung to rung. She landed in a darkened room with a low ceiling and a few sticks of furniture. The only light came from a handful of candles.

"Who's there?" called a startled voice. It was a voice she recognized.

The Narn sat up in his bed and stared at her, his red eyes glowing as brightly as the candles in the room. "Oh, it's you."

"You're looking well," said Ivanova, "for a dead man."

Above them came the sound of angry voices and a struggle. G'Kar rose to his feet and bellowed, "It's all right! I am coming up! Don't harm them."

He looked at Ivanova. "I have meditated about what to do. I am glad you decided for me."

G'Kar grabbed the ladder and started climbing upward. Ivanova scrambled after him, and she reached the upper deck just in time to see him step into the corridor and confront Garibaldi, Na'Toth, Captain Vin'Tok, and half-a-dozen armed crew members. Without so much as a hello, Na'Toth stepped forward and punched the ambassador in the stomach.

He doubled over, and spittle drooled from his mouth.

Two crew members grabbed Na'Toth, but G'Kar waved them off and croaked, "Leave her be. I deserved that."

"You certainly did!" said Na'Toth. "I have never heard of an action so despicable. So cowardly!"

"Is it cowardly to want to live?" he asked, still gripping his stomach. "Would you like to go through life always looking over your shoulder? Wondering when the next murder attempt will come? Wondering if it will be the last?"

He looked at Captain Vin'Tok and his crew. "Leave us now, Captain. You have fulfilled your debt to me. I should have known that I could not fool these people—they know me too well."

"Are you certain?" asked Vin'Tok.

"Yes," said G'Kar. "I will explain to them how I involved you on short notice, as a debt of honor."

The captain motioned to his crew, and they followed him to the intersection and up the ladder.

Garibaldi crossed his arms. "G'Kar, you've got a lot of explaining to do. First of all, was that data crystal real?"

"Absolutely. That's what drove me to these desperate measures. That, and the dreams I have of the last murder attempt."

He turned to Na'Toth. "Even you do not know about that one. It occurred when I returned to Homeworld to speak at the university. I was ambushed by hired assassins and nearly killed. I hushed it up, for obvious reasons." G'Kar narrowed his eyes at her.

"It is all right," said Na'Toth. "They know. When Mr. Garibaldi found the data crystal, I had to explain to them about the Du'Rog family."

"Everything?"

"Yes," said Ivanova, "including the way you falsely accused Du'Rog of selling arms to your enemies. You destroyed a whole family just to do a little social climbing."

G'Kar lifted his chin, and the old arrogance returned.

"Seceding to the Third Circle is more than a little social climbing. But that is in the past, and there is nothing I can do to change it. Believe me, I have suffered for my actions. I thought Du'Rog would be temporarily disgraced—I never dreamt he would be thrown off the Council and his family stripped of their wealth and rank. When Du'Rog sent the first assassin, Na'Toth saved me. I thought that was the end of it, not the beginning of something worse."

Ivanova shook her head in amazement. "How on Earth did you expect to pull this off? How were you going to come back from the dead? Say it was all a dream?"

G'Kar scoffed. "That was the simplest part of my plan. I would be found in an escape pod, a survivor after all. These things happen in the vastness of space—people are found alive after being presumed dead. As long as I return to the living before the official period of mourning is over, I can reclaim my ambassadorship, my holdings, everything. You were the only witnesses to the explosion—everyone else heard about it secondhand. I assumed they would believe my story, and that you would be glad to have me back."

"You assume too much," said Garibaldi. "So let's get this ship turned around and get back to B5."

"No." G'Kar shook his head firmly. "The danger is still real. Mi'Ra, T'Kog, Ka'Het—these people have vowed to kill me! They have given up on assassins and have pledged to kill me with their own hands." He turned to Na'Toth. "Did you explain to them about the *Shon'Kar*?"

"I tried, but they had a difficult time understanding, especially Captain Sheridan. What were you going to do? Kill them yourself, or have me kill them?"

G'Kar stiffened his broad shoulders. "It is still my duty to attend to this problem. I am sorry you were involved, but you have been ordered to appear before the Kha'Ri, and you must do so. I hope that will give me enough time."

"No," said Ivanova. "We may not have any legal

ground to stand on, but we're not going to stand by and watch you or anyone else commit murder. Isn't there some other way you can mend things with these people?''

G'Kar scowled and shook his fists at the ceiling, as if he were dealing with children. ''Why don't you *meet* the Du'Rog family, and then you can tell me how to deal with them. As far as Mi'Ra is concerned, I think a blade to the throat is the only option, but I am willing to be talked out of it.''

Na'Toth shook his head. ''The danger to his life is very real. If we do nothing, they will come to the station and try to fulfill the *Shon'Kar.*''

''All right,'' said Ivanova, ''I am willing to meet with them, unofficially, and warn them against ever coming to the station to cause trouble. I think that's about all we can do.'' She looked at G'Kar. ''But you have to agree to come back to life.''

''Of course,'' said the ambassador. ''Do you think I want to remain a nonentity? I would prefer that we wait until our return to Babylon 5, so that I can be discovered alive in the escape pod. While I'm on Homeworld, I will wear a disguise.''

Garibaldi laughed. ''A disguise? Give me a break.''

''It fooled you.''

''What?'' said Garibaldi.

''Yes, I passed you this morning in Down Below. I was wearing the crude robe of an acolyte of the Eighth Circle. You looked right at me.''

''I'll be damned. That was *you*?''

''None other.''

Ivanova shook her head. ''The whole purpose of this trip is to meet with your Council. We're not going to lie to them about you being dead.''

''Please,'' said G'Kar, ''don't lie to them, but don't tell them that I accompanied you on this ship. If you want to say you have new evidence that I may be alive, so be it, but give me a chance to move freely. Give me at least a day.''

She gazed at him. "Will you try to kill her?"

"Not if you are with me," the Narn promised.

"Wait a minute," said Garibaldi. "There was an attack on one of my men in Down Below. Did you have something to do with that?"

"I have a disguise," insisted G'Kar, "complete with identicard. Why should I need to attack anyone?"

They heard a sound, and they turned around to see a crew member drop off the ladder into the intersection. He glanced suspiciously at them for a moment, then went down another corridor.

"There are dangers other than the Du'Rog family," said G'Kar in a low voice. "The Du'Rog family may be the most vocal of my enemies, but they are not the only ones. I thought being dead would give me freedom, but instead it has made me a prisoner."

"Yeah," said Garibaldi, "it's not much of a crime to kill a man who is already dead."

The Narn started back into the hatch, then turned around. "I will not see you again until we reach Homeworld. Believe me when I say that it means a great deal to have you here, willing to help me."

"We're not promising anything," said Ivanova. "There may be nothing we can do."

G'Kar smiled. "At least I am not facing them alone." He ducked through the hatch and slammed it shut behind him.

Dinner that night in the Narn mess hall consisted of some rather evil-smelling meat simmering in a greasy gruel. The Narns used their fingers to eat, shoveling the food directly from their bowls into their mouths, but they gave their guests some tarnished spoons. Garibaldi sampled some of the gruel and pushed the meat around in his bowl, while Al Vernon dug in and ate with considerable gusto. The merchant even used his fingers to eat in the Narn fashion. Ivanova drank a lot of coffee and smiled a lot, but didn't eat much. The humans were seated at a table with Na'Toth, Captain Vin'Tok, his first mate, Yal'Tar, and the military attaché, Tza'Gur.

"Delicious *lukrol*!" Al Vernon announced, licking his fingers. "My compliments to your cook. Oh, I have missed Narn cooking—the pungent spices, the zesty meats, the crunchy grains—it is truly the tastiest food in the galaxy."

Captain Vin'Tok beamed. "We have *mitlop* for dessert."

Al clapped his hands. "*Mitlop!* How wonderful! Made from fresh tripe?"

"Of course," answered the captain.

The merchant slapped his palms on the table. "Captain, can't we add an extra day or two onto our journey?"

Vin'Tok chuckled. "I'm afraid not. You have a memorial service to attend."

Thus far, noted Garibaldi, nobody had mentioned the fact that G'Kar was actually alive and well in the hold of the ship. He didn't know how many of the Narns knew about it, but he suspected that all of them did. It was as if G'Kar had come down with some terrible illness that nobody could bring themselves to discuss. Of course, Al Vernon didn't know G'Kar was alive, but he was probably the only one on the entire cruiser.

"Tripe for dessert?" asked Ivanova doubtfully.

"Sure," said Al. "You have to marinate it in *pakoberry* juice overnight. At least, that is the traditional method. It's tasty and pleasantly chewy."

Ivanova gulped. "You know, traveling always takes away my appetite."

"Not mine," said Al, going after another handful of *lukrol*.

Garibaldi thought it was time to broach a subject he'd been wondering about. "Captain Vin'Tok," he asked, "are you planning to wait for us, then take us back to Babylon 5?"

The Narn fixed him with a meaningful gaze. "The *K'sha Na'vas* is at your disposal for as long as you need her. We will remain in orbit, while a shuttlecraft will meet us and take you to the surface."

"Okay," said Garibaldi, feeling a bit better about things. He didn't want to be stuck on the Narn planet for weeks, waiting to find a public transport headed to B5. On the other hand, he knew that Vin'Tok owed his allegiance to G'Kar and the Narn Regime, not Earthforce. If they wanted to leave and G'Kar wanted to stay, they could be stuck.

Garibaldi rubbed his eyes, wondering how he had managed to get sucked into this situation. Preventing a murder, especially that of one of B5's ambassadors, was a noble goal, but how much hope did they have? The Narns themselves were oblivious to murder when a Blood Oath was involved, so maybe this was an exercise in futility. What would the Du'Rog family do when they found out they had been duped and G'Kar was still alive? For that matter, what would Captain Sheridan do? They wouldn't be able to contact the captain until they came out of jump.

He looked up to find Na'Toth studying him. "Mr. Garibaldi, you haven't eaten much."

"I don't think I feel too well," he answered, holding his stomach. He looked at Captain Vin'Tok. "May I be excused?"

"Certainly, Mr. Garibaldi. I understand. It's been a stressful time."

"No kidding," said the chief, rising to his feet. "I'll see you later."

"May I have your *mitlop*?" asked Al Vernon cheerfully.

"Sure, Al, knock yourself out."

Garibaldi nodded to the crew members in the mess hall and shuffled out. As the crew quarters were on the same deck, it was a short walk to his cabin, but he still had to pass the corridor that led to the hold. The guards were back on duty, and they gazed resentfully at him, perhaps because he had already had dinner and they hadn't. Or maybe they knew their watch was pointless, because the secret was out. At any rate, he saluted them and wandered on to his room.

The security chief was lounging in the upper bunk of the cramped cabin, almost asleep, when his roommate came home. Al announced his presence with a large burp, then began to rummage around in his luggage.

"Are you awake, Garibaldi?" he asked.

"Yeah. How was the *mitlop*?"

"Actually, not as good as they serve on Homeworld, but what can you expect from a galley cook? I didn't tell the captain that, of course."

"Of course," said Garibaldi. He leaned on his elbow and looked over the edge of his bunk. "What are you looking for?"

"We still have thirty-some hours to travel, don't we? As a rule, Narns only eat twice a day, so we have to have something to pass the time. Ah, here it is!"

He produced a small cardboard box. "My deck of cards. What's your game? Gin rummy? Bridge? Naw, you look like a poker player to me. I'm afraid I haven't got enough money to do much gambling, but maybe the Narns have some matchsticks."

Garibaldi frowned at his colorful companion. "I'm not going to regret bringing you along on this joyride, am I?"

Al grew thoughtful for a moment. "I have to be true to myself, Mr. Garibaldi. The Narns have a saying—'you can only run so far from yourself.' I've always thought that was a way of saying that we have to face up to the consequences of our actions."

"What consequences do you have to face?" asked Garibaldi.

The portly man smiled and held up the deck of cards. "Shall we start with gin rummy?"

# CHAPTER 9

The Narn shuttlecraft plunged through the atmosphere of Homeworld, heating up the cabin only a bit but causing a glorious light show outside the small porthole windows. Garibaldi leaned forward to get a better look. Despite an entire career spent on hostile planets and space stations, he was still a tourist when it came to space travel. He still gawked while Al Vernon, for instance, snoozed noisily across the aisle from him.

The shuttlecraft sat eight passengers in two rows of single seats with an aisle between them, so everyone sat alone. There were only the four of them, and Ivanova and Na'Toth sat in the front row, conversing in low tones. They were probably discussing how they should behave at the memorial service when they knew perfectly well that the deceased wasn't deceased. He guessed they would spend a lot of time looking grim and nodding somberly.

True to G'Kar's word, they hadn't seen him since their first day on the Narn vessel. The chief hoped that G'Kar had enough sense to stay on the *K'sha Na'vas* and not go looking for trouble on Homeworld, even with his disguise. Garibaldi rubbed his hands nervously. This was only a day trip, he reminded himself, to attend the service, answer questions, and head back to the *K'sha Na'vas* for the night. Still, it felt funny to be descending upon an alien planet, unarmed.

Suddenly, the flames outside the porthole vanished, and the shuttlecraft banked toward the surface, affording Garibaldi his first view of the Narn Homeworld. There wasn't a cloud anywhere in sight, and the sky had a washed-out color, not the vibrant blue of Earth's sky. He wondered whether that had anything to do with the giant red sun that anchored the solar system.

The terrain that he could see had a rose-copper color, like the Black Hills gold his mother used to collect. He could see mountains, giant canyons, landing strips, and occasional patches and circles of green that he assumed were crops. As they swooped lower, he could make out grids of rectangular buildings and covered domes; smoke spewed into the air from what might have been a power plant or a smelter. Numerous low-flying aircraft dotted the sky.

Homeworld wasn't quite as barren as Mars, but it was hardly a flowering paradise. This was only one part of the planet, he told himself, but he knew Homeworld had very few bodies of water. Polar icecaps and underground streams supplied what little water the Narns needed. It wasn't like flying down to Earth, when all you could see were shimmering horizons of blue liquid. Garibaldi also reminded himself that the land had been stripped bare by the Centauri. They had withdrawn only after a war of attrition, when the Narn resistance had begun to cost them more than they were getting from the depleted resources and slave labor.

The shuttlecraft banked again and took a dive that left his stomach in flux. Al Vernon blinked awake beside him. "Are we there yet?" he muttered.

"I don't know," answered Garibaldi. "I don't know where we're going."

"Hekba City is quite a lovely place," said the merchant. "I believe it was G'Kar's hometown, although it's also one of the most hospitable cities for humans. You know, the temperatures on Homeworld can fluctuate wildly in the course of a single day."

Garibaldi lifted the heavy coat from his lap. "I know. But why should Hekba City be better than anyplace else?"

Al smiled. "You'll see. By the way, since you owe me five hundred thousand matchsticks, I expect you to buy me lunch."

"I think those cards of yours were marked," grumbled Garibaldi. Nevertheless, he owed Al something for making the days aboard the *K'sha Na'vas* pass fairly swiftly.

He stared out the porthole and could see that they were circling an immense canyon, and he feared for a moment that they were going to try to land inside it. At the last moment, the pilot veered toward a landing strip that skirted the rim, and he made a perfect three-point landing in the tiny craft.

"Hekba City," came a flat voice over the ship's intercom, "on the rim of Hekba Canyon."

"Is this shuttlecraft going to wait for us?" asked Garibaldi of no one in particular.

"No," answered Na'Toth. She showed him a small handheld device. "I have the codes to summon another one."

The hatch opened with a clank, and a blast of scorching air flooded the cabin. Within milliseconds, Garibaldi was bathed in sweat, and his lungs felt as if they were on fire. He groaned out loud.

Ivanova rose slowly to her feet and stretched her arms. "Time to change into your speedo," she told Garibaldi.

"No kidding," he muttered. "Feels like a Swedish sauna."

"On the contrary," said Al Vernon, "this is quite pleasant." The portly man was dripping in sweat, but then he was always dripping in sweat. "Make sure you drink fluids whenever you have the chance."

Na'Toth was the first out of the craft, followed by Al Vernon, who seemed to be in an exuberant mood. Ivanova and Garibaldi staggered out after them. If the heat didn't take their breath away, the sight that greeted their eyes certainly did. A vast canyon yawned before them, and its walls were lined with a honeycomb of dwellings carved directly into the cliff. Some were the copper color of the rock, but most were painted in muted shades of red and rust. Garibaldi inched toward the rim of the canyon, but he couldn't see either the bottom or the end of the buildings.

"They go all the way to the bottom," said Na'Toth, as if reading his mind. "Our reptilian ancestors clung to the rocks, and so do we. At the bottom of Hekba Canyon is some of the most fertile farmland on the planet, with numerous hot pools and geysers."

"I doubt if I'll be going all the way to the bottom," said Garibaldi with a gulp.

Al Vernon chuckled. "You will want to go down there, once the cooling starts on the surface."

Garibaldi splashed the sweat from his brow. "The cooling can start anytime, as far as I'm concerned."

"Come," said Na'Toth, leading the way toward a rock staircase with a wrought-iron railing. Al waddled eagerly after her, leaving Garibaldi and Ivanova to bring up the rear. Behind them, the shuttlecraft roared away, giving the security chief an uneasy feeling of being deserted.

Ivanova raised an eyebrow. "It's a nice place to visit, but I wouldn't want to live here."

"I'm not even sure it's a nice place to visit," said Garibaldi, gazing up at the blazing red sun.

He had to admit, though, that Hekba City was fascinating. The Narns apparently didn't mind living like termites on a tree trunk, because people swarmed along the narrow walkways and the death-defying bridges that spanned the crevasse. The Narns glanced curiously at the humans whenever they passed them in close proximity, but Garibaldi saw a number of other off-worlders in the city, including several Drazi. As on Babylon 5, the Drazi appeared to be a worker class.

Na'Toth stopped to study some markings carved into the cliff face. "The sanctuary is on this side of the canyon," she said.

Garibaldi glanced at one of the swaying bridges. "Good."

In due course, they reached what seemed to be an older section of the city, formed of natural caves and indentations in the rock, with facades added later to afford privacy. In the yawning mouth of one of the caves, they saw a clutch of people who were milling about, waiting, making strained small talk. As the Terran delegation approached, Na'Toth put her fist to her chest in the Narn salute, and Al Vernon did likewise.

An elderly Narn in a crimson robe stepped forward to meet them. He bowed formally. "We welcome our friends from Earth, friends of G'Kar."

"It is our honor," said Al Vernon with a bow. "You are Y'Tok of the Second Circle."

"Yes," said the Narn with surprise. "Have we met?"

"I saw you give the convocation at the Blood of the Martyrs Ceremony," explained Al. "That was many years ago, but I have never forgotten it. Al Vernon is my name."

Y'Tok nodded, clearly impressed by the human's memory and knowledge of Narn affairs.

Na'Toth broke in, "Holy One, this is Commander Susan Ivanova of Earthforce, and Michael Garibaldi, Chief of Security on Babylon 5."

"We are honored that you chose to bring us here," said Ivanova.

"We did not honor G'Kar enough when he was alive," replied the priest. "It is our duty to honor him now that he is gone. We have a few moments—permit me to show you the sanctuary."

Y'Tok led them into the wide fissure in the rock, and Garibaldi was surprised to find that it widened even more into a natural cathedral complete with stalactites and stalagmites. The air felt several degrees cooler inside, which was a welcome relief. For a holy place, the sanctuary was remarkably austere, with only a few weathered stone benches for furnishings and smoky torches for light.

"This is one of the oldest sites of our civilization," explained Y'Tok, his voice echoing in the chamber. "Our ancestors lived in this cave tens of thousands of years ago. But it only became a sanctuary during the Centauri invasion, when freedom fighters held out here for one thousand days—before starving to death. All such places where the Martyrs sought sanctuary have been given the status of holy sites."

"Even the Centauri revere this place," said Al Vernon. "They call it the Vase of Tears because of all the lives they lost here."

Na'Toth looked askance at the human. "I didn't know you were a Centauri scholar as well."

"I am well traveled, nothing more," answered Al.

A young Narn in a crimson robe came running up to Y'Tok. "Holy One, Mistresses Ra'Pak and Da'Kal are here."

Y'Tok nodded in acknowledgment, then turned to his guests. "One more thing—I have been instructed to tell you that a committee from the Kha'Ri will meet with you in two days' time."

"Two days' time?" asked Garibaldi. "What's the matter with right now?" The priest glared at him. "I mean, after this?"

The old Narn held up two fingers. "You will be our guests for two more days. Is it so bad?"

"That's fine," said Ivanova with a game smile.

The priest nodded and strode through the crowd, somberly greeting everyone he met. When the aged Narn was out of earshot, Ivanova turned to Na'Toth. "Who are Ra'Pak and Da'Kal?"

The Narn woman lifted her chin. "Ra'Pak is a member of the Inner Circle. It is a mark of considerable respect for G'Kar that she is present. Da'Kal is . . ." She hesitated. "Da'Kal is G'Kar's widow."

"Hmmm," murmured Garibaldi. He couldn't say anything more because Al Vernon was standing a meter away, listening intently to their conversation. He wondered if Da'Kal knew the truth about her late, lamented husband.

Mourners began to filter into the dingy recesses of the cave, filling every corner and even the spaces between the somber stalactites. In fact, the columns of calcified minerals seemed like especially respectful mourners, ghostlike aliens from eons long forgotten. Despite the crowd, it was cool and quiet inside the sanctuary, and Garibaldi began to feel an odd kind of peace. He wasn't much given to religion or sentimentality, but he could almost feel the presence of the long-departed Martyrs, granting their approval to this solemn occasion.

His reverie was short-lived, however, as acolytes in crude robes began to move around the cavern, sprinkling pungent incense on the torches. The young Narn in the crimson robe began to bang on a copper gong, and the chamber resonated with the metallic tone. Then the procession began.

In the lead came Y'Tok in his flowing robe, and he was holding a bronze circle that was so old it was discolored with green and white spots. Very quietly he tapped the circle with a metal stick, and it provided an odd counterpoint to the loud gong. Behind Y'Tok came a plain-looking Narn woman who was bare-breasted and wearing rags. In fact, she kept ripping away at her clothes as if they offended her. Garibaldi felt embarrassed, but he couldn't bring himself to turn away from the sight of the distraught woman. He knew without being told that she was the widow, Da'Kal.

Behind the widow walked a regal woman with an attendant holding her black robe off the dusty floor of the cave. That must be the Narn royalty, thought Garibaldi, Ra'Pak of the Inner Circle. Following her came several members of the Narn military, distinguished by chests full of jeweled medals. The procession circled the immense cavern, passing within a meter of the humans. Garibaldi felt himself getting angry at G'Kar—that ingrate didn't deserve the two fine memorial services he had gotten. Coming back from the dead was going to be anticlimactic after this.

The procession moved toward the mouth of the cave, and the mourners pressed forward, carrying Garibaldi, Ivanova, Na'Toth, and Al Vernon with them. They emerged into the scorching daylight in time to see the grieving widow toss her rags over the cliff. They fluttered downward, swirling around in the thermal updrafts. Then an acolyte handed her a small animal which looked something like a piglet. Da'Kal held the squirming creature over her head and screamed something into the wind. Then she tossed the animal over the cliff, and it plummeted a kilometer or so to its death.

Al Vernon whispered in his ear, "In the past, a Narn widow was expected to die with her husband. Today, the animal dies instead."

An attendant came forward and wrapped a black robe around the widow's shoulders and led her away. Y'Tok beat on the discolored circle while the other priest banged on the gong, and a low moan rose from the gathered mourners. The moaning and drumming reached a crescendo at the same time, and Y'Tok ended the ceremony by dropping to his knees and bowing to the canyon.

While Garibaldi looked on in a daze, someone pulled urgently on his sleeve. He turned to see Ivanova, and she was pointing toward someone in the crowd of mourners. He saw a young Narn woman wrap a cloak around her slim body and dash away. He recognized her in an instant.

It was Mi'Ra, daughter of Du'Rog.

"Wait here," he whispered to Ivanova, stuffing his coat into her arms. Before she had a chance to answer, he shouldered his way through the crowd and set off down one of the narrow walkways. His instincts told him that he might not get another chance to talk to this avenging angel, and he had two things to say: First, that he knew she didn't kill G'Kar, and second, that she had better stay away from Babylon 5. She'd find out the reason for that warning later.

Mi'Ra slipped through the crowd like a wraith, glancing over her shoulder as if she knew she was being followed. Garibaldi staggered after her like a man who knew if he lost his footing he would join the sacrificial animal at the bottom of the canyon. But he had an advantage in that the Narns on the ledge made way for him, realizing he was a stranger.

At various intersections, the walkway sloped downward to a lower level of dwellings, while steps continued upward to the original level. Without hesitation, Mi'Ra went lower at every opportunity, and Garibaldi plunged after her. His clothes were soaking with sweat, and thirst burned in his throat—but this young Narn had threatened to kill one of the ambassadors in his charge. Had she come to the memorial service to make certain G'Kar was dead? Or had she come because she suspected he wasn't dead? It didn't matter—he was on an unfamiliar planet, and this was the one person he wanted to talk to the most. He wasn't going to lose this opportunity.

Suddenly, he realized that he couldn't see Mi'Ra anymore. She had escaped. He quickened his pace and found himself on a stretch of walkway where many doorways were blocked off with rocks and pedestrians were few. He tried not to look over the narrow railing at the certain death that waited below. His senses were acutely on edge, and he saw the boot whip out of the doorway a microsecond before it struck him in the knee.

Garibaldi yelped with pain and stumbled toward the abyss. He grabbed the railing, pushed off, and fell hard onto his back; a knife flashed through the air. He caught her arm as the dagger kissed his throat. The young Narn woman fought like a commando, using every ounce of her wiry body to drive the knife home. He couldn't help it if she was pretty—he smashed her in the jaw with his fist and sent her crashing against the rock face. He heard her grunt as the air rushed out of her body, but she still had enough strength to draw a PPG and level it at him.

"Don't!" he warned, trying to sound calm. "I just want to talk."

Her corseted chest heaved as she struggled to regain her breath, and her red eyes drilled into him with hatred and suspicion. Garibaldi had seen enough criminals to know when he was confronting someone with nothing left to lose. Mi'Ra had been kicked around so much in the last few years that she didn't care about life anymore. She only cared about death. He could plainly see the yellowish scar on her forehead where she had drawn blood to seal her *Shon'Kar*.

"I just want to talk," Garibaldi said. "I saw the data crystal, and I know about your *Shon'Kar*."

"If you intend to take me back to your Earth station, I might as well kill you now." She hefted her weapon and seemed to be deciding where to put a hole in him.

Very slowly, Garibaldi lifted himself to his elbows. "I know you didn't kill him, and I couldn't take you back even if you did. But we need to tell you and your family to stay away from Babylon 5."

"Why?"

"Babylon 5 is under Earth administration, and we don't recognize the *Shon'Kar*."

Mi'Ra spat on the dry walkway. "Yes, I was deprived of my *Shon'Kar*. G'Kar deserved to be roasted to death over a slow fire, with a spit stuck through his gut, and I'm sorry he died quickly, before I could get my hands on him. Do you know what he did to my family?"

Garibaldi swallowed. "Yes, I do. I believe he was sorry for it, in the end."

"Ha!" scowled the attractive Narn. "He was a pathetic excuse for a Narn."

Garibaldi decided not to argue with her and her shiny PPG. Keeping the weapon trained on him, Mi'Ra scrambled to her knees to reclaim her knife. She stuck the knife in a shabby leather sheath and looked thoughtfully at Garibaldi, as if deciding how to dispose of him. He flinched, expecting to have his chest turned into melting goo, but the young woman tucked the PPG inside her tight-fitting waistcoat and rose to her feet.

She looked down at him with pity. "G'Kar was the type to betray everyone, including his friends."

Garibaldi wasn't likely to argue with that point, but there was one more thing he had to know. "Did you send assassins after him when he was on Homeworld a few months ago?"

Mi'Ra frowned. "I thought they were professionals. I will never make that mistake again."

"Were they also Thenta Ma'Kur?"

The Narn woman smiled slyly. "If you have any brains at all in your hairy skull, you will stay far, far away from the Thenta Ma'Kur."

Garibaldi picked himself up and dusted off his pants. "That's what I've heard, but G'Kar defeated them on their first try."

The slim Narn scowled at him. "Go home now, Earther, before you get hurt. This is not your affair."

With that, Mi'Ra tossed back her cloak and sauntered away, giving him a good look at her athletic backside. Garibaldi sighed, being a fan of rear actions in motion. Two more days he had in this vertical village, and he would also like to meet Du'Rog's widow, to see if she was as headstrong as her daughter. His eyes wandered over the railing into the bottomless canyon. It must have a bottom, he told himself, but it was so far down he couldn't see it.

He took a few steps after her and called out, "Where can I find you?"

"The border zone," she shot back. "But you aren't brave enough to go there."

# CHAPTER 10

"Where have you been?" growled Na'Toth when Garibaldi finally straggled back to the sanctuary, perched upon the cliffside of Hekba City.

Ivanova studied her comrade, noting his dirty pants and the way he limped slightly. "I think he's been exploring."

"Yeah," muttered Garibaldi, "but not too successfully." He glanced around. "Where is Al?"

"Where we should be," answered Ivanova, "out of this heat and getting something to drink." She used Garibaldi's coat to dab the sweat off her face, then she shoved it into his hands.

Garibaldi lowered his voice to report, "After you saw Mi'Ra in the crowd, I chased her down. Well, sort of. Actually she ambushed me and nearly killed me. She's quite a piece of work."

"Unfortunately," said Na'Toth, "it is G'Kar's fault that Du'Rog's family is so bitter. I am losing much of the sympathy I had for him."

"Mi'Ra lives in a place called the border zone," said Garibaldi. "Where is that?"

Na'Toth said, "Do you remember how I told you about the regimentation of Narn society? The caste system applies to entire cities. For example, only those of the Eighth Circle or above may live here in Hekba City, which is one of our oldest and most revered places. Plebeians and others may work here, but the plebeians have cities of their own. Between these cities there are areas where our poorest people live—those who are thieves, prostitutes, and outcasts. If Mi'Ra and her mother and brother live in a border zone, then they have truly fallen to the lowest stratum of our society.''

"Do you know which place she's talking about?" asked Ivanova.

"I have an idea," said Na'Toth. "There is a large border zone that is fairly close to here."

Garibaldi's jaw tightened. "I warned Mi'Ra to stay away from B5, and I'd like to warn the entire family, if possible. Sooner or later, they're going to find out that G'Kar is alive, and I don't want to go through a bunch of memorial services all over again."

The security chief turned to Na'Toth. "Are you sure there's no way to talk Du'Rog's family out of their Blood Oath? We talked you out of the one you had on Deathwalker."

The Narn woman scowled. "That was very difficult for me, and I draw great contentment from knowing that Deathwalker died anyway. To correct matters between G'Kar and the Du'Rog family will take more persuasion than you and I have to offer."

Ivanova let her attention drift from this futile conversation, and she heard somebody clear his throat. She turned to see a tall Narn male with unfamiliar spots on his head and bland brown eyes. He was dressed in the simple garb of a crewman from the *K'sha Na'vas*. He smiled at her and put his finger to his lips.

"Do I know you?" she asked, having the distinct feeling that she did, if only from the ship.

Garibaldi leaned toward the Narn and whispered, "Are you crazy?"

Na'Toth stiffened and stared at him. "Yes, he is."

The stranger held out his hand to Ivanova. "The name is Ha'Mok. Please address me as such."

*That voice!* She blinked at the Narn in amazement. His real name sprang to her lips, but she caught herself before she said it. "You *are* crazy," she agreed. "What are you doing here?"

"Enjoying shore leave," answered the man who had been G'Kar and was now Ha'Mok. He kept his head bowed as if addressing his betters. "How was the memorial service?"

"Better than you deserved," hissed Na'Toth.

"Why are you here?" Ivanova demanded again.

"Two things. First, the *K'sha Na'vas* received a delayed transmission from Babylon 5. Captain Sheridan has been trying to reach you." He lowered his voice to add, "The captain is no fool. Perhaps he has found out what I did."

"Can we contact him?" asked Garibaldi.

"Not from here. When we return to the *K'sha Na'vas*."

"You didn't come here to tell us that," said Ivanova.

"No," admitted G'Kar. "Most importantly, I want to see Da'Kal, my wife. She lives in this city, on the other side of the canyon. I want you to come with me."

"Why?" asked Ivanova.

"You may have to protect me in case she tries to kill me."

"I'm not sure we would," said Ivanova. She rubbed her lips and peered up at the blazing red sun. "Before we get deeper into this mess, we humans need to get something to drink. Where did you say Al went?"

Na'Toth pointed to a doorway about twenty meters away. "He said there was a tavern down there, and he went inside as soon as the service was over. We haven't seen him since."

"Who is this Al person?" asked G'Kar. "Can we trust him?"

Ivanova fixed the dead man with a stare. "Can we trust *you?* We have to wait two full days before meeting with the Kha'Ri. You didn't have anything to do with that, did you?"

G'Kar shrugged. "I am trying to make amends, but I must have time."

"You can start by buying us some drinks," said Garibaldi, heading for the tavern.

The party of two humans and two Narns ambled into a doorway that looked no different from any of the others, except for three gashes carved into the wall above the door. After the intense sunlight, the darkness inside the shelter momentarily blinded Ivanova. She could see nothing, but the sounds of laughter and voices convinced her that she was indeed inside a public tavern. Na'Toth and G'Kar brushed past her, apparently having no difficulty with the change in light.

She bumped into a customer and decided to stand still until her eyes adjusted to the darkness. Once they had, she saw a low-slung bar against one wall; it seemed to be carved directly from the rock. Stepping closer, she saw the bar had deep holes dug into it, from which strange aromas and curlicues of steam rose toward the ceiling. There were no bar stools that she could see, but she couldn't miss Al Vernon, who was sitting on the floor, his back against the bar. He was drinking from what appeared to be a bag made out of animal skin.

"Here you are!" he said happily, bounding to his feet. He pointed to a sickly-looking Narn who could only be the proprietor. "These are my friends. They will pay my bill."

"Wait a minute," grumbled Garibaldi. "How much is his bill?"

The proprietor appraised him with cool red eyes that looked like embers about to burn out. "One hundred credits."

"A hundred credits!" snapped Garibaldi. "You should be able to rent a room for that!"

Ivanova swallowed dryly and held out her creditchit. "Give us two more of whatever he's having."

Garibaldi added, "Make mine a Shirley Temple."

The proprietor blinked at him. "Pardon me?"

"No alcohol in mine," answered the chief.

The old Narn nodded and took the card. Then he produced two flat skins and dipped them into separate holes in the bar. When he brought the skins up, they were plump and dripping with steaming liquid. He handed the pouches to the visitors and processed Ivanova's chit. The skin was sticky, and whatever was inside was highly aromatic. It wasn't a terrible smell but oddly redolent of mincemeat pie, truffles, and English cooking.

"This is crazy," muttered Garibaldi. "When I'm thirsty, I want something cold."

Ivanova replied, "It's a fallacy that something cold quenches thirst better than something hot. In fact, whenever I'm really thirsty, I drink coffee."

"You always drink coffee," countered Garibaldi. Wrinkling his nose, he put the skin to his lips and took a cautious sip. "Hmmm," he said with surprise. "Sort of tastes like mulled wine and beef broth."

Ivanova took a sip, and the warm liquid did indeed taste like a combination of cloves, raisins, and the drippings from a roast. It warmed her insides while the condensing steam cooled her face.

Al Vernon chuckled. "Do you want me to tell you what's in it?"

"No!" Ivanova and Garibaldi answered in unison.

"Listen, Al," said Ivanova, "we fulfilled our part of the bargain and got you here. If we're going to pay your bills, too, then you had better stick with us."

"I told you where I was going," said Al. "When Mr. Garibaldi ran off after that attractive Narn woman, I assumed he would be gone for a while."

Garibaldi lowered his drinking skin and said, "We've

got two more days here. What do you know about the border zone?''

"Oh, no," replied the portly human, looking grim. "You aren't planning to go to a border zone, are you?''

"We have to," said Garibaldi. "We have to talk to someone there.''

"You don't need a guide, you need a bodyguard." Al took a long swig from his pouch.

Ivanova cleared her throat. "Another Narn from the ship is going with us, so there will be five of us.''

"That's too few," said Al. "Let's get the whole crew to go with us.''

Ivanova looked at Garibaldi. "Maybe he has a point. If we really want to go traipsing around this planet, we ought to talk to Captain Vin'Tok about having an escort. It might keep us out of trouble.''

Someone tapped her on the shoulder, and she turned around to see the disguised Narn who was going by the name of Ha'Mok. "I want to attend to that errand we talked about," he said insistently.

To see his wife, recalled the commander. She had no objection to telling people that G'Kar was still alive, and the sooner the better! They might as well start with his poor widow, and Ivanova hoped she would punch him in the stomach, the same way Na'Toth had.

Before she could reply, Al butted in. "Hello, I don't believe we've met. I'm Al Vernon, formerly of Homeworld.''

"Ha'Mok," lied the Narn. "Your friends need to come with me. You can stay here.''

Al sighed. "I'm afraid, sir, I am currently short of funds, and this establishment won't extend me credit.''

G'Kar grabbed the human's pudgy hand and dropped some black coins into it. "That should hold you until we get back.''

"Indeed it should!" said Al. "Thank you."

"Finish your drinks," ordered the Narn. "I'll be over there with Na'Toth." He strode into the dim recesses of the tavern.

Al cocked his head thoughtfully. "He's rather bold for a simple crewman, isn't he?"

"Yes," said Ivanova, gazing after him, "and I've had just about enough of it. But we may need him, just as we may need you. Wait for us here, please."

"Have no fear," said Al pleasantly. "I have no intention of letting any of you get away from me."

A few minutes later, Ivanova and her party were hundreds of meters in the air on a swaying bridge with only a few ornamental cables supporting it in the middle. She lifted her eyes toward the red sun to avoid looking down, but her wobbly legs and staggering gait forced her to watch where she put her feet. That the bridge was constructed of metal cables and planks didn't do much to lessen her fear, and it didn't help that G'Kar and Na'Toth were striding ahead of her, making the bridge sway even more. She took some comfort in the fact that Garibaldi was even more frightened than she was. He inched along behind her.

"The next time Captain Sheridan orders us to a weird planet," he muttered, "will you remind me to resign?"

"No," she answered. "But I will make sure someone else goes instead of me."

Fear paralyzed her legs every time the bridge swayed. Adding to her discomfort was the miserable heat, the sweat drooling down her back and chest, and the fact that she was still carrying her coat. Ivanova brushed sweaty ringlets of hair from her face and her eyes wandered downward. The canyon floor looked like the primordial ooze she had always read about. It was a bubbling cauldron of murky water, and the putrid smell of sulfur rose hundreds of meters into the air. Nevertheless, she could see a few strips of farmland among the geysers and pools.

*Keep going,* she told herself. It wasn't much farther. But it was, as they were barely a third of the way across the bridge. Ivanova had the irrational urge to turn around and run back to the tavern, seeking safety with Al Vernon, but she forced herself to keep moving. They had traveled billions of kilometers in order to honor G'Kar and confront his murderers—only to end up with *no* murder and a frightened ambassador in disguise. Now they were going to hold his hand as he broke the news to his wife that he was still alive.

Ivanova had to remind herself that this planet harbored a family of would-be murderers who would not be pleased to find out that G'Kar was still alive. Plus, there was a league of assassins—the Thenta Ma'Kur—who had contracted to kill G'Kar and failed. Even if a murder had yet to be committed, it wasn't for lack of trying. Thinking about these various parties gave her the impetus to quicken her step and make her way across the swaying span.

Na'Toth and G'Kar waited for her at the other end, and she nearly dove into their outstretched hands. "That wasn't so bad, was it?" asked G'Kar.

"Yes," she breathed.

Garibaldi was almost crawling by the time he reached the end. When they helped him off the bridge, he sank against the rock wall and panted for a few seconds.

"Damn," he said. "Is there anything you Narns are afraid of?"

"Wives," answered Na'Toth with a sidelong glance at G'Kar.

"Yes," he admitted, "that is true. I sincerely appreciate the help you are giving me. The home I share with Da'Kal is on this level, only a few doors away."

They were doing G'Kar such a big favor, and he was in

so much trouble, that Ivanova felt the normal boundaries between them were all but gone. "Why haven't you ever brought Da'Kal to the station?" she asked.

G'Kar shrugged his broad shoulders. "I'm not sure she would come. You have no doubt realized how ambitious I am. Marrying Da'Kal was the most ambitious act I have ever taken, more so than what I did to Du'Rog. She is extremely well placed, with friends in the Inner Circle, such as Ra'Pak. I was a young soldier, a dashing war hero, when I met Da'Kal; and she was a few years older. She was very much in love with me. My success was ensured when I married her."

"Are you in love with her?" asked Ivanova.

G'Kar fixed her with his altered brown eyes. "I am in love with the *idea* of her, and I owe her more than anyone in the universe. But love? I doubt whether I have ever loved anyone but myself. Follow me."

With G'Kar leading the way, the odd party of two Narns and two humans strode down the peaceful walkway. There was less hustle and bustle on this side of the canyon, as if it was a better neighborhood, and the facades of the dwellings were uniformly painted in muted brown and rust shades.

Na'Toth hung back to whisper to the humans, "Narns are not strictly monogamous. It is quite possible that Da'Kal has had lovers, and may have lovers now. A marriage is like two businesses joining forces—for the purpose of creating wealth and children—but they maintain their separate identities. Do I make myself clear?"

"You do," answered Ivanova. "What should we expect?"

Na'Toth shook her head. "I have no idea."

G'Kar stopped in front of a dwelling that was distinguished by its pinkish color and a heavy metal door. He turned to the humans and said, "This is our home. I suppose you would have reason to discuss my death with

Da'Kal, as you know more about it than anyone. Simply ask her: Would she be happy or angry to learn that I am alive? Depending on the answer, you may come to fetch me.''

"You're going to owe us big-time for this," warned Garibaldi. He pushed the door chime, and the two Narns backed away.

The door opened, and a wizened old Narn peered at them. "Who are you?" he snarled.

"We're from Babylon 5," said Ivanova. "If Mistress Da'Kal is available, we would like to talk to her about her husband."

"Hmmm," grunted the servant. "Come in."

He ushered them into a narrow foyer that was decorated in a typically masculine Narn style, despite the fact that the man of the household had lived elsewhere for years. The walls were gilded with a copper-colored metal and decorated with tapestries, antique weapons, and family crests of bloodstone and exotic fabrics. A clay vase held dried flowers and reeds, and the floor was tiled in orange and brown. Beyond the foyer, Ivanova could see a sumptuous sitting room with heavy metal furniture, and she could hear feminine voices. The windowless dwelling had the oppressive feeling of a cave, or a space station.

"Wait here," growled the wizened servant as he shuffled toward the back of the house.

Garibaldi took a deep breath and whispered to Ivanova, "I've had to tell people their spouses were dead, but I've never had to tell anyone their dead spouse was alive."

"I hope we don't regret this," said Ivanova. "I'd feel a lot better if we called her from back on B5."

"I'll drink to that," muttered Garibaldi.

Ivanova took a moment to wipe the sweat off her brow. At least it was considerably cooler inside G'Kar's home than outside in the open air.

A few moments later, two women appeared. One of them was the regally dressed woman from the Inner Circle, Ra'Pak, and she glanced disdainfully at the humans as if they were stains on the wall. The other woman was Da'Kal, who was dressed in a simple beige tunic, knotted at her waist. For a Narn, she was short and delicate, almost fragile. Ivanova found it difficult to tell age in a Narn, but Da'Kal had the look of a woman who had aged considerably in the last few days.

"Then I will see you at the reception," Ra'Pak said, making it sound like an order.

Da'Kal nodded. "I will try, my friend. Thank you so much for being here."

Ra'Pak tilted her head. "It's the least I can do when your husband never was."

Da'Kal took her friend's hand. "I know you are thinking of me, always."

"I will be staying at the villa if you need me," concluded Ra'Pak. She swept toward the door, and the servant rushed to open it for her.

Once the noblewoman was gone, Ivanova stepped forward. "I am Susan Ivanova, and this is Michael Garibaldi. We're from Babylon 5."

"Yes, I saw you at the service," said Da'Kal, twisting her hands nervously. "My husband mentioned you in his messages, and he was very impressed with you. Thank you for coming so far to honor him." She motioned toward the sitting room. "Shall we make ourselves comfortable?"

Ivanova glanced at the aged servant. "We would prefer to speak to you alone, if we could."

"Of course. He'Lok, I believe we need some things from the market."

"Yes, my lady." The servant bowed and shuffled out the door.

"Come," said Da'Kal, leading them into the sitting

room of the small but elegant house. The furnishings in this room were surprisingly bright and cheerful for a Narn household, with ivory-hued curtains gracing most of the walls and several vases of dried flowers and plants. The furniture was dark and massive, but some brightly colored cushions gave it a feminine touch. The widow seated herself on the edge of a small sofa, still twisting her hands. The humans sat in high-backed chairs.

Ivanova glanced at Garibaldi, and he looked at her helplessly. Apparently, he was going to let her do all the talking. Although Ivanova felt rather lacking in the tact department, she resolved to do the best she could.

"We're sorry to bother you at a time like this," she began.

"How could it be otherwise?" asked Da'Kal. "But I must warn you—I know very little about my husband's affairs. Certainly it's no secret to you that we didn't see each other very often."

"Yes, we know," said Ivanova, lowering her eyes with embarrassment. "Did you know a man named Du'Rog?"

The distress that swept over the woman's face made it very clear that she did. "Of course I knew him. He was on the Council—a former associate of G'Kar's."

"Were you aware that Du'Rog hired an assassin from the Thenta Ma'Kur to kill your husband?"

The woman's jaw hung open for a moment, then she nodded with realization. "Ah, that is what happened to G'Kar."

"No," said Ivanova quickly. "That murder attempt was unsuccessful, and so was one other."

Da'Kal leaped to her feet. "I knew nothing of any of this. Oh, that fool! Why didn't G'Kar come to me for help? I am not without influence, even among the Thenta Ma'Kur. But G'Kar was so stubborn! He thought he was master of his own fate, when he never was."

Ivanova sighed. It was becoming woefully clear to her that G'Kar had kept his wife in the dark about almost everything for the last few years. Da'Kal must have known what her husband had done to succeed to the Third Circle, but she didn't seem to know anything beyond that. The commander had only two more questions before she tackled the big one.

"Do you know Du'Rog's family? Ka'Het is the widow's name, and Mi'Ra and T'Kog are his children."

Da'Kal stopped pacing and bent over to rearrange one of her dried flower arrangements. "I already told you that I knew Du'Rog. Of course I know his family. If you are trying to make trouble for me . . ."

"No," insisted Ivanova. "What's in the past is in the past, except as it relates to the incident that brought us here. Did you know they vowed the *Shon'Kar* against your husband?"

Da'Kal's back stiffened, and she gazed into the distance. "That is within their right. If you are expecting that I will seek revenge against them, let me assure you, I will not. Nor will I help you to persecute them. The family of Du'Rog has suffered enough. The *Shon'Kar* is now ended."

Ivanova took a deep breath. There was just one more question to ask. "Would you be happy or angry to learn that G'Kar is still alive?"

The woman whirled around, her red eyes blazing in their bony sockets.

G'Kar and Na'Toth stood on the walkway about thirty meters beyond Da'Kal's doorway. They pretended to admire some golden goblets on display in a shop window, but the proprietor was beginning to look at them suspiciously. G'Kar lowered his head and motioned to his aide, and they began to walk slowly toward Da'Kal's house.

"What is taking them so long?" seethed G'Kar.

"It's only been a few minutes since your servant left," said Na'Toth. "We were lucky that neither he nor Ra'Pak recognized you."

"That old witch," muttered G'Kar. "She has always hated me. I doubt if the years have changed her mind very much."

The door of the pink dwelling opened, and G'Kar froze in his steps. He had confidence that his disguise would fool a cursory inspection from most of his acquaintances, especially humans, but he harbored no illusions that it would fool his wife. He held his breath until he saw that it was Ivanova and Garibaldi. They left the door open and approached him.

"She's waiting for you," said Ivanova. "We'll wait for you in the tavern where we left Al."

G'Kar swallowed and gave them a brief nod. "I thank you."

"Don't thank us yet," said Garibaldi. "She may have a rolling pin in her hand."

The Terran reference flew over G'Kar's head as he strode toward the door. He carefully entered the doorway, bowing his head respectfully. The first thing he noticed were the vases of flowers, an addition since he had lived here. Then he saw her standing in the next room, a small but proud woman dressed in the traditional beige of mourning. Shadows and shock obscured her face.

Her voice was like ice. "G'Kar—is that really you?"

"Yes," he said. A dozen words of endearment sprang to his mind, but he could force none of them onto his tongue. He was sure she would believe none of them.

She stepped toward him and peered into his eyes. He bent his head downward, pushed on his eyelids, and let the brown contact lenses fall into his hand. Then he slowly peeled off the skullcap that had changed his appearance so much.

"By the Martyrs!" she gasped. "What made you do this thing?"

"Fear," he answered. "Desperation. Most of all, shame."

"You could have come to me for help."

He shook his head. "You could not have helped without revealing what I did to Du'Rog and his family. When I received word that they had vowed the *Shon'Kar* against me, I was afraid. My first instinct was to hide, and my second was to kill Mi'Ra. I could accomplish both by pretending to be dead. The Earthers discovered the truth before we reached here, and now I feel mostly shame for my actions. This is my first step in reclaiming my life."

Da'Kal stepped forward and held out her trembling hands. G'Kar took them in his, and they were both calm. The ambassador looked down at the woman who had shared his bed and his life for so many years, and it seemed as if their years apart were nothing but a long, dark night. He needed Da'Kal more than ever, but he had no idea if she still needed him. He feared to ask if she still loved him.

She insisted, "You must make amends to Ka'Het and her children. I don't know how you can do this, but you must try."

"I know," he answered. "Believe me, I know how wrong I've been. If I had to do it over again, I would wait forever to succeed to the Third Circle. I would do so many things differently."

Da'Kal pulled her hands away from his. "We cannot wait—we must do something!"

She strode into the sitting room, and G'Kar rushed after her. This was the dynamic woman he remembered, before apathy and ambition had weakened their marriage. Da'Kal went to the wall and pulled on a cord, and a curtain opened to reveal a sophisticated computer terminal. As her delicate fingers touched the controls, the screen blinked on.

"Ka'Het and her children are living like animals in the border zone," she said. "I have been as cruel as you—I knew their circumstances, yet I have done nothing to help them. Like you, I have been afraid to reveal the past. It is time to be brave and do the honorable thing. You can only run so far from yourself."

"What are you doing?" asked G'Kar, suddenly worried despite his good intentions.

"I am transferring funds to the Du'Rog family. I know that Ka'Het still maintains an account that is dormant. I can't restore their social status, but I can do what I must to help them be comfortable. Whatever we do for them, it is long overdue."

As her fingers plied the controls, G'Kar paced nervously. "Won't they know where the money is coming from?"

"What difference does it make? If we haven't the stomach to destroy them, we must help them. Go bolt the front door."

"Bolt the front door?" asked G'Kar numbly.

"Yes, before my servant returns home. It is a signal we have used before. If he finds the front door bolted from the inside, he knows I am entertaining. He won't return until summoned." Da'Kal turned to her husband and smiled slightly. "You have been gone a long time, G'Kar."

He nodded and rushed to bolt the front door. There was a romantic, dreamlike quality about all of this—returning to his home in disguise, seeing Da'Kal after ignoring her for years, and bolting the door against the outside world. It was as if the years were melting away and they were young again, sneaking behind their parents' backs. Could the clock really be turned back? Could they return to a simpler time, before his life had been consumed with ambition and intrigue? He walked back into the sitting room and found Da'Kal shutting the curtain on the computer terminal.

"It is done," she said with a sigh. "This won't begin to make up for what you did to Du'Rog, but at least his family won't have to live like animals anymore."

"And us?" asked G'Kar in an urgent voice. "What is to become of us?"

As Da'Kal approached him, she untied the beige tunic from around her waist. "I am no longer in mourning."

She slipped the garment off her shoulders, and it fell to the floor. "This is twice today I have bared myself for you, G'Kar. No other woman would do that for you. You once owned every molecule of this body. Do you still want it?"

"Yes," he said hoarsely, as he lifted her in his powerful arms and pressed his face to her flesh.

# CHAPTER 11

Mi'Ra waited solemnly in line with the servants and tradespeople of the lower castes who were leaving Hekba City for the day. The line wound into a tunnel on the third level, where a series of moving walkways, called outerwalks, allowed them to travel many kilometers in a short time. With hunched shoulders and weary expressions, the plebeians stepped upon the conveyor belts and began their long march home.

The young woman tried to hold her head high, knowing she didn't belong with these commoners, but it was difficult. She knew that most of them were returning to better homes than the hovel she shared with her mother and her brother. They had jobs and at least some station in life, even if it was a lower one. She had nothing but her bitterness and the weapons stuck in her belt. Mi'Ra had believed that the memorial service for G'Kar would in some way cleanse her, or please her, but the finality of his death had just the opposite effect. Her father was dead, his tormentor was dead, and she felt dead, too. Without the *Shon'Kar* and the hatred which fueled it, her purpose in life was gone.

Perhaps, thought Mi'Ra, it was time to get away from Homeworld, time to explore the galaxy. The concerned human who had pursued her down the walkway had made her realize that there were other races out there, other places where no one cared about the *Shon'Kar,* the Kha'Ri, or the arcane aspects of Narn culture. She was an outcast here, but she would merely be an alien there—and that would be preferable. Mi'Ra knew she would be young and attractive for many more years. She had too much pride to stoop to prostitution, but there must be someplace in this wide galaxy where she could carve a new life.

For example, what was this Babylon 5 like? After a lifetime spent among her own kind, she couldn't imagine a place where humans, Narns, Centauri, Minbari, and a dozen other races lived together. Surely, in a place like that, the sins of the father made no difference to anyone. But why would the human warn her to stay away. Prejudice? It didn't seem likely that a prejudiced, close-minded person could live and work in such an environment. Perhaps she merely frightened him—and that thought made her smile.

Mi'Ra had to consider her mother and her brother, though when she did her rosy dreams vanished like the stretch of tunnel behind her. They were helpless without her. She couldn't leave them in the border zone, destitute and outcast, while she went off to seek her fortune among alien races. And both of them would be useless on such a grand adventure. Mi'Ra had expected to fulfill her *Shon'Kar* and die young, in a blaze of glory. Now she would do neither. Instead she would grow old, caring for her impoverished family, all hope of a better life dashed forever.

Mi'Ra stood numbly on the frayed belt of the moving walkway, watching the plebeians shuffle past her. She looked up at a naked lightbulb, barely illuminating the dark tunnel. This retreat from Hekba City was characteristic of her life—a journey from wealth and position into poverty and despair. She had nothing to look forward to but a swift descent into a dark tunnel.

There was one other possible path for her, one she had been considering since hearing of their recent success. Mi'Ra considered joining the Thenta Ma'Kur, the league of professional assassins. She had the qualifications: a complete disregard for her own life, beauty and poise that would help her travel in disguise, and the most important qualification—a deadened soul that was prepared to kill. She was a perfect candidate, and perhaps she could make enough money as an assassin to send her mother and brother to Babylon 5, or someplace far removed from the bitter memories and daily reminders. They could open a shop and have lives that were at least respectable, if not privileged.

The thought of this plan cheered her slightly as she reached an intersection where three outerwalks branched off. Most of the plebeians took the right-hand walkway, headed to their homes in the city of Jasba. A few lucky ones took the left-hand walkway to a neighborhood reserved for members of the Outer Circle. She took the least-traveled outerwalk to the area in between, the border zone.

Mi'Ra had been deprived of everything—her birthright, her station, her inheritance, and now the glory of the *Shon'Kar*. Even the pitiful humans seemed to dismiss her. She was disappointed that the tall human in uniform hadn't put up more of a fight on the walkway. He hadn't even offered her the chance to die fighting. But why should he? He knew she wasn't the murderer—he simply had a desire to speak with her before returning to his life among the stars and planets. She understood—the military were a privileged class in her society, too.

The tunnel grew darker, narrower, and more neglected, and eyes peered at her from the shadows. They were the eyes of animals and Narns, those who were so downtrodden they made the tunnels their homes. They were chased out of other tunnels and neighborhoods, but not this one. They were chased *into* the border zone. The tunnel denizens scurried furtively about as the outerwalk shuddered further into the netherworld.

When she had lived among the privileged, Mi'Ra had never given much thought to the unlucky, the poorly born, the classless. Forged by slavery, the Narn were a hard people who admired the victors in any struggle and shunted the losers to the bone pile. Those who knew their place got to keep their place, and that was struggle enough for the plebeians and Outer Circle. For the fallen from grace, there was a special netherworld.

Mi'Ra recalled how her mother's estate had been seized by the government as proof of illicit profits on those ludicrous arms-dealing charges. Like most of his peers, Du'Rog occasionally pulled a shady deal—a few of them with G'Kar as his partner—and kept less than scrupulous records. But no one could have predicted the fall he was about to take. The military had nearly tortured General Balashar to death, and they needed to produce him in court to name his contact for the horribly potent biological weapons. The weapons were especially successful on Narns, as if they had been formulated for them in the first place. Despite holding high rank in the Kha'Ri and the Fourth Circle, Du'Rog was embraced as the scapegoat.

The military executed Balashar posthaste, and G'Kar installed his family in a life of splendor on a distant colony—while her father died from the stress of fighting the unjust charges. Then the scavengers moved in, expecting easy pickings. Mi'Ra had to grow up fast in a short time, and she wasn't able to ward them off. The creditors and opportunists had picked her father's skeleton clean before she was strong enough to fight them. As part of the supposedly generous settlement, she and her mother and brother had gotten the deed to a house in this pit, the border zone.

The outerwalk deposited her in another pit, a so-called station where the stairs to the surface were covered with dirt and garbage. You literally had to climb out to reach the slum. There was a newsstand in the pit, but it had long been boarded up with adobe bricks and barbed wire. The only reason they kept the walkway running was that they didn't want anyone to have the excuse that they couldn't get home. If you didn't belong in Hekba City, then there had to be a way to get you out of there at the end of the day —to wherever you did belong.

Mi'Ra drew her PPG and dug in the toes of her boots as she scaled the garbage pit. She finally found a few clear steps where dust devils had strayed down the stairs, and the ascent got easier. There was nothing easy, however, about the sight of the border zone, with its depressing row houses. Each was two stories tall, although some had sunken on their poor foundations and looked no more than one-story. They were built quickly, then forgotten quickly, left to rot with the firm knowledge that anyone who had sunk to this level had lost his place in Narn society. For a Narn who didn't know his place, there was no hope.

Mi'Ra stepped cautiously into the wind that blew across this treeless plain ninety percent of the time, or so they said. No one could remember the ten percent when it allegedly wasn't blowing. The decrepit row houses were supposed to be offset by impressive walls and archways that mirrored preinvasion architecture. But the constant feeling of running into walls made it seem like a maze, a place where society observed its freaks. At other times, the walls seemed like a prison, which is what they really were, thought Mi'Ra.

There were murders every night, but no one saw anything over the damn walls or the fear. The border zones were conveniently unincorporated, patrolled by rangers from the Rural Division, who showed a determined lack of interest in solving most crimes. In the ones they decided to solve, they acted as police, judge, jury, and executioner. Mi'Ra had finally realized that a race that could be cruel to other races could also be cruel to itself.

She skirted a familiar wall, trying to stay out of the light. There were cheap clay candles swaying in the archways and on a few porches. The government left candles and boxes of food at certain intersections every day, and a few conscientious people tried to light the border zone. Most just ignored the cheap candles, and the sand was littered with sooty clumps of pottery that had once been candles.

The young Narn padded down a hill and paused before an archway. A lone traveler could never tell what might be waiting in one of those infernal archways; at least this one had a clay pot burning. She was young and attractive, and her greatest fear was that some street pack would capture her alive. Mi'Ra slowed cautiously and put her PPG away in favor of her knife. In close quarters, she had more faith in her knife to inflict damage without risking a war.

Mi'Ra was still annoyed that a human had managed to deflect her attack so easily today. Of course, she could have killed him, which gave her some satisfaction. The young Narn gazed up at the top of the wall, wondering if anybody could be hiding up there. She knew from experience that footing was treacherous atop the crumbling structures. No one in his right mind scampered around up there. The ground was littered with chunks that had fallen from the ornamental walls.

The smell of burning rubber, the only available fuel for some downtrodden souls, assaulted her nostrils, and she felt like turning back. But her mother and brother were waiting for a full report on the memorial service. Even though G'Kar's death brought them no immediate relief, at least it had exorcised one ghost. They no longer anguished over the fact that G'Kar enjoyed a soft life built from the hide of their father's corpse.

Mi'Ra stopped again to listen, and she thought she heard someone moving on the other side of the wall. She darted through the archway, slashing her knife, but her would-be attacker was only a dust devil, unable to find its way around the wall. It whipped and whirled in frustration.

She moved swiftly away from the light, not wanting to

draw attention to herself. There was still enough daylight left that this trip home shouldn't be torturous. She could see some young Narns at the bottom of the hill, burning the tread from a mining vehicle and cooking rodents over the flames. But they were often there and had never tried to pursue her. Still, she kept a safe distance and was poised to run if they even stood up too quickly. Mi'Ra had no delusions about the dangers of the border zone. Some people down here were mentally unhinged, not fit for Narn society or any other society; some had become addicted to drugs the Centauri had introduced. Many were just unlucky, like herself, and it was cruel to mix the misfits with the misfortunates.

Narns prided themselves on having few prisons, as if this was some indication that Narns accepted their rigid caste system. But Mi'Ra had decided that Narn culture was nothing more than a series of prisons, expanding ever outward. Even G'Kar had not managed to escape from it.

She heard a sound, and she broke out of her careless reverie to see two dark figures rise out of the shadows. As they had already seen her, she decided to let them see everything. She stepped back near the archway and let them see the light glinting off her knife, then she slowly made her way across the alley to the first row of dreary houses. Mi'Ra wanted to let them know that she intended to steer clear of them and hoped they would do likewise. The two shadowy figures watched her go, although they grunted something to each other and laughed.

When Mi'Ra was well beyond them, she sheathed her knife and dashed through an opening in the houses without alerting anyone. She jogged down the middle of the street, knowing the ground was fairly level and not too badly littered. A few residents poked their heads out of their doorways to watch her pass. Even though most of them knew who she was, no one greeted her. People in the border zone were faceless and wanted to stay that way.

Mi'Ra could see the lighted clay pot swinging on her mother's porch. At least T'Kog had done something he was supposed to do. As she approached the dreary house, she could hear the people who lived upstairs fighting; one of them was a dust addict, and the other one was a pickpocket who worked the tunnels. Mi'Ra hated to have to rent out the upper floor, but that was the only steady income they had. Besides, this hovel and its hideous surroundings had never seemed like their real home. It was just the cell to which the Du'Rog family had mistakenly been condemned until the magical return of the good life. That's how Ka'Het and T'Kog looked at it, thought Mi'Ra angrily. The only *V'Tar* that burned in them was the minimum it took to survive, plus the useless hope that their father's name would someday be cleared.

She tried to tell them that they had been put in the border zone to be forgotten, to die. The only glory awaiting them was to achieve the *Shon'Kar*—to fulfill their father's dying wish to know that G'Kar was dead. At least that goal had been attained, even if it was another's hand that held the glory. That was honest cause for celebration, so Mi'Ra tried to put on a cheerful face as she walked up the crumbling steps. But she still felt empty. The fire of revenge had gone out, and she had nothing to replace it with.

The neighbors' fighting was a common sound, but the next sound she heard was highly unusual. It was her mother laughing! That couldn't be possible, thought Mi'Ra, it had to be another woman laughing; but what woman would be in the border zone, laughing? Even through the cheap tin door, it sounded like her mother. The hand on the hilt of her knife, she inserted a keycard and pushed the door open.

It was her mother, the downtrodden martyr to G'Kar's ambition, and she was roaring with laughter—for the first time in years! T'Kog, her strapping but spineless brother, was doubled over in laughter, gripping his sides.

Mi'Ra scowled. "I know G'Kar's death was a major event, but I don't understand this much levity."

"Oh, you will!" gasped T'Kog. He waved a finger at Ka'Het, who was so dejected earlier that morning that she couldn't get out of bed. "Tell her, Mother!"

The older woman usually looked gaunt and beaten, but today she heaved with joyous gasps. "We are rich, my dear! We are back in the good life again! As you said we never would be."

"Father has been absolved?" asked Mi'Ra, beaming at the thought.

That thought sobered Ka'Het. "Ah, no," she admitted. "This has no official effect on his case, but maybe that will change, too. We have the next best thing, which is *money*! Transferred directly into our old account. The banker sent an armored courier to tell us!"

"How much money?"

"Four hundred thousand Old Bloodstone!" gushed T'Kog.

"Keep your voice down," Mi'Ra hissed. "And who provided this windfall?"

T'Kog stopped laughing for a moment. "What does it matter? It's the same blackguards who stole it in the first place."

"Who was it?" Mi'Ra demanded of her mother.

The older woman looked away and straightened her ragged housedress. "It was G'Kar's widow, Da'Kal. I wondered when she would come through. She used to be one of my best friends, you know."

"Mother," said the young Narn woman, trying to remain calm, "that's only money. That was probably one year's housekeeping money in the old times. Nothing changes—we'll still be outcasts with no station in life, and Father will still be considered a traitor.''

"But we'll get out of *here*!" Ka'Het snarled. "With that much money, we can get some kind of life back. What do you think it will buy?"

Mi'Ra was thinking. It would not buy her silence, she knew that. It would buy the services of several mercenaries, and it might buy more creature comforts, but it wouldn't buy them respect. And how long would it really last? If she knew her mother, not very long.

"What do you plan to do with the money?" she asked matter-of-factly.

"Buy a home on the Islands, or some resort where the circles are allowed to mix. I think we'd be accepted in a place like that, even with our past."

*Our past,* Mi'Ra thought bitterly. They hadn't done anything wrong, yet her mother was still suffering guilt! "A house on the Islands," she observed dryly. "There goes most of the money."

T'Kog jumped to his feet and stared at his older sister. "You never want anything good to happen, because you're too obsessed with revenge. Whether you like it or not, *two* good things have happened, and I say we should rejoice! I'm with Mother. Let's get back to civilization."

Mi'Ra knew when to bide her time, and she bowed her head respectfully. "Mother, of course you are right. And may I suggest that you and my brother go on a house-hunting excursion to the Islands. But don't be hasty and grab the first thing."

"No, never!" said her mother. "If this experience has taught me anything, it's to be practical." She pulled at her rags. "Of course we'll have to buy some new clothes. Are you saying you wouldn't come with us?"

"No, you two go. I will stay and look after what we have here."

T'Kog laughed disdainfully. "We have nothing here, Mi'Ra. You're the only one who thinks we do. But I'm glad you agree with us."

"I want to get out of here as much as anyone," Mi'Ra assured her mother. "Now I'm going to lie down and take a nap."

"We splurged and bought some dry fish," said Ka'Het. "There is some in the pantry."

T'Kog moved lazily toward the door. "Mi'Ra, how was the memorial service?"

"Quite touching," she answered with all sincerity. "You would have thought he was a great man. Ra'Pak was there, and so were several Earthers from the place where he died, the Babylon 5 station. They can't arrest us, but they may want to ask us questions."

"In the name of the Martyrs, why?" asked Ka'Het. "Should we try to leave before they come?"

"No. They must have found the data crystal we sent to G'Kar, and they want to meddle."

"I knew that was a bad idea," said T'Kog righteously.

Mi'Ra narrowed her red eyes. "You agreed at the time, dear brother. We have never gone anywhere near Babylon 5, so they can't implicate us. We don't know anything about G'Kar's death, except that it wasn't us and it wasn't the Thenta Ma'Kur. Are we agreed?"

"Of course, my dear," said Ka'Het, patting her daughter's spotted hand. "You worry too much. We know what to say, and we *are* innocent. Do you suppose we should offer them a bribe? One never knows with humans."

Ka'Het touched her mother's hand and smiled. "No, Mother. Just be yourself. I think the Earthers are quite fascinated with us. I was told there is one among them who was married to a Narn."

T'Kog winced. "That's disgusting."

"This is the future," said Mi'Ra. "It may be our future,

too. On a Terran station such as Babylon 5, we would be exotic aliens with no past and only a future. Old Bloodstone could be rare on an Earth station, and our money might last longer. We should consider this.''

''We will,'' said Ka'Het. ''But I'm not sure I want to leave all my friends.''

*The same friends who haven't spoken to you in three years!* thought Mi'Ra angrily. She held her tongue. Her mother hadn't spent any of the money yet, and Mi'Ra had firstborn power of access. She could make withdrawals from this suddenly valuable account.

Truly, G'Kar's widow had done a noble thing, but it would be an empty gesture if the money were wasted. They could easily end up back in the border zone, more bitter and more estranged from society. Despite her mother's elation, this was not the answer to their problem. Plus, Mi'Ra was suspicious of this money. Why? And why now? What kind of silence was it supposed to buy? Whose guilt was it supposed to salve? Narns weren't known for experiencing much guilt.

When the Earthers arrived, decided Mi'Ra, she might have a few questions for them.

With hardly a whimper, the big red sun ducked behind the rim of Hekba Canyon, chased away by the blackest shadows imaginable. The shadows stretched like demons into the deepest crevices, stealing the heat as they went. Susan Ivanova must have sweated off ten kilos during the day, but now she was shivering and unable to stop, even wrapped in military-issue fleece. She was expecting the drop in temperature—she understood how thin atmosphere, low humidity, and weak air pressure could have this effect —but she still wasn't prepared for the reality of night on Homeworld. The commander could swear that her breath formed ice crystal bridges over the glaciers that used to be her cheekbones. The temperature must have plunged sixty degrees.

"Whose bright idea was it to come outside?" shuddered Garibaldi, pounding his arms against his chest in a futile attempt to keep warm. At least he wasn't complaining anymore about having to drag his coat with him.

"I told you, we can't stay on this high level," answered Al Vernon, glancing over the railing to the depths below. "We need to get lower into the canyon. In fact, all the way to the bottom."

Ivanova wanted to look over the edge of the railing, but she couldn't make her frozen muscles move. She unstuck her face long enough to ask, "Is it really that much warmer d-d-down there?"

Na'Toth scowled. "I don't see what you thin-skinned humans are complaining about. It's perfectly pleasant up here. I say, we go back into the tavern and wait for Ha'Mok as planned."

"It's been *hours*!" protested Ivanova. "What could he be doing?"

Al shook his head. "I don't know why we should be worrying so much about a simple crewman. Let Ha'Mok find his own way back. If he's not of the right circle, the rangers will probably catch him and send him packing, anyway. Na'Toth, if you want to stay and wait for him, that's okay with me, but we can't stay on this level. Humans *are* thin-skinned, and we don't have much insulation."

Al chuckled and patted his ample stomach. "When I lived here, I tried to pack on extra insulation, but it didn't help much."

Ivanova pried her frozen lips apart enough to ask, "Can we wait a little longer?"

Al squinted at his fellow humans. "You two can stay here and freeze to death—and it's going to get colder yet—

but I didn't sign on for that. I'd rather take a five-minute lift ride and be sitting down there beside a nice, bubbling, hot spring, dabbing the sweat off my brow. You can call the *K'sha Na'vas* from down there, can't you? Why do we have to wait for Ha'Mok—he's just a crewman, isn't he?''

Na'Toth glanced back at the tavern door, as if considering going back to wait. But Ivanova didn't think the Narn wanted to wait indefinitely in the tavern by herself. Not only had the establishment gotten substantially colder with the fall of darkness, it had gotten rowdier with an infusion of privileged young Narns who thought they owned the universe. Besides, it was beginning to look suspicious that they should be so concerned over a simple crewman. More than once, Ivanova had almost called Ha'Mok by his real name. If they weren't careful, Al Vernon was going to learn their secret.

Na'Toth finally slumped her shoulders. ''Yes, we can contact the *K'sha Na'vas* from the bottom. There is no way to predict how long Ha'Mok will be, and I can't force him to be sensible. Therefore, lead on, Mr. Vernon, I believe you know this city better than I do.''

''With pleasure,'' said Al. He swung his pudgy arms and headed off down the walkway. Garibaldi and Ivanova fell in step behind him, with Na'Toth bringing up a watchful rear. It felt good to be moving, thought Ivanova, with blood pumping to the outer extremities again. Growing up in Russia, she thought she knew what cold was, but Homeworld was causing her to rethink her most primal memories.

''We don't have to cross the bridge again, do we?'' asked Garibaldi with a shudder.

''I don't think so,'' said Al. ''The lifts don't begin here until half-a-dozen levels down. This is the commercial section—they want you to walk, giving you time to pass the shops and shop.''

Ivanova nudged Garibaldi. ''We can't forget about Captain Sheridan. To contact him, we have to return to the *K'sha Na'vas* sometime soon.''

''Maybe not,'' said Al, overhearing them. ''You won't find public screens with interstellar links on every corner, but this is a wealthy neighborhood, and they've got lots of interesting stuff behind closed doors. We'll ask around, *after* we get someplace warm.''

Ivanova was not about to argue with Al's priorities, not with icicles encasing her spine. The chill would have been worse, she marveled, without all those broth drinks she had consumed in the tavern. She hadn't tasted much alcohol in the drinks; if they were at all intoxicating, the freezing air must have snapped her right back into sobriety. Ivanova felt nothing but cold, creeping numbness all over her body, and she could barely remember that the same air had felt like a blast furnace a few hours ago. It felt as if Homeworld had been mired in the Ice Age for eternity.

In the dim light, Al Vernon walked down a level to check the markings on a newer section of dwellings. As if some kindly sensors realized he needed more light, green light filaments suddenly ignited all along the handrails and the swooping bridges that spanned the crevasse. Ivanova swiveled her head and stared in awe at the giant spiral of light. She felt as if she were inside a fluorescent, tubular spiderweb. The effect was quite startling, until she realized that the handrail filaments gave off little actual light and no warmth. If anything, the cool, impersonal lights made Ivanova feel even colder.

''Excellent,'' said Al. ''We shouldn't have any difficulty finding the lift now.''

He picked up the pace and lumbered confidently down one walkway after another. When he finally ducked inside a small cavern illuminated by blue lights, Ivanova almost kissed him, but her lips were stuck together. It was still bone-chilling even inside the cavern, and she ran to catch up with Al, mostly to keep warm. She could see his destination at the end of the corridor—a tiled alcove with an oval booth constructed from copper and black metals.

Garibaldi was right behind her, muttering to himself and flapping his arms. He tried to say something, but it just came out gibberish through his frozen lips. They huddled around Al, who was looking at a map—an elegant mosaic embedded in the walls of the chamber. It was barely illuminated by reddish pilot lights glimmering on the lift booth.

"Remind me to bring a flashlight next time I come here," said Garibaldi, his teeth chattering. "This whole trip is beginning to remind me of a camp I went to as a kid. Camp Windigo, upstate New York. That's the only place colder than this."

Ivanova smiled, afraid her face would crack. She turned to see Na'Toth saunter in. Dressed in her usual attire and a lightweight cape, the Narn had yet to notice the cold. She stood behind them and studied the mosaic map.

"There's an inn at the bottom," she pointed out. "They probably cater to you thin-skinned types."

"Maybe we should just return to the ship," said Garibaldi. "Then we'd have beds and be able to contact B5."

Al Vernon shook his head and shivered. "I'm afraid you waited too long to do that. The only place their shuttlecraft can land is up on the rim, and there's nothing there but desert. You think it's cold here, you should go up there and stand in the wind! We wouldn't last two minutes, I assure you. No, I'm afraid we can't go back to the *K'sha Na'vas* until daylight."

"Why didn't you tell us this?" snapped Garibaldi.

Al blinked at him. "Hey, it was you idiots who wanted to wait around for Ha'Mok to come back! I didn't know what was going on. Who is this Ha'Mok, anyway? Why is he so important?"

Ivanova, Garibaldi, and Na'Toth looked guiltily at one

another, knowing that one of them would probably reveal G'Kar's secret sooner or later. But it wasn't going to be right now, Ivanova decided.

"He's a special investigator," she lied. "One of our team."

The merchant shook his head. "I don't know what he's doing, but he cost us our chance to get off this planet tonight. I can't say I mind, though. This is exactly where I want to be."

Al Vernon pushed part of the mosaic, and the entire map lit up like a stained-glass window, sketching a path from their position on the sixth level to the very bottom, three hundred levels away. They heard a shuddering sound as a car rose from the bowels of the canyon to fetch them.

"You'll like it down there," Al assured them. "Although I hope your creditchits are good. Non-Narns pay extra for boarding and food."

"Great," muttered Garibaldi. "The captain still hasn't approved my expenses from the last trip I took."

Na'Toth frowned. "I still say this is pointless. We should stay where we agreed to stay."

Ivanova clutched her own shoulders and shivered. "Please, Na'Toth, none of us agreed to freeze to death."

To their considerable relief, the lift arrived at their level, and the doors whooshed opened. The humans jammed in, and Na'Toth entered reluctantly. The doors shut with a jolt, and Al warned, "These lifts are fast. Watch for changes in pressure."

A second later, Ivanova was close to screaming after what seemed like a sheer drop to the bottom of the shaft. Her stomach churned, her ears ached until they popped, and she could see Na'Toth yawning. The lift finally began to slow, and it deposited them gently at the bottom level of the canyon.

Following Al Vernon, Ivanova staggered off the plat-

form. The first thing she felt was the thick humidity, like
steam pouring from a hot shower. Then she smelled the
sulfur, magnesium, and other bitter minerals in the air. As
her eyes grew accustomed to the dark, Ivanova stepped
around a small geyser that bubbled on the slate floor and
shot gusts of steam around her ankles. It was soothingly hot
and sticky in the cavern, and Ivanova loosened her collar as
she followed Al Vernon through the dusky fissure.

She heard the voices and clink of glassware before she
even emerged into the grotto. Plump vines stroked her hair
as she ducked under a natural archway, and she found herself surrounded by sweaty vines, stretching high overhead.
Plants and steam seemed to flow in equal measure from the
moss-covered walls of the grotto. There were dining tables
set at spacious intervals, each with a collection of elegantly
dressed Narns seated at it. They regarded the humans with
suspicious looks but returned swiftly to their dinners and
conversation. Al Vernon plunged ahead as if the diners
weren't there. He seemed to have a destination in mind.

The civilized setting and warm humidity was beginning
to relax Ivanova, and she let down her guard as she wandered out of the grotto into a rock garden of geysers, bub-
bles, and sulfuric smells. She gasped as an intense current
of icy air sliced along her path and clutched her spine. Her
mind short-circuited, but her reflexes caused her to stumble
away and find a warm pocket of air. She stood perfectly
still in the gases of a hot pool, hardly minding the unctuous
smells of sulfur and methane. At least the methane was a
familiar smell.

As she stood in the hot mist, forcing her body temperature back to normal, Ivanova surveyed the primordial land-
scape at the bottom of Hekba Canyon. As above, the only
light came from green fibers embedded in the walkways.
Paths wound around uneven terrain, jagged rock outcrop-
pings, and assorted geysers, pools, and springs. The bottom

of Hekba Canyon had been left in a natural state, she decided, except for a few isolated strips of crops, plus elegant restaurants and inns. Polite laughter mingled with the gurgling and spitting of the hot springs. Thank God for geothermal energy, thought Ivanova, even in its natural state.

Garibaldi and Na'Toth had paused to inspect the grotto, and Al Vernon was out of sight. She hoped that he hadn't deserted them. She finally decided that no human was likely to wander far away from this place during the middle of a Narn night.

"Watch out for cold spots," she cautioned Garibaldi as he emerged from the grotto with what looked like strands of seaweed in his hair. The security chief glanced around warily, as if he could actually see a cold spot.

"You'll know when you hit one," she assured him.

Na'Toth's eyes narrowed. "Where did Mr. Vernon go?"

"Beats me," said Ivanova. "But this is an awfully warm spot where I'm standing, and I'm reluctant to move."

Garibaldi wrinkled his nose. "Smells like my old high school locker room down here."

"I was going to say it smells like chemistry class," said Ivanova. "Listen, if Al never does anything else but lead us down here, I'm grateful for his help. But we do need a plan. Where *are* we going to spend the night? Everything down here does look fairly expensive."

Na'Toth held up a small communications device. "Captain Vin'Tok gave me his direct link before we left. He said we could contact the ship and send for a shuttlecraft. I don't care what Mr. Vernon says, maybe there is a way to get you off the planet tonight. I'm sure you would be more comfortable spending the night on the *K'sha Na'vas*."

"Yeah," agreed Garibaldi, "and we'd be able to call the captain. Let's try it. I say we ditch both Al and good old Ha'Mok."

"Go ahead," said Ivanova.

Na'Toth activated the device and waited until it beeped. "Attaché Na'Toth to the *K'sha Na'vas,*" she said. "Come in, Captain Vin'Tok." When there was no response, she repeated, "Attaché Na'Toth to the *K'sha Na'vas.* Come in, Captain Vin'Tok. This is top priority—come in!"

She tapped the device. "It acts like it's working, and I've used these compact units before. Because they're encoded for one frequency, they are usually very reliable."

"Maybe we're too deep inside this canyon," suggested Garibaldi.

"That shouldn't make any difference." In frustration, Na'Toth tried again, saying the same words and achieving the same results, with one difference. This time, she studied the readouts on the device's tiny screen.

"Out of range," she said with confusion. "This device is telling me that the *K'sha Na'vas* is out of range. There's only one explanation for that. It's left orbit."

"Why would they leave orbit?" asked Garibaldi with disbelief.

Na'Toth squared her shoulders. "I don't know."

# CHAPTER 12

G'Kar nestled in Da'Kal's bosom, trying to tell himself he didn't have to get up, he didn't have to leave. But he knew it was a lie. He knew as surely as his name wasn't Ha'Mok that he was neglecting urgent business, including friends who were taking risks for him. He had come to Homeworld to squash his enemies, not take pity upon them and bequeath a substantial amount of cash to them! Yet that is precisely what had happened, all because he was soft and couldn't resist a woman's arms.

Quite a woman's arms they were, he had to admit. Many men would never have neglected a prize like Da'Kal for any amount of promotions and honors, but G'Kar wasn't many men. If he had been, he doubted whether Da'Kal would have wed him. He was not an ideal choice for her—a young Narn from a lesser circle with nothing to show but war medals—but she had been an ideal choice for him. Under her tutelage, he had learned how to curry favor and rise in the circles, and he had quickly surpassed her in ambition and ruthlessness. She took pride in his accomplishments, but she also maintained a distance, as if he were an experiment gone awry.

Da'Kal never seemed surprised at what he did, even this latest ploy. Despite all the other women, she was truly the only one for him, but she was never enough to keep him from his destiny. He had a role to fulfill on Babylon 5 that went beyond the petty concerns of Narn society; every day he spent there convinced him of it. However, his career seemed less important than ever at this moment.

G'Kar pressed himself against Da'Kal's compact body,

and she moaned at his touch but remained asleep. Despite his resolve to leave, he didn't want to. He had to admit that even G'Kar of the Third Circle, Ambassador to Babylon 5, the most important diplomatic post in the Regime—even he needed comfort and forgiveness. G'Kar welcomed the blissful amnesia of lovemaking, which had always been so satisfying with Da'Kal. Every molecule of her body had belonged to him once, and he knew how to please each of them. This night reminded him of their earliest nights together, when she had taken him in, and he had been the grateful one.

For an instant, he wondered if he and Da'Kal could simply run away together, leaving the rigid society and impossible commitments of the Narn Regime far behind them. They could be like this—a plain man in love with a plain woman—and maybe then he and Da'Kal could really build a life together. But he worried that his selfishness and ambition were too deeply ingrained. He was already plotting how to escape.

In her sleep, she twisted away from him, and he used that moment to slip his arm free and rise to his feet. It felt odd to have to steal away from his own bedroom, but G'Kar hadn't earned the right to remain here. He scooped up his clothing and dashed into the sitting room. As he pulled on his pants, he remembered that he was officially dead; if there was ever a time to start a new life, this was it. Then he shook his head. G'Kar had too much to live for, and the sooner he set matters straight with the Du'Rog family, the better.

He desperately hoped that Da'Kal's blood money would mollify the Du'Rog family, but he didn't think it would. When they found out he was alive, they would want more money, or his hide, or both. He had to meet face-to-face with that angry daughter, offer her a settlement that was good enough, or a threat that was strong enough. If he didn't have the courage to kill her, he would have to live with her. As tempting as it was, it wasn't possible to lie in Da'Kal's arms and ignore the past.

"Don't forget your disguise," said a voice. He turned around to find Da'Kal standing in the doorway, her robe hanging open. She tossed the spotted skullcap to the floor.

"It's not that I want to go," he said apologetically.

She smiled wearily. "You never *want* to go—it's always business, duty, or necessity."

"In this case, it's all three," said G'Kar, pulling on a boot. "But I'll be back when this is over."

"I suppose so. But will I be here when you come back?" Da'Kal shut the bedroom door softly, not slamming it, just shutting it.

With one boot on, G'Kar hobbled to her door and began to knock. Then he realized that he had nothing more to say to his spouse. She had heard all his excuses and rationalizations many times, and they didn't register anymore. She truly knew him better than anyone, his equal parts bravery and bluster, his independent, selfish streaks. One thing they had in common—they were both people of action. He marveled at the way she had moved decisively to appease the Du'Rog family, while he had let the situation fester for years. Physically, emotionally, socially, and in every other way they were suited to each other, yet he kept running off at moments when they could be getting closer.

That was the great gamble of their marriage, the risk he took whenever he left Da'Kal. Would she be there when he returned?

G'Kar sat down to pull on his other boot. Then he picked up his skullcap from the floor and carefully smoothed it over his real cranial spots. He reinserted the brown contact lenses that gave his face such a bland appearance. Once again, he was Ha'Mok, a simple crewman from the *K'sha Na'vas*.

He went again to Da'Kal's door, wondering if he should give her a parting word. But he still had nothing new to say. In the end, neglecting Da'Kal could be the worst mistake of his life, much worse than smearing Du'Rog. One day, he knew, he would have to answer for his neglect of his marriage along with everything else.

He took a final glance at his disguise in the mirror and was satisfied. The Narn crewman pulled back the bolt, opened the door, and hurled himself into the blustery night. He put his head into the wind and strode down the walkway toward the bridge. He had told Na'Toth and the humans to wait for him in the tavern, but he had no desire to spend much time in a public place. He had taken enough risks already. The puny humans were probably cold by now, so they shouldn't mind returning to the *K'sha Na'vas* as soon as possible.

Figuring that he might as well summon the shuttlecraft, G'Kar took a small device from his belt. He pressed it, waited for the beep, then began to talk. "This is Ha'Mok to Captain Vin'Tok aboard the *K'sha Na'vas*. Come in, Captain Vin'Tok aboard the *K'sha Na'vas*. Respond, please."

When no one answered, he studied the device and shook it in his ear. "Bah!" he muttered. "The Earthers make better links than this." He tried contacting the ship again, and this time he watched the readouts.

*Out of range?*

How in the name of the Martyrs was that possible? G'Kar tried to stay calm. He and Vin'Tok had talked about the possibility of the *K'sha Na'vas* being reassigned, or having to respond to an emergency. Both prospects seemed remote, given the *K'sha Na'vas*'s high position in the fleet. Still, it would seem as if the *K'sha Na'vas* had left orbit; there was no other logical explanation for their being out of range. Under normal circumstances, G'Kar would have a dozen options, ranging from ordering another shuttlecraft to commandeering quarters in the nearest inn. Unfortunately, the options of a dead man were limited at best.

Troubled, G'Kar put the device away and strode across the swinging bridge. This was a temporary inconvenience, he assured himself. The *K'sha Na'vas* might have left orbit to refuel, take on supplies, ferry crew members, or any number of errands. It didn't mean he was stranded here.

The soothing darkness on the bridge helped to calm his fears, and G'Kar convinced himself that his disguise was almost foolproof. Especially at night. Even Narns who knew him personally were not likely to pay much attention to him. All he had to do was find his friends, and they could put their heads together and decide how to proceed. The ambassador stepped determinedly off the bridge and headed for the tavern where he had left his comrades.

Laughter and raucous voices poured from the tavern and gave G'Kar a moment's hesitation. Then he reminded himself that Hekba City was a civilized place, without the usual riffraff. He puffed up his chest and entered the dusky tavern, thinking that he would have little difficulty locating three humans in this crowd. Even though he peered into every corner of the establishment, he saw only young Narns, the privileged sons and daughters of the ruling circles. In his youth, he had tried to run with a crowd like this, but he had never been immature enough. He couldn't spend entire evenings frittering away his time, as they could.

"Are you lost?" a young aristocrat asked snidely. "This is no spaceport."

G'Kar started to scowl at him, then he remembered that they weren't seeing G'Kar of the Third Circle—they were seeing a common crew member, a plebeian. He bowed apologetically and held out his hands.

"I was told there were human passengers in here. Has anyone seen my human passengers?"

"The humans left hours ago!" shouted the proprietor.

"And you will, too," added a customer, "if you know what's good for you!"

Now the raucous laughter was at his expense, but G'Kar kept smiling and bowing. He had spent so much time on Babylon 5 that he had forgotten how lower classes were unwelcome in certain neighborhoods after dark. G'Kar kept bowing politely as he backed his way out the door, which caused him to run into a large Narn in a black uniform.

"Watch it there!" said a ranger from the Rural Division, shoving G'Kar aside. "Get back to your ship."

"Just leaving," G'Kar assured the ranger, almost scraping the ground with his bow. To demonstrate, he hustled up the walkway toward the rim of the canyon, and the ranger nodded with satisfaction and ducked inside the tavern. G'Kar did an immediate about-face and slipped past the tavern, headed deeper into Hekba Canyon.

Now he was worried. It was not a good sign that both the *K'sha Na'vas* and his comrades were gone. True, he had lingered much too long in Da'Kal's bed, and he couldn't blame the humans for not waiting hours for him in a slight chill. Plus, the clientele of the tavern had turned rather unpleasant. The humans had probably returned to the ship, G'Kar told himself. Yes, that was a logical explanation to one mystery, but it didn't explain why Na'Toth was gone. Na'Toth should have realized his precarious position and been there waiting for him.

G'Kar halted in the middle of his step. What if they hadn't gone back to the ship? Where would the humans go? To the warmer bowels of the canyon, he imagined, someplace he would not dare to go. They could get away with going down there, because they were off-worlders, but in his crewman's garb he would stand out like a Centauri's hair. Plus, he had no money, having given his emergency funds to Al Vernon. He could imagine his friends and acquaintances dining late in the grotto, by the warmth of the hissing geysers. Perhaps they were making a toast to his departed soul.

He looked up at the stars glimmering over the great slit in the planet, and he wondered what madness had brought him to this point. Alone, penniless, unrecognized in his hometown, and wearing the disguise of a simple crewman —he must have been atoning for some terrible sins. The idea of coming out in the open, revealing all of his secrets, was beginning to appeal to G'Kar. What worse could Narn society do to him than he had done to himself? He was in a netherworld, neither dead nor alive, caught between the clay and the heavens.

G'Kar tried to mold into the shadows along the cliff face, hoping he could avoid the authorities for an entire night. He trusted Na'Toth to eventually return to the tavern, the place they had agreed to meet. Plus, he saw no reason to stray too far from Da'Kal's house in case he needed a genuine sanctuary. He thought about going back there now, but his pride wouldn't let him. If need be, he had his fake identicard and his excuse to be looking for human passengers.

G'Kar settled into a crevice in the rock, hoping the Earthers were passing a better evening than he was.

Outside the grotto, Ivanova, Na'Toth, and Garibaldi stared sullenly at each other. They were tired of discussing what they should do. Na'Toth wanted to return to the tavern to look for G'Kar, and Ivanova wanted to contact Captain Sheridan. Al was still missing in action, so he couldn't be polled. Garibaldi was content to stand near a sputtering little geyser that stunk like a skunk but shot warm steam around his legs. All three of them wanted to contact the *K'sha Na'vas,* but that didn't seem to be an option. Even if they did contact the *K'sha Na'vas,* neither human wanted to brave the plunging temperatures at the top of the canyon.

"We can't abandon G'Kar," whispered Na'Toth, reviving her favorite argument.

Ivanova sighed. "We've gone out on plenty of limbs for G'Kar. Maybe it's time we started thinking about *our* mess instead of G'Kar's mess. We've been out of contact with our superiors for days, we're out of contact with the *K'sha Na'vas,* and we're aiding and abetting a fraudulent death scheme. Homeworld at night is colder than humans can stand, and we seem to have wandered into a ritzy nightclub section."

Garibaldi cut in. "Plus we lost Al, and he's my responsibility. Which way did you say he went?"

Ivanova sighed. "I told you, he took a right turn out of the grotto, and I lost him when I hit that cold spot."

"Right." Garibaldi's gaze drifted toward a Narn couple who were walking among the bubbling pools, and his gaze followed them into the grotto. Now he understood where G'Kar's overly mannered style came from; it was de rigueur among this class of people. Deeper inside the lush grotto, a colorful blimp moved among the aristocratic Narn, looking completely alien, like a parade flag slicing through a sea of bronze statues.

"Excuse me," Garibaldi told the ladies, as he took off at a jog. "Al! We're over here!"

"Garibaldi!" shouted the merchant, waving his stubby arms. The Narns regarded the uncouth humans through lizard-lidded eyes, but the two men converged and began to speak in low tones. The denizens went back to polite repartee.

"Where have you been?" said Garibaldi, suspecting that Al had given himself some extra time to conduct personal business.

"I've been trying to find us a place to stay." The merchant sounded hurt at Garibaldi's accusatory tone. "And I've been successful, although it won't be cheap."

"Why am I not surprised?" Garibaldi scowled and turned around to see Na'Toth and Ivanova approaching. Neither one of them looked particularly pleased to see Al, and they regarded him with sullen faces.

"You're our guide, and we need some guidance," said Ivanova.

Na'Toth crossed her arms. "I am going to the top and wait for our missing comrade."

"Hold on just a minute," said Al. "Let me tell you what *I've* arranged. There are several inns here, but this is the social season, and they're all filled. However, I have prevailed upon an old associate, the manager of the Hekbanar Inn, to give us his second-best suite. I believe there are two chambers, and we can make the same sleeping arrangements we had on the *K'sha Na'vas*."

Garibaldi cleared his throat. "How much of a cut are *you* getting out of this?"

"My friend," protested Al, "you cut me to the quick! If you can make better arrangements, please do so. We're not going up to the rim tonight, so logic dictates that we have to spend the night down here. The sooner you accept that fact, the sooner we can make ourselves comfortable." He winked at Na'Toth. "Besides, this is the most romantic time of year in Hekba City."

"I'm not staying," said Na'Toth. "I intend to look for Ha'Mok and contact the *K'sha Na'vas,* as was our original plan."

"Oh, yeah!" Al produced a fresh newspad and squinted at it. "I don't read Narn as well as I used to, but I take it there's been an alert at one of the colonies. Every ship in the Golden Order was summoned, including the *K'sha Na'vas*."

"That's highly unusual," said Na'Toth, grabbing the pad from his hand. "The Golden Order is the personal fleet of the Inner Circle, what you might call our last line of defense. This is terrible luck for G—'' She started to say his name and caught herself on the first syllable. ''Just everybody,'' she finished.

''Is the *K'sha Na'vas* really gone?'' Ivanova asked.

Na'Toth flipped to another page on the pad and nodded her head slowly. ''She's gone. Although the action would seem more a ceremonial show of force than an all-out battle. I suppose if you wanted to show somebody what a Narn fleet looked like, the Golden Order would be an impressive choice.''

Al clapped his hands. ''Let's not be so glum, shall we? I can tell you from experience, there are worse places on Homeworld to spend the night than the bottom of Hekba Canyon. And far worse lodgings than the Hekbanar Inn. And tomorrow, if you still want to go to the border zone, I'll take you there. Early morning, the temperature will be perfect, and that should be a safe time to go there. We don't need a shuttlecraft—there is public transportation.''

''Is that right?'' Garibaldi asked Na'Toth.

Na'Toth nodded her head absently. ''We have excellent public transportation on Homeworld. After hearing this news, I am more determined than ever to find Ha'Mok. Hold the room for us—we will meet you at the Hekbanar Inn.''

Al cleared his throat. ''Are you sure you want to bring a common crewman down here? You know better than I . . .''

Na'Toth scowled. ''We'll be careful.'' With that, the determined Narn strode off toward the grotto. Garibaldi watched her until she ducked under some dripping vines and vanished inside the cavern.

''Lead on,'' said Ivanova with a resigned sigh.

An ebullient Al Vernon led them down the walkway, past the grotto, and through a stretch of classy boutiques, gaming parlors, and sidewalk cafes, interspersed with hissing geysers and smelly pools. The fancy watering holes were indeed packed, with Narns who were as stiff and well behaved as mannequins. Garibaldi had to remind himself that these effete-looking snobs were ruthless conquerors who ruled dozens of solar systems and claimed vast expanses of space. A few generations back, they had been slaves. The Narns took stock of their visitors as they walked past, but they seemed fairly blasé about the sight of off-world dignitaries.

Garibaldi was actually getting used to the idea of spending the night in the lap of luxury. After all, luxury wasn't a condition in which he found himself very often. Maybe he shouldn't go kicking and screaming against the idea. Let Captain Sheridan deal with his expense account.

"You there!" He heard a deep-voiced shout.

All three humans stopped in their tracks and whirled around. Garibaldi spotted three Narns standing on a second-story balcony that overlooked a small cafe. The Narns in the cafe regarded the Narns on the balcony and nodded approvingly at them. Two of the Narns on the balcony were broad-shouldered males, but the third one was an elegant woman wearing a black gown and golden jewelry.

"Earthers, may we talk with you?" spoke the deep-voiced man, this time sounding more polite.

Garibaldi shrugged. "Why not." He led his tiny party through the cafe to the patio beneath the balcony.

The two men stepped back, as if deferring to the woman, and she leaned over the balcony to study them. Now Garibaldi recognized her—it was the noblewoman who had attended G'Kar's memorial service, the same one who had been visiting G'Kar's widow when they showed up there.

"I am Ra'Pak," she said pleasantly. "And you are the delegation from Babylon 5. We have met twice today, but we didn't have the opportunity to talk."

She hadn't seemed very interested in talking to them either time, Garibaldi recalled, but they had her attention now. Before he could speak, Al made an exaggerated bow.

"Your Highness, I am Al Vernon, a former resident of this lovely planet. This is Commander Susan Ivanova and Security Chief Michael Garibaldi. It is an honor to address a member of the Inner Circle."

Ra'Pak nodded at the compliment. "I had no idea you would be spending the night in Hekba City. I simply want to make sure your needs are being met. Is there anything you require?"

Ivanova answered quickly. "We need to contact our superior on Babylon 5. The ship that brought us here was called away, and now we're not sure where to go."

The elegant woman straightened up and spoke to the man standing to her left. He nodded solemnly and went inside. Ra'Pak leaned over to say, "My cousin, who owns this villa, has consented to let you use his netlink. He's coming down to let you in. I hope you have a pleasant stay with us." With that, Ra'Pak glided back into the party room.

Garibaldi turned his attention to a door beneath the balcony; it looked like stained glass and twinkled eerily. He finally saw what made the strange twinkling lights when a tall Narn opened the door and held out a candelabra filled with white candles.

He bowed politely. "Won't you come in?"

Al Vernon started to push past Garibaldi, but the security chief held out his hand. "No offense, Al, but we've got to talk privately to the captain."

"That's fine with me," said Al, pointing upward. "I'll be upstairs. When you get a chance to hobnob with these people, you do it."

Al brushed past him, and Garibaldi shrugged at Ivanova and followed him inside the villa. The foyer reminded the chief of a carnival fun house, because the walls were decorated with some sort of mirrored surface that reflected the candlelight and made it appear as if flickering candelabras stretched into infinity. There were also gently pulsating lights in the ceiling and floor, which were both disorienting and oddly relaxing. He had to look away from the hypnotic flashes and concentrate on his host's face.

"I am R'Mon of the Third Circle," said the man with a somber bow.

"Terrible about Ambassador G'Kar, isn't it?" said Al morosely. "He was in his prime."

"He was gristle," said R'Mon.

"Yes, he was gristle," agreed Al, as if they had been close personal friends.

"Excuse me, sir," interrupted Garibaldi, "the lady said you had a netlink?"

"Yes." R'Mon bowed. "I am conducting a considerable amount of business with Earth companies these days, so I'm on your central net. I am certain all your codes will work. Right this way."

He led them through a darkened boudoir that had faint echoes of fading comets streaking across the sky. They came upon a mirror that made Garibaldi look as chubby as Al Vernon, and R'Mon pushed the door open to reveal a well-appointed office.

Al stopped at the doorway. "Excuse me, sir, but I couldn't help smelling the *tagro*. Do you think I could have a sip of that ambrosia before we leave your splendid villa?"

The Narn smiled. "Certainly, Mr. Vernon. Please come upstairs with me." He motioned to Ivanova. "Take your time, and when you are done please come upstairs. Join us in a toast to G'Kar."

"Thank you," said Garibaldi, looking doubtfully into the dimly lit room. "Excuse me, are we going to have privacy in here?"

"It is my *private* office," the Narn assured him. "My business depends on privacy."

The Narn motioned to Al, who was happy to lead the way out of the bedroom and toward the party. Garibaldi followed Ivanova into the office, which was austere in comparison with the rest of the exotic furnishings. The terminal was a universal type that Ivanova had no trouble deciphering. Garibaldi stood watch at the door and finally just shut it, thinking that if there were listening devices in the room there was little he could do about it. They had to trust R'Mon of the Third Circle, and they still had to be careful.

"The link is going to take a few minutes," said Ivanova, studying the board, "but the request is going through."

Garibaldi stuffed his hands in his pockets. "How do you want to handle this from here?"

The commander rubbed her eyes. "Provided we get a good night's sleep, I say we head off for the border zone first thing in the morning, like Al suggested. I'm almost inclined to tell Du'Rog's family the truth, so we can make it very clear why we don't want them to get near B5."

"That's fine with me," agreed Garibaldi. "But what are we going to do with Ha'Mok?"

"I don't know." Ivanova yawned, then gave him a smile. "Sorry."

"I understand. It's warm in here, and it's making me sleepy."

She was still yawning when Captain Sheridan's square-jawed face appeared on the central viewer. "There you are!" he said with relief. "There's a possibility that G'Kar may not be dead."

"We know all about it," said Garibaldi, leaning over Ivanova's shoulder. "This is not a secured channel, so let's not go into the gruesome details."

The captain nodded. "All right, but there's enough

funny stuff in this matter that I'm recalling both of you. Get the *K'sha Na'vas* to bring you back immediately.''

''The *K'sha Na'vas* got sent on a mission,'' said Ivanova, ''and we still haven't talked to the Kha'Ri. We're sort of marooned for the night, but I think we'll be okay.''

Garibaldi gave the captain a shrug. ''Provided you'll approve our traveling expenses.''

''Yes, yes, as long as you're trying to come back as soon as possible. I'll have Earthforce send a ship for you, but that will take a few days. If you can find any way to get home sooner, do it. Don't worry about how much it costs— I'll take it out of your bonuses.'' The captain forced a smile, telling them that he was worried and wanted to see them come home.

''We'll see you as soon as possible,'' Ivanova promised. ''Considering this new information, we feel we should pay a visit to the Du'Rog family and warn them about staying away from B5. Believe me, we don't want to spend another night on Homeworld. Garibaldi says it's colder than upstate New York.''

''That's cold. Be careful.''

''We're trying.''

# CHAPTER 13

G'Kar shifted uncomfortably from one leg to another, wishing he could at least find a place to sit down. But there were no benches on the narrow walkways of Hekba Canyon, only wind, darkness, and an occasional passerby to hide from. At intervals he tried to contact the *K'sha Na'vas,* with no success. His lonely vigil was all the more irksome because he could think of dozens of places where he would be welcome for the night, if only he were G'Kar again. The novelty of being dead had definitely worn off.

He continued to marvel at the popularity of the seedy tavern a few doors away, especially among young Narns of a certain breeding. He watched them come and go, wondering if he had ever been as shallow and arrogant as that. He supposed so, which was a depressing thought. Having never been on the outside looking in at the upper circles, he had never realized that the malcontents had a point. Who was to say that the vagaries of birth alone should determine a person's future?

There had to be plebeians who were more deserving of the jobs for which these spoiled youngsters were being groomed. They would never get the chance, however. The best they could hope for would be an assignment aboard a starship like the *K'sha Na'vas,* where they would see something of life outside Homeworld before they died, unsung, without a fancy memorial service.

G'Kar heard voices, and he turned to see two large figures approaching him from a lower level. As they mounted the staircase to reach his level, he again pressed himself into a crevice in the cold rock and tried to look invisible.

For a plebeian, it seemed to be distressingly easy to look invisible, he mused. But not this time.

One of the men shined a light directly into his face, blinding him and forcing him to raise his hands. The other one stepped forward and knocked his hands down. G'Kar tensed for a fight, then realized that they were rangers and he was in the wrong place, dressed the wrong way.

"We had complaints about a person loitering on this level," said the one who had knocked his hands down. "Let us see your face."

"Yes, sir," answered G'Kar, turning his face from side to side and squinting into the light. "Anything else?"

"Yes. What are you doing here? This isn't a place for shore leave."

"I am crewman Ha'Mok of the *K'sha Na'vas*," said G'Kar, trying to sound proud of his lowly station. "I am here, awaiting my passengers."

"Isn't the *K'sha Na'vas* in the Golden Order?" asked the other officer.

"Yes," said G'Kar hesitantly, wondering why that should be notable.

"Then your story doesn't fit. Your fleet was called away on a mission. Do you have an identicard?"

"Yes," G'Kar answered with a nervous gulp. He fumbled in his waistcoat for it, thinking how much trouble he was in. If they took him to a processing center, he would be searched and his secret revealed, and he didn't know whom he could trust in the Rural Division.

Smiling pleasantly at his tormentors, he handed them his identicard. One of the rangers snatched it from him and ran it through a small handheld device. They both stared menacingly at him while they awaited the results.

"I am Ha'Mok of the *K'sha Na'vas*," he assured them.

"This is a funny place to wait for passengers," remarked

the ranger with the light. "Especially when your ship is light-years away."

G'Kar shrugged and tried to smile, but his confidence was waning. He could remember times when he had reported suspicious people loitering in Hekba City, and he wondered if they had been treated as contemptuously as this. He supposed so, as the lines of Narn social behavior were tightly drawn.

"His identicard checks out," reported the ranger, sounding disappointed. "I still say we bring him in. His conduct and story are both suspicious."

"My story is true!" he protested. Nevertheless, the two rangers grabbed his arms and hauled him rudely to the edge of the railing. For a moment, G'Kar feared they would throw him over.

"So there is my servant!" called another voice. The three men whirled around to see a tall Narn woman striding toward them. When the ranger shined his light in her face, G'Kar was never so relieved to see another Narn in his entire life. It was Na'Toth!

He bowed down to her. "Good evening, my liege. I explained to them that I was waiting for you."

The rangers peered suspiciously at Na'Toth, and one of them growled, "Who are you?"

She grabbed his hand and directed the beam of light toward the insignia on her chest. "Na'Toth, diplomatic attaché to Babylon 5 and aide to Ambassador G'Kar."

"Oh!" exclaimed the ranger, straightening to attention. "We had reports of a suspicious person . . ."

"I was delayed," explained Na'Toth. "This crewman was following my orders to the letter by waiting for me."

"But his ship has left . . ."

"Temporarily and very suddenly," said Na'Toth. "You know that the Golden Order doesn't stay away long from Homeworld. Crewman Ha'Mok is my shuttlecraft pilot.

Come along." She pushed G'Kar ahead of her, and he shuffled gratefully down the walkway.

The rangers stood and watched for a while, but they didn't pursue. Nevertheless, G'Kar and Na'Toth put considerable distance between themselves and the uniformed authorities before they stopped to talk.

"That was close!" said G'Kar. "Where have you been?"

Na'Toth raised a hairless brow. "I could ask you the same question."

"All right," muttered G'Kar, "now we're even. What happened to the humans? Did they make it back to the *K'sha Na'vas*?"

"The *K'sha Na'vas* left before any of us knew about it," said Na'Toth. "We're on our own, and that includes the humans. At least they find it habitable at the bottom of the canyon."

G'Kar shook his head miserably. "I was counting on Vin'Tok. Do you notice, as soon as anybody starts to help me, they disappear! I've almost decided to confront the Du'Rog family and tell them the truth."

"Before we do anything really foolish," said Na'Toth, "let's get you out of sight. We supposedly have a room at the Hekbanar Inn."

G'Kar scowled. "That pesthole?"

At the party, Ivanova had commenced shivering again. She could tolerate the temperature, but there was a noticeable difference on the second story of the villa compared to the ground level of the canyon. The temperature wasn't the only thing that was chilly. The Narns seemed little interested in talking to them, although they cast a reptilian eye her way. To be fair, she wasn't feeling very sociable either, and she was content to watch the cultured guests float in and out of the party. She had seen R'Mon briefly but

Ra'Pak not at all since coming upstairs from the netlink in the office.

She could see Al Vernon, flitting about from one congregation of Narns to another, running into a few old acquaintances, most of whom were polite but noncommittal about meeting him again. That was okay for Al; he was content to work the room and introduce himself. Maybe he was looking for his wife or someone who knew her, mused Ivanova; he certainly seemed to be enjoying himself. There came Garibaldi chasing after him, trying to get him away from the party.

With reluctance, Al made another round of handshakes and let Garibaldi push him to the staircase. Ivanova was right behind them.

"You're missing a great opportunity," Al lectured them. "You might never meet these kind of people anywhere else."

"I meet Narns every day," growled Garibaldi. "And I want to meet two of them back at this hotel you keep talking about. So lead on!"

They tromped down the stairs and out into the exotic geyser pit, with its softly lit walkways trodden by cultured Narns. Al now acted like he was in a hurry, and it was all she and Garibaldi could do to keep up. It was evident that he knew the bottom of the canyon well, and he led them past four very similar-looking inns dug from the cliff only to arrive at the fifth, the Hekbanar Inn.

The lobby of the inn looked like a boudoir, with lounging sofas, soft music, and twinkling lights. The men seemed intent upon negotiating with the proprietor, so Ivanova let them have their fun. That way, Garibaldi would have to produce his creditchit first.

Ivanova sat down in one of the luxuriant sofas and stretched her legs. The hypnotic blips of light in the walls and ceilings seemed to form some sort of pattern, and she lay back to study the shifting vectors on the ceiling. She was blissfully asleep by the time the men returned.

"There are cheaper rooms than the one we're taking," grumbled Garibaldi.

"The best thing about the suite is it's on ground level," insisted Al. "There are natural hot springs to lie around in, to keep it warm and cozy, and you wouldn't believe the laser show!"

"Let's take it," said Ivanova, dragging herself to her feet.

As the dust devils frolicked on Street V'Tar, Mi'Ra carefully shut the front door of her mother's house. She had to double-check that it was locked, because the persistent wind had sent the clay candle crashing to the porch. Her mother and brother were still celebrating the windfall of Da'Kal's money, and they were poring over advertisements in old newspads that Ka'Het had saved. The only ones she saved, thought Mi'Ra angrily, were stories of her father's fall from greatness and his pathetic attempts to clear his name.

Ka'Het had no collection of his triumphs, only his failures, as if Du'Rog was totally defined by his fall. Her mother's fatalism and insipid belief in things getting better on their own drove Mi'Ra crazy. Many nights she just had to get away from her.

The young Narn hated to be cynical, but she was. She just couldn't believe that Da'Kal's money came with no strings attached. If she had learned anything in her young life, it was that the bill for everything came due sooner or later. It had come due for her father, for her, and even for G'Kar. They would learn eventually what Da'Kal needed from the Du'Rog family in exchange for this blood money. Until then, she would reserve judgment on Da'Kal's generosity.

Mi'Ra stepped into the street, heeding her instincts that she was not alone on this blustery night. No one was in sight, but some people in the border zone never walked in the open. She kept moving, with no real destination in mind, except the thought of the illegal taverns on Street Jasgon. They were holes in the clay, where one might obtain illegal drugs, stolen goods, sex, and even conversation, if one wasn't too picky. She should have been afraid to go to Street Jasgon, but she wasn't. Mi'Ra wasn't afraid of the evil she knew, but she was afraid of the rustling in the dark, the shadow that moved when she moved.

She whirled around and dropped to a crouch, aiming her PPG at a water barrel that was cracked and dusty. "Who's there? I'll shoot!"

"Please!" came a tiny voice. "Don't shoot, I'm only following orders!" Behind the water barrel, two scrawny arms shot into the air.

"Is that you, Pa'Ko?" she asked.

"Yes, yes!" cried the boy. He ran out from behind the water barrel and did a cartwheel in the middle of the street, landing perfectly on his thin, bare legs. Mi'Ra had never been able to peg Pa'Ko's age exactly —he was small for a Narn and looked no older than ten full cycles. But he often acted older, especially in the way he stayed up all night and never left the streets. She supposed that everyone who lived in the border zone aged prematurely.

She holstered her weapon. "What do you mean, you were following orders?"

"I mean, a man paid me to find you." With awe, Pa'Ko reached into a threadbare pocket and held out two black coins.

"To find me?" Mi'Ra asked with alarm. She stopped and surveyed the windblown street, wondering who else was lurking in the shadows.

The lad did another cartwheel and landed right beside

her. He barely came up to her shoulders. "The man asked me if I knew where you lived. I said I did, but I wouldn't show him your house—that could be dangerous. I only agreed to watch for you and give you a message."

"What is this message?" asked Mi'Ra warily.

"At the north end of Street Jasgon, a shuttlecraft is parked. You are to go there and meet him." Pa'Ko smiled and held out his hand, cocking his head from side to side. "Now you will give me a reward, too."

"Get out of here!" scoffed Mi'Ra. She took a mock swing at the youngster, but he deftly dodged it. "Who is this man?"

Pa'Ko shrugged. "Do I look like I know people who fly around in fine shuttlecrafts? It is parked there now. I would go see him, if I were you."

"It wasn't a human, was it?" asked Mi'Ra.

The boy laughed, and it was a surprisingly joyous sound. "A human from Earth? That is even more rare than a shuttlecraft!"

"Some humans will be looking for us tomorrow," said Mi'Ra thoughtfully. "If you spot them first, you might have a chance to make some more money."

"Critical!" yelled the young Narn. Pa'Ko stared into his hand at his newfound riches, then ran off down the street, a collection of gangly limbs. He darted between two houses and was gone.

Mi'Ra took a deep breath and thought about going back to the house to get her brother, to back her up. But T'Kog wouldn't flex a muscle now that he had money again, however briefly. The only place he would be willing to go would be an expensive vacation, or house hunting. More than ever, she felt alone and shut out from everything—her family, her birthright, even her revenge. Besides, this mysterious stranger hadn't sent the boy to look for her whole family, just her.

She stuck to the center of Street V'Tar for as long as she could, then she pulled out her knife and slipped into the alley. There were people burning debris, but they were a good hundred meters away. She skirted along the wall until she reached the archway, then she dashed through, slashing her knife. Only the dust devils took notice of her heroics, and they swirled around her admiringly.

Mi'Ra decided not to walk directly down Street Jasgon, knowing she might meet people she knew. It was the hour of the night when almost anyone might be walking the streets of the border zone, and the attractions of Jasgon were not unknown in the upper circles. Mi'Ra hoped this stranger wasn't some playboy having a joke at her expense, hoping to get his way with a woman who had fallen from grace. She wasn't that desperate to brush up to power again. Mi'Ra had endured countless propositions since moving to this hovel, but she had entertained none of them. The daughter of Du'Rog wanted to get back into the upper circles, but she wanted to do so on her own terms. Her father's reputation had to be rehabilitated at the same time, and she tried to ignore how unlikely that was to happen.

The young Narn kept to the walls and alleys, passing a few people but doing it too swiftly to be noticed. She could be very lizardlike when she wanted to be, darting away from danger, holding perfectly still, moving in spurts with little wasted energy. In dashes from wall to wall and building to building, she reached the end of Street Jasgon without having set foot in it. Just as Pa'Ko had foretold, there was a gray, unmarked shuttlecraft sitting in a windblown field, crushing a few scraggly stalks of grain.

Mi'Ra walked slowly toward the sleek craft, her hand on her PPG. It was, indeed, a very fine shuttlecraft, better than the military or rangers had. Mi'Ra noticed movement in the small cockpit, and a light flashed for a second. She wondered whether an image had been taken of her. So what if it had? She wasn't a fugitive, and her likeness and history were well known, even if her existence was determinedly ignored in certain circles. Let them see that she wasn't afraid or ashamed of facing them, as they were of her.

As she drew closer, the hatch door opened upward. She froze with her hand on her weapon, waiting. A man dressed in evening finery, as if he were about to dine in the grotto, stepped off the shuttlecraft. He looked around the area, making sure she hadn't been followed or molested, then he nodded to her. When she stepped closer, he motioned inside the expensive shuttlecraft.

"A lady would like to speak with you," he said.

"A lady?" She stared at him warily. "Da'Kal, the widow?"

The man smiled with amusement. "No."

"Come in," called a woman's steely voice. It was the kind of voice that brooked no nonsense, and Mi'Ra climbed aboard the shuttlecraft without further hesitation. This was a royal summons, and she was still Narn enough to obey.

Seated at the navigator's station was a woman wearing a long, black gown, with her legs crossed seductively. Mi'Ra recognized her immediately, having seen her earlier that day. It was Ra'Pak of the Inner Circle. The young Narn had the sinking feeling that she was going to get the bill for Da'Kal's gratitude before even a single coin had been spent. If this was a warning for her to keep her place and keep her mouth shut, Mi'Ra was going to give this woman an earful.

"You are angry all the time, aren't you?" observed Ra'Pak.

"Yes," answered the younger woman. "I'm waiting for a reason to be content."

"I'm afraid I can't give you that." Ra'Pak suppressed a smile. "Seeing as how you're already angry, I don't feel too badly about telling you something that will make you even angrier."

"That would be difficult."

"I don't think so. What if I told you that G'Kar had faked his death and was still alive?"

"What?" Mi'Ra was trembling.

"You heard me, and it is the truth. I suspected something was amiss with G'Kar's death, and the Earthers confirmed it just tonight."

"They helped him fake his death?" asked Mi'Ra, thinking that the human she had met didn't seem the type for underhanded fraud.

"No, they only discovered what he did a short time ago themselves. I eavesdropped when they were talking with their commander on Babylon 5. It is definite— G'Kar is alive. If you don't believe me, you can wait for a few days, and the news will come out on its own."

Still in shock, Mi'Ra ran her hands over her cranium. She could feel the scar where she had sealed her *Shon'Kar*. "If he lives, then I will not be denied."

"Oh, he lives," Ra'Pak assured her. "And you won't be denied if you move swiftly. My spies believe he is on Homeworld now—he may even be traveling with the humans, wearing a disguise. This is the time to strike, while he is supposedly dead and is still within easy reach."

Mi'Ra growled and shook her fist. "That blasted Thenta Ma'Kur—they lied to me!"

Ra'Pak shrugged. "It isn't the first time they've taken credit for something they didn't do. They are snakes."

"But why would G'Kar do this thing?"

"Fear of you."

The young Narn smiled, feeling the blood surging within her breast, flowing to her brain and muscles. Her message to G'Kar had gotten through, and not only would she kill him, she would make him suffer for his treachery. It pleased her to know that he had already suffered enough to fake his own death. Then she realized that Da'Kal's blood money might have come from G'Kar, with his blessings! He couldn't buy his way out of this, but she wouldn't stop him from trying. Maybe they could have his money *and* his blood.

Ra'Pak nodded with satisfaction. "I see that you were the right person to inform about this chicanery."

"And why did you tell me?"

The noblewoman's face hardened into a ghastly mask of hatred. "You and your family are not the only ones he has hurt. He has hurt someone very dear to me, and I want to see him pay for it. Unfortunately, he has never committed a crime against the Narn Regime, so I am powerless. But no one could deny the honor of your *Shon'Kar*."

"No one will," vowed Mi'Ra. "Can you help me?"

"I have already helped you. His confederates who brought him here are gone, and he is cut off from any outside help. His aide, Na'Toth, might still be loyal to him, and she could be a problem. As for the humans, they strike me as inconsequential."

"I'm not so sure of that," said Mi'Ra. "But if they are helping G'Kar, then they are like his arms and legs and must be broken! Anyone who stands in the way of my *Shon'Kar* is the enemy."

"You could use the humans to get to G'Kar," suggested Ra'Pak with a twinkle in her ruby eye. "But I leave the details up to you."

"Thank you, mistress." Mi'Ra put a fist to her chest in salute. "You have trusted the right person with this news. I will never forget this."

"Just do the job," said Ra'Pak gravely.

Mi'Ra nodded and backed out the door. The man waiting in the field gave her a nod, as if it was safe to proceed, then he climbed back into the shuttlecraft. Mi'Ra jogged away, quickening her step, when she heard the engines of the shuttlecraft go into a burn. She reached the first building of Street Jasgon just as the thrusters clicked on, and she turned to see the shuttlecraft lift gracefully into the night sky and zoom toward the stars. As she watched the craft turn into just another shooting star, she wondered if she was saying good-bye to that life forever. Was her mother right? Was there a way back to the privileged circles?

No, thought Mi'Ra, there was only degradation and glory. She had had enough degradation, and now it was time for the glory.

As Mi'Ra walked down Street Jasgon, a million details crowded her mind for attention. One by one, she told herself, she would take care of the details, because a thorough assassin plans well.

"Pa'Ko!" she cried. "Pa'Ko, if you're around, come out here!"

The boy sprang out of a stone gutter and did a somersault in front of her. "At your service!" he said, bounding to his feet.

Mi'Ra lowered her voice to match the wind. "I will pay you *five* coins if you simply make sure that the humans— and the Narns who accompany them—arrive at my mother's house tomorrow. They will come to the border zone tomorrow, I'm certain."

"Critical!" replied the boy. "This is a lucky time for me!"

"For me, too, I hope," said Mi'Ra. Without another word to the boy, she strode to the most infamous of the illegal taverns, called simply the Bunker, because it was housed inside an old bunker built by the Centauri for guard duty. Even back then, this part of Homeworld had housed the unwanted, the troublemakers.

There was a husky guard at the door of the Bunker, but he knew her. He might or might not let her in, because he knew she was often bad for business. At least she never indulged in the kind of business everyone wanted from her. She brushed past the guard, giving him a shoulder that knocked him back into his seat.

When she reached the dark recesses of the Bunker, she could tell there were a fair number of reprobates and cutthroats, exactly the kind of people she wanted to see. When they saw her, standing in the entrance with her hands on her slim hips, they gave her the usual rude remarks, followed by slurred laughter. But tonight, she had a comeback for them.

Mi'Ra yelled, "Are there any sniveling cowards from the Thenta Ma'Kur in here?"

That silenced the ribald conversation very quickly and won her everyone's attention. "If the Thenta Ma'Kur is here and they aren't hiding behind their fathers' aprons, let them meet me in the alley. As for you others, I am hiring good fighters for one hundred Old Bloodstones a day!"

That lifted the conversation to a fevered level of good cheer, eliciting cries of, "I'm your man!" and "I'd kill my own kids for that!"

"I'll be back," she promised them. She walked past the guard at the door, and he gave her a quizzical look but didn't challenge her. For one hundred Old Bloodstones, thought Mi'Ra, he was probably considering joining her.

Mi'Ra strode into the alley and slumped against the wall to get out of the wind. She crossed her arms, hiding the PPG in the crook of her elbow, and waited. She didn't think it would be long, considering the advanced communications of the Thenta Ma'Kur, and it wasn't. She felt him crawl up beside her, like a lizard seeking warmth. Having nothing to cover his face with, he kept to the shadows.

"Are you causing trouble for us again?" he asked.

"I'm only beginning to cause you trouble," she promised. "First you botched my father's contract, and now you've lied to me about killing G'Kar!"

"Did we now?" sneered the assassin. "Then who did kill G'Kar?"

"Nobody! He's still alive!"

The dark figure bolted upright, and his impressive chin jutted into the light. "Are you serious, girl? If you are trifling with the Thenta Ma'Kur . . ."

"A plague on the Thenta Ma'Kur! I have more to fear from the dust devils than you lazy buffoons. *You* are trifling with *me!* I just want you to know that I am finished with you. I will show *you* how it's done."

She started to leave, but the man gripped her arm. He held tightly, painfully, almost pinching off her blood supply. "If this is true, we will fulfill that contract," he vowed. "We will be there when you have failed."

Mi'Ra yanked her arm away and howled with laughter. She didn't care if she sounded insane, because in this terrible world what good did sanity do? She sauntered away from the assassin, laughing into the wind. The Thenta Ma'Kur were only for insurance, in case she failed; they were angry enough to do the job properly this time. She still intended to kill G'Kar herself, and his guardians if need be.

The costly suite in the Hekbanar Inn was all that Al Vernon had promised, complete with a natural spring bath carved out of sheer rock. The bath was in one of the bedrooms, and Ivanova kicked the men out, stripped off her clothes, and immersed herself. The rotten-smelling water was almost unbearably hot, but she found a cool current flowing from one small fissure and planted herself there. Currents of two contrasting temperatures flowed around her body, and Ivanova lay back and passed her hand over the panel on the edge of the tub. At once, the ceiling was engulfed by twinkling patterns of subtle lights cast against what looked like the black velvet of space.

Their luggage was on its way to some far-off Narn colony, but she had her uniform, a heavy coat, and now a bath. With those elements, she could survive any journey, thought Ivanova, although she knew she would miss the coffee aboard the *K'sha Na'vas.*

On the other side of the door, Al Vernon threw himself into a plush couch with a dozen striped pillows. He and Garibaldi were in the common room of the suite, between the two bedrooms. When Al began lowering the lights and bringing up weird patterns in the ceiling, Garibaldi interrupted him. ''Before you make yourself too comfortable, we've got to find the other two people with our party.''

''The innkeepers are Narns,'' said Al. ''They know everybody who comes and goes, especially down here. They'll know who Na'Toth is the moment they see her, and they'll send her along. I'm a little worried about that other one, Ha'Mok, but if you say you need him, then you need him. Me, I'm going to relax.''

He put his hands behind his back and closed his eyes. ''Believe me, Garibaldi, on this planet you could be in worse places than this.''

The security chief was pacing, trying to tell himself that he should go to the lobby and at least sit watch for Na'Toth and Ha'Mok, when the chime on the door sounded. He rushed to the panel that opened the door, and he was extremely relieved to see Na'Toth and the ambassador, still wearing his disguise. Garibaldi's initial relief turned to anger as he thought about all the wasted days G'Kar had put them through with this stunt. Garibaldi was about to bawl G'Kar out when he remembered Al Vernon sitting there, grinning innocently.

''I am sorry,'' apologized G'Kar as soon as the door

shut. "For being late, for bringing you here, for subjecting you to this. Where is Commander Ivanova?"

Al pointed a fat thumb at the rear door. "Don't feel sorry for her, she's taking a bath. But we were a little worried about you, Ha'Mok. They aren't friendly to the lower classes around here—better watch your step."

G'Kar rubbed his eyes. "Can we continue this conversation in the morning? I think it's a good idea for all of us to get some sleep."

"I'm comfortable here," said Al Vernon. "You fellows can have the male dormitory."

Na'Toth suddenly stepped toward the pudgy merchant and stared down at him. Al flinched as if he was about to get slugged, but Na'Toth bowed respectfully. "You have done well, Mr. Vernon, finding these quarters. I for one am very pleased that you are a member of our party." She glanced at Garibaldi. "If it were up to me, I would take you into our confidence."

Al leaped to his feet and took her hand. "Thank you, dear lady. Coming from you that is quite a compliment. Don't worry about taking me into your confidence. I've always found that when people start telling you their secrets, it's because they want something from you. We have an amenable relationship, and Mr. Garibaldi says we only have one destination tomorrow before my duties are finished."

"The Du'Rog family?" asked G'Kar.

Garibaldi nodded.

"Good. I have something to say to them." G'Kar strode through the bedroom door and slammed it shut behind him.

Al leered at Na'Toth. "After tomorrow I'll be a free man and can get on with my love affair with Homeworld. This is a wonderful time to be in Hekba City—I don't suppose you could arrange to stay for a few days?"

Na'Toth shook her head. "We'll have to see what happens tomorrow."

"Just so," agreed Al. "Before we make any plans, let's see what happens tomorrow."

# CHAPTER 14

Garibaldi had to admit that the pickled eggs were pretty tasty, but he didn't want to ask what kind of animal they came from. At any rate, the breads, broth, and eggs seemed to appeal to everyone in the suite, although Ivanova complained that there wasn't any coffee. Dawn had broken half an hour ago, and at Garibaldi's insistence they were getting an early start.

"What kind of place is this border zone?" he asked of no one in particular.

Na'Toth and G'Kar looked at one another as if they weren't eager to answer that question. G'Kar, who was still wearing his Ha'Mok disguise, lowered his head.

Al piped up, "It's the slums, the ghetto, the end of the line. You can't get any lower than that. You wouldn't think a civilized society would tolerate such a place."

G'Kar pursed his lips. "It's much like Down Below on B5."

"Then it's dangerous," said Garibaldi, gazing at the Narns. "Since we're stupid dignitaries, we came here unarmed. What kind of weapons do you have?"

Na'Toth took her PPG pistol out of the holster on her waistcoat. "Standard issue."

G'Kar looked thoughtful for a moment, as if trying to make up his mind about something. He finally frowned and pulled a hidden belt from under his tunic. It had two PPGs on it and two small incendiary devices.

Garibaldi nodded appreciatively. "Good. Why don't you hang on to one PPG and give the other one to Commander Ivanova. I'll take the grenades."

Reluctantly, G'Kar handed one of the pistols to Ivanova, then he handed the belt with the two grenades to Garibaldi. The chief inspected the devices and was satisfied that he could use them in an emergency, a very dire emergency.

He glanced at Al. "You don't mind not being armed, do you?"

Al shrugged. "If I can't talk my way out of a situation, I probably can't shoot my way out either. We're just going to pay a courtesy call, aren't we? What's the danger in that?"

All eyes, white and red, turned to G'Kar. He scowled and rose to his feet. "Mr. Vernon, you don't have to go if you don't want to. I'm sure Na'Toth and I can find our way through the border zone. I've been there a time or two."

"Oh, no," said Al, springing to his feet, "I insist. You folks have been wonderful to me, putting me up in the grotto, feeding me—I want to do my share. Once you get to know me, you'll find that I always fulfill a contract."

"That's very commendable," said Na'Toth. "Our intent is not to put ourselves in danger, but Mr. Garibaldi is correct. This is a dangerous section of the city—with thieves and cutthroats—and we don't want you to take unnecessary risks."

"I haven't been to the border zone very often," Al said. "I may never get a chance to go there again with fellow humans. But I can guide us to the outerwalks. That is how we're going, isn't it?"

G'Kar scowled. "Without a shuttlecraft, we have no choice."

Al opened the door and stepped into the corridor, with the others trailing behind him. Garibaldi took the rear position, feeling like a human time bomb with the grenades strapped to his chest. Under normal circumstances he wouldn't have been worried about a simple interrogation, even if it was on an unfamiliar planet. However, the unspoken consensus was that they should end the charade of

G'Kar being dead. A logical place to start would be by
telling the Du'Rog family.

G'Kar had told Garibaldi about the cash that had been
settled upon the disgruntled family, and his hopes that it
would soften up their hatred. But Garibaldi wasn't sure it
would work on that spitfire, Mi'Ra, who had nearly cooked
him on the walkway yesterday. She was going to be a handful no matter what, he had a feeling.

They wound their way through the dimly lit lobby and
stepped into blinding sunlight that was streaking down the
canyon walls and leaking into doors and caves. Garibaldi
squinted into the light and took a deep breath of bracing
dawn air. The air was nippy but not frigid, and the giant red
sun promised more warmth soon. The heat probably
wouldn't become gruesome for another five or six hours
yet, thought Garibaldi.

"This is more like it," said Ivanova, smiling at the sun.
She took off her coat and tied the sleeves around her slim
waist.

Al pointed along the strip of boutiques and cafes, most
of which were deserted at this early hour. "We need to take
the lift to the third level. As I recall, that's where the
outerwalks are."

"Correct," G'Kar confirmed. The fake crewman looked
as if he wanted to take the lead, but he lowered his head
and followed behind Na'Toth, as befit his station in life.

They wound their way through the geysers and springs,
which by daylight looked more like a bubbling swamp than
a romantic playground for wealthy Narns. Wordlessly, they
strode through the grotto and ducked under the glistening
vines. They filed quickly down the corridor toward the inner chamber that housed the lift. Al Vernon bent down and
touched the map, illuminating the path to the third level
and the outerwalks. The doors opened immediately, and
they stepped into the car.

The rapid rise left Garibaldi's stomach around his ankles, but he managed to ask Al, "Do we have to cross the bridge?"

"I'm afraid so," answered Al. "But at least there's not much wind this morning."

There was nothing to see as they rose through sheer rock within the canyon wall. The upper lift chamber looked exactly like the lower one, until they stepped out on the walkway and saw a vertical drop of a kilometer or two. Garibaldi took a deep breath, thinking that spending much time in Hekba City would give him permanent vertigo. As the small band marched along a narrow walkway, he stuck close to the wall.

Al and the two Narns stepped briskly onto the first bridge they came to, and Garibaldi forced himself to emulate them. That left Ivanova bringing up the rear. Garibaldi didn't exactly dash across the swaying bridge, as Al and the Narns did, but he did tell himself that it was safe. He even snuck a look between the metal slats to see the greenish bog at the bottom of the canyon. It seemed impossible that they had just been down there a few moments ago. From this angle, the bottom of the canyon looked pristine, as if untouched by civilization.

Despite his calm, he was relieved to get off the bridge and onto land, even if it was only a ledge on the side of a cliff. They were about six levels below the rim, Garibaldi estimated. Al, Na'Toth, and G'Kar climbed to the next level, as he waited to help Ivanova off.

She looked at him, ashen. "I'm not going to miss those bridges. I don't see how they can live here."

Garibaldi shrugged. "Some people think we're crazy for living on a space station."

"Yeah," said Ivanova, "but you can't fall that far on a space station, like you can here. This damn gravity will kill you."

They caught up with the others just as they reached a widemouthed cave on the third level. Workers were already filing out of the cave for the day shift, but no one was filing in. The Narns gave them apathetic stares, looking heavy-lidded and half-asleep. Garibaldi was reminded of dead-end workers on Mars headed to the mines and factories.

"Looks like we're going against the traffic," said Al cheerfully. Once again, the stubby human led the way into the darkness, with Na'Toth and G'Kar trailing closely after him. After the bright sunlight, the clammy darkness of the cave was both disconcerting and depressing. The cavern also preserved the chill from the night before, and Ivanova was forced to put her jacket back on. Garibaldi walked slowly until his eyes grew accustomed to the dimness, and he finally saw the outerwalks, which were decidedly low-tech and no-frills. But the conveyor belts looked efficient enough. The incoming walkway continued to disgorge workers, while the outgoing one rolled away empty.

After making sure that they hadn't lost the Earthforce contingent, Al, Na'Toth, and G'Kar stepped upon the outerwalk and were whisked away. Ivanova and Garibaldi hurried to catch up, but they couldn't see well in the darkness. They were on the belt before they knew it, and Garibaldi was almost thrown off his feet by the jolt. Ivanova doubled over the handrail and hung on.

"Damn," muttered Garibaldi. "When they want you out of Hekba City, they want you out fast!" He could barely see the others ahead of him, but they appeared to be walking on the belt, moving twice as fast. He was content just to hang on.

"We need to check commercial transportation back to B5," said Ivanova. "I want to leave right after we talk to the Council tomorrow. But first, let's tell the Du'Rog family that G'Kar is still alive."

"But back on B5," Garibaldi interjected.

"Yes. We'll tell them in no uncertain terms to stay away from Babylon 5. G'Kar recently gave them a nice piece of change, so maybe they'll be sensible."

Garibaldi scowled. "Nobody's been sensible yet. What makes you think they'll start now?"

Ivanova said nothing, and nervous energy had the chief walking briskly down the conveyor belt. Once he got into stride, he was covering ground at a fast clip, and he could see ceiling bulbs flying past over his head. He was starting to unwind his long legs and really stretch out when the belt abruptly stopped and pitched him forward. Strong arms caught him before he could do much damage.

"Mr. Garibaldi," said Na'Toth, "you must learn to watch your step. We aren't on a space station, and you can't go charging about."

"Oh, sorry." Garibaldi looked around with confusion. He was no longer on a moving walkway, but he was surrounded by them.

"We have to branch off here," explained Al Vernon. "There's a nice middle-class neighborhood off that way, and a lower-class neighborhood this way. We're going to the ghetto between them—the border zone."

"You and Na'Toth go ahead," said Garibaldi. "I want to talk to Ha'Mok while we wait for the commander."

"We'll wait for you at the other end." Al took Na'Toth's arm and led her toward the middle walkway. "Come, my dear. Let me point out the sights."

G'Kar scowled impatiently at the security chief. "What do you want, Garibaldi?"

"I don't know what you're thinking inside that spotted skull, but I want you to keep your disguise on. I want you to let us do the talking. We're going to tell them you're alive—don't worry about that—but we're going to tell them you never left B5. And we're going to make it very

clear that their clan had better *not* come to B5 looking for
you. You just keep a low profile, all right, Ha'Mok?''

"Don't tell me what to do," said G'Kar.

Garibaldi got right in his face. "We've come this far for
you, against our better judgment if we ever had any. So for
once, you're going to do what I tell you to do! Don't test
our friendship too much."

"Friendship?" asked G'Kar with amazement.

"I couldn't be this stupid out of a sense of duty," muttered Garibaldi. "It has to be friendship."

Ivanova stepped off the walkway behind them. "Trouble?" she asked.

"Just a conversation," answered Garibaldi. "I was just
telling Ha'Mok that he should keep out of the way and
remember who he is, and who he isn't."

"But I know the border zone so much better than you,"
said G'Kar. "I've lived in Hekba City for years."

"And you've made frequent excursions here," said Ivanova. "I'll remember that, but you're to remember who's
in charge of this party. *Me*."

The Narn nodded somberly. "All right, I agree. Out of
*friendship,* I will obey your orders. Remember to take the
middle walkway." With that, the Narn stepped onto the
belt and was whisked away.

Garibaldi held his stomach and looked at Ivanova. "I'm
beginning to think this is a big mistake."

"Maybe it's the pickled eggs," she suggested. "Let's
deliver our message and go home."

She strode onto the walkway ahead of him, and Garibaldi followed her at a distance. He simply rode the con-
veyance without trying to walk at the same time. There
wasn't anyone traveling in the opposite direction, and he
guessed that people in the border zone didn't hold jobs in
Hekba City. The belt rumbled down a dreary corridor,
where every other lightbulb in the ceiling was burned out.

No one had tried to make this part of the tunnel look natural—it simply looked endless and depressing.

Finally he spotted the others waiting for him in a tumbledown alcove at the end of the line. He stepped off the walkway deftly this time and marveled at the pit in which they found themselves. There was some kind of boarded-up stand, and the stairway leading out was covered with dirt and garbage. At the top of the stairs, swirling dust devils were in the process of blowing more dirt down.

"Welcome to the border zone," said Al. "I suggest we all try to remember where this station is. Things aren't well marked here."

"How are we going to find the Du'Rog family?" asked Ivanova.

"We can ask around," said Na'Toth. "They must be known, even in this place."

"Did they really kill G'Kar?" asked Al, sounding doubtful. "It doesn't seem as if they would have the wherewithal to kill someone on B5, living in this place."

G'Kar replied, "Never underestimate the power of the *Shon'Kar*."

"Come on," said Garibaldi, leading the way up the hill of debris.

The view at the top of the stairs was even worse than down in the pit. It was truly a slum—a dreary, unending grid of decrepit row houses that made the worst parts of Brooklyn look pretty good. Unlike Hekba City, no effort was made to allow the architecture to fit the natural beauty of the place. Of course, there was no natural beauty—just a rolling, arid plain with decayed buildings and crumbling masonry walls that tried to disrupt the wind.

Garibaldi would have thought the place was deserted, but he heard the shouts of a domestic quarrel and then a scream. The cop in him wanted to take off toward the sound, but he told himself that he was on a mission, and it didn't include saving the border zone from neglect and apathy. He wished that G'Kar hadn't mentioned Down Below in the same breath as this foul place, but he knew that every society had a bin in which to put its refuse.

G'Kar stood beside him, turning his disguised cranium into the wind. He squinted his eyes, protecting his brown contact lenses. "It isn't a pretty place to sentence a family, especially when they have done no wrong."

Ivanova was scouting around the perimeter, her hand on her PPG. Al and Na'Toth were busy trying to read signs and debating which way to go. So Garibaldi lowered his voice to say to G'Kar, "It's about time you felt some guilt."

"Oh, I feel guilt, Mr. Garibaldi, about many things. I'm good at feeling it. I'm not so good at knowing what to do about it."

From the corner of his eye, Garibaldi spotted movement. It wasn't aggressive enough to cause him to reach for a grenade, but there was very clearly a person dashing around corners, ducking under steps, and drawing closer to them. Ivanova worked her way toward Garibaldi, and she nodded in the same direction he was looking.

"Somebody's watching us."

"I saw him," said Garibaldi. "It's just one."

Suddenly, their pursuer came charging into the street, whereupon he executed an exuberant flip and landed on bowed, scrawny legs. He bowed comically and folded that action into a somersault, once again bounding to his feet.

"Have we encountered the natives?" Al asked cheerfully.

"He could be useful," said Na'Toth.

Garibaldi motioned to the boy, whom he judged to be roughly equivalent to a ten-year-old on Earth. "Come on over. We'd like to talk to you."

The boy charged toward them, all bony elbows and

knees, then did a graceful cartwheel and landed beside Na'Toth, gazing into her red eyes. "Hello, fair lady. I am Pa'Ko, the greatest guide in all the border zone! Just tell me where you wish to go, and the streets will open like a magic walkway."

Na'Toth cocked her head and smiled at the cheeky boy. "Do you know the Du'Rog family? Ka'Het, Mi'Ra, and T'Kog."

"Good friends of mine," the boy claimed. "They used to be rich, you know. I think a very bad man stole their money."

G'Kar cut in. "Can you take us to them?"

"Are you friendly?" Pa'Ko asked innocently.

"Yes," said Na'Toth. "We won't do them any harm." She looked at Garibaldi as if trying to get some confirmation of that.

"And how much will you pay?" Pa'Ko smiled expectantly.

"I was expecting that," said G'Kar. "Mr. Vernon, do you have any of those coins left I gave you?"

"Well," muttered Al, "I suppose I do have one or two."

"Give him two if you've got them."

Al dug deep into his pockets to produce two black coins, which he tossed into the air. The boy snagged one in each hand and grinned. Pa'Ko's scrawny neck and hairless head made him look anemic, thought Garibaldi, but he would give anything to have reflexes and coordination like his.

Pa'Ko set off at a jaunty walk down the middle of the street, making sure that Na'Toth followed closely. It was almost comical to watch Pa'Ko and Al Vernon vying for her attention. Garibaldi had never considered Na'Toth to be all that attractive, but he guessed he was missing something. Mi'Ra, on the other hand, he could see fighting over, but he'd be scared to death to win.

G'Kar walked respectfully behind Na'Toth; although his

head was bowed, his eyes flashed back and forth, missing nothing. Ivanova walked a few meters to the left of G'Kar, and she watched him like he was a child about to run off. Garibaldi did his best to keep watch on all of them, but the deserted street and the warm sun were beginning to lull him into complacency. He warned himself that this wasn't the ghost town it seemed, and the sun would soon turn on them. Then he caught a shutter moving as someone peered out at the passing parade.

Garibaldi did his best to remember their route as they cut between houses, across streets, through archways, and down alleys, but he doubted he could find his way back to the outerwalk without help. That was a depressing thought, and it made him feel for the grenades strapped to his chest, just to make sure they were there.

Finally, the oddball group of three humans, two Narns, and their young guide reached the top of a small hill, where an old street sign hung creaking in the wind. The sign read "Street V'Tar" and Garibaldi's mind flashed back to the data crystal in which Mi'Ra had recorded her infamous *Shon'Kar*. She had used that same word—*V'Tar*—and Garibaldi didn't think it was a coincidence. He knew without being told that this forlorn street was where she lived.

He tried to imagine what it would be like to go from Hekba City to this—permanently. Even though the two places were only a few kilometers apart, they were different worlds that bred different creatures. Was Mi'Ra more a product of this place, or those snobbish watering holes for the rich? The answer might determine how successful they would be in warning her off.

"Down there," said Pa'Ko, pointing toward a dip in Street V'Tar. "Where the street is red from the running water. Brown door on the right."

"You aren't coming with us?" asked Na'Toth with surprise.

Pa'Ko waved his hand. "I see them often. I will be watching for you, fair lady." He kissed her hand, performed a cartwheel, landed at a dead run, and kept running. With a childish chuckle, he ducked out of sight.

"The ingrate," muttered Al. "Not even a thank-you for the coins. We'll never see him again, I daresay."

"Until we need to find our way back," said Ivanova. She started down the hill and waved them forward. "Let's go."

"Remember," Garibaldi told G'Kar, "let us do the talking."

"Very well," grumbled the ambassador. "Tell them, if they cooperate, there will be more money."

"You really do want to make this right, don't you?" asked Garibaldi.

The Narn nodded. "Death is not the answer. I found that out. So we must choose life."

Stepping over the broken candles on the porch, Ivanova reached the brown door first. Garibaldi came up behind her and gave her an encouraging smile. He glanced back to see that Na'Toth, Al, and G'Kar had remained in the street, with G'Kar keeping a respectful distance and his head bowed. Ivanova pressed the chime button. When no sound came, she knocked softly on the dented metal door.

They heard a bolt being pulled back, and both of them took a deep breath. The door opened, and Mi'Ra stood before them. She was dressed in what appeared to be purple gauze that flowed over her youthful figure. Did it matter that the material was threadbare at the sleeves and hems? Not to Garibaldi it didn't, as he forced his eyes upward to her dazzling smile and ruby eyes. She looked radiant and very pleased to see them.

"You make me look like a soothsayer," said Mi'Ra with amusement. "I told my family you would come today. Enter, please."

"There are others in our party," said Ivanova, glancing back at the three in the street.

"They are welcome, too," offered the young Narn.

Al stepped forward importantly. "I'm Al Vernon," he proclaimed, "a visitor to your planet, but I once lived here."

"A pleasure." Mi'Ra bowed politely.

Na'Toth climbed the steps after Al, but G'Kar didn't move. "My servant will wait outside," she explained.

"As you wish," said Mi'Ra through a clenched smile. It was the first sign to Garibaldi that she was struggling a bit to be civil. He resolved to watch her during the conversation, an assignment he was happy to give himself.

They entered a simple sitting room, which was overcrowded with massive furniture that looked as if it belonged in a palace. Or a museum, it was so tattered and chipped. Perched on a couch like a queen sitting on her throne was an older Narn woman. The matriarch was working hard to appear regal, but Garibaldi could tell she was rusty at it, not like those Narns down in the grotto. They probably snored regally. Pacing the back of the room was a young Narn male who tried to look nonplussed but only succeeded in looking nervous.

"My mother, Ka'Het," said Mi'Ra smoothly, "and my brother, T'Kog."

Ivanova handled the introductions for their side—herself, Garibaldi, Na'Toth, and Al Vernon. She didn't bother to introduce the simple crewman who was listening on the porch. Despite the friendly behavior of the Du'Rog family, nobody offered them anything to eat or drink, or even a place to sit down.

"We need to establish something right away," said Ivanova. "Did all of you vow the *Shon'Kar* against G'Kar?"

"I did," declared Mi'Ra proudly. "That snake deserved it."

Garibaldi caught the angry glare that passed between Na'Toth and the younger Narn woman, and he hoped they would both be cool.

Ka'Het laughed nervously. "It was a symbolic sort of gesture. You must understand that G'Kar completely destroyed this family. When I tell you what he did to us, your sympathy will be entirely on our side."

"They know all about it," said Mi'Ra with a sneer. "They still take his side."

Ivanova leaned forward. "Look at it from our point of view. It's our job to protect the ambassadors on Babylon 5, which was built specifically so that they could have a neutral place to meet. Your *Shon'Kar* may be acceptable to Narns, but to us it's a death threat against one of our most important dignitaries."

"What difference does it make?" asked T'Kog, striding into the center of the conversation. "G'Kar is dead, and the fact is that we didn't have anything to do with it! We weren't anywhere near Babylon 5 when it happened."

"We know that," answered Garibaldi. He looked pointedly at Ivanova and Na'Toth, making sure they were all in agreement. "We're warning you for the future, because it turns out G'Kar isn't really dead."

"Ooooh!" shrieked Ka'Het, swooning. T'Kog rushed to her aid, and Garibaldi whirled around to find Mi'Ra staring at him, judging his reaction instead of the other way around. She averted her eyes, but it was too late. Garibaldi had the distinct impression that she knew G'Kar was still alive, and that set off warning bells inside his skull.

T'Kog fanned his mother and scowled angrily. "If this is some kind of a jest . . ."

Garibaldi found himself talking, trying to say anything that would do some good. "It's no jest. We don't know all the details, but we think he has been discovered in a rescue pod, still alive. At any rate, we know you've gotten some money from his estate, and we know you'll get more if you just drop this *Shon'Kar*.''

Mi'Ra laughed harshly and crossed in front of Garibaldi, fixing him with her blazing red eyes. ''My mother and brother are foolish enough to think that money means something. But it doesn't mean anything while my father's reputation is stained. What can Earthforce do about that?''

''Nothing,'' admitted Garibaldi, ''but I'll tell you one thing Earthforce can do. If you show up on Babylon 5, looking to kill one of our ambassadors, we can slap you into irons, and we can shove you out an air-lock in your birthday suit. Whatever the worst thing you can imagine is, that's what we're going to do to you. And I'm serious, lady.''

Mi'Ra stopped in front of him and looked him up and down. ''I believe you are serious, Mr. Garibaldi. You would like to shove me somewhere in my birthday suit.''

''Mi'Ra!'' snapped her mother, making a remarkable recovery. ''You stop threatening them. What they've brought us is disturbing news, but we will have to make the best of it. Attaché Na'Toth, you are the ambassador's aide?''

''I am,'' answered the Narn.

''The Earthers said something about more money. If we were to negotiate this amount with you, perhaps you could take the figures back to your superior.''

Na'Toth sighed. ''I could. In return, we will want you to disavow the *Shon'Kar*.''

Mi'Ra was silent, although her jaw worked tensely.

''We can talk about it,'' her mother said pleasantly. ''Everything is negotiable.''

During the ensuing conversation, Garibaldi backed away from Mi'Ra and opened up his collar. The day was already starting to get warm. While the women negotiated, nobody was paying any attention to Al Vernon, so the merchant gave Garibaldi a jaunty wave and wandered out the door. Garibaldi wished he could join him—a little fresh air sounded good about now. He tried not to look at Mi'Ra, because it amused her every time he did.

Sitting on the porch, G'Kar was startled by the door slamming shut and Al's heavy footsteps. Al smiled at him and breathed a huge sigh of relief.

"I can't believe it," whispered the human. "They actually told that crazy family that G'Kar is still alive! Can you imagine?"

"But it seems to be working out all right, doesn't it?" asked G'Kar hopefully. "I've been listening, and it sounds as if they've agreed to make peace."

Al grinned. "All except that luscious daughter of his. She wants dice made out of G'Kar's vertebrae. But it does sound promising, which is fine with me. I was afraid I would have to step in."

G'Kar laughed derisively. "You could end a *Shon'Kar*?"

"You never know how a *Shon'Kar* will end," observed Al. He patted his ample stomach. "My work is done here —maybe I should return to Hekba City."

"Come back with us," insisted G'Kar. "I'm feeling in a very magnanimous mood, and we owe you something for everything you've done. Remain with us—I think we can prevail upon G'Kar's wife to give you something extra for your trouble."

Al tugged at his sport coat, as if that were his intention all along. "Of course, I wasn't planning to leave just yet." He gazed around. "The street is awfully deserted, isn't it? I mean, people *do* live here. Have you seen anything suspicious?"

"I haven't see anything at all," grumbled G'Kar. "But I haven't been looking around. I suppose I should."

"Let's not make a big deal of it," said Al. "I'll just take

a look off to the right here, and you take the left. Like we're biding our time.''

G'Kar whispered, "Do you think this could be some kind of a trap?"

"I've been down here before during the day, and I never remember it being this quiet. Where are the people?"

"There's one of them," said G'Kar with his sharp vision. But he didn't point; he turned and smiled at the stocky human. "He just ducked down behind a water barrel. That's rather suspicious behavior, isn't it?"

"Indeed it is," agreed Al, sneaking a look in that direction. "That's the way we would go back to reach the outerwalk. You're sure about what you saw?"

"Yes, I am. Of course, it may have been that confounded boy."

"No." Al pointed out, "He wasn't foolish enough to come down this street, remember?"

Their troubling conversation was interrupted by the door squeaking open and the exit of their bedraggled party from the Du'Rog house. Garibaldi charged out, gasping for air as if the atmosphere inside the house had been stifling. He was followed by Ivanova and Na'Toth, neither of whom looked overjoyed at what had transpired. Weariness and relief showed in their faces in equal measure. The mission was over, thought G'Kar, and it was a success. The dreaded Du'Rog family had been cornered in their lair, told the truth, and settled with. They should all be overjoyed that it was over. But was it over?

Mi'Ra stepped out on the porch after them, and she did look quite fetching in her filmy gown. She pointed up the hill. "If you want to get back to Hekba City, the outerwalk is that way."

"Yeah," said Garibaldi, "we should get going. I hope you won't be offended if I say I never want to see you again."

"Too bad," said Mi'Ra playfully. "I think we could have been friends.

"Okay, let's get going," said Ivanova, making it an order.

"No!" G'Kar blurted out. Then he remembered to bow his head and act obsequious. "Mr. Vernon and I have been talking, and we feel another route is better."

"Yeah," said Al, wiping the sweat off his brow. "There's something we want to see in the other direction."

Garibaldi got the message. "I'll go wherever you two want. It's your territory."

Mi'Ra got angry. "That's absurd. The quickest way is to the south." She stepped off the porch and stared in that direction.

G'Kar strode off determinedly in the northern direction, hoping the others would get the idea, and Al was not far behind him. G'Kar had always found that humans had fairly good senses of danger—there was still some reptile left in their brains—and he hoped it would kick in soon.

A clay pot crashed somewhere, and Ivanova whirled around, which spooked an assailant hiding up the hill. He leapt to his feet and cut loose with PPG fire that streaked over Ivanova's head and raked a house across the street. Ivanova dropped to one knee, rested her elbow, and took aim; she cooked the gunner with a short burst of her PPG. Everyone else fled, including Mi'Ra, who vanished into the house.

G'Kar drew his own weapon and hoped that would be the end of it, but Mi'Ra burst from the house toting a PPG bazooka. "Kill them!" she shrieked. Her voice was drowned out by the roar of her own weapon.

Behind G'Kar, an entire house blew into flaming cinders. When he tore his eyes away from that horrible sight, he saw an army of thugs pouring from the buildings up the street. They came charging down the hill, howling like drunken, bloodthirsty lunatics.

"Retreat!" screamed G'Kar.

# CHAPTER 15

Ivanova ignored the wild PPG fire that pulsed over her head. She guessed she had one more shot before the army of thugs figured out they had to stand still to shoot well, so she took careful aim at the figure in the purple dress.

"Don't kill her!" shouted Garibaldi far behind her. But she ignored him, too, and squeezed off a burst.

The bazooka in Mi'Ra's arms lit up like a toy laser sword, and she shrieked as she flung it to the ground. She was burned and her dress was singed, but the bazooka was no more. Ivanova leaped to a crouch and ran northward down the street, with the raging mob in close pursuit. Her small band was strung out ahead of her, fleeing for their lives.

"Artillery!" G'Kar yelled over the din.

Garibaldi got the message, and he stopped in his tracks and whirled around. Ivanova passed him as he pulled the first grenade off his belt. "Nice shooting!" he called.

"She's next," warned the commander.

But she didn't think Garibaldi heard her, as he concentrated on arming the grenade. With great accuracy, he lobbed it underhanded into the mob, and the blast was ferocious, engulfing a dozen of the ragtag army in a scorching fireball. Their screams were chilling as the dying Narns crumpled to the ground or staggered away like torches with legs. The grenade had the desired effect of slowing up the mob and forcing most of them into cover, but it enraged some of them, who cut loose with PPG fire that blew away porches and huge chunks of the street. It was war now.

"Fall back!" shouted Ivanova.

She ran for her life along with the others, and she found G'Kar organizing their forces at the end of the street. There was nothing beyond it but a neglected field. They were being fired at but not chased, and Ivanova crouched on the ground behind a cracked wall.

She stared at G'Kar. "How do we get out of here?"

"First of all," he answered, "you put me in charge. We need to move like a squad, and I can command a squad. By the way, that was good shooting back there."

Ivanova shook her head in exasperation. "Okay, you're in charge. Now get us out of here!"

G'Kar motioned to Na'Toth. "You and Al on the left side of the opening. Ivanova and Garibaldi on the right side. We've got to make it look like we'll make a stand."

Their assailants were also regrouping, although a few kept up their indiscriminate firing. Na'Toth shot back at them.

"Don't fire unless they're in range," ordered G'Kar. "We have to conserve those PPGs; they won't last forever."

"We need a plan," said Ivanova. "Is there any other way to get back to the outerwalk?"

"No," answered G'Kar, "they're between us and the only transportation we have to get out of the border zone. Here are our options: We could run east or west to the plebeian villages, but they're a lot farther than the outerwalk. We could make a stand, but they would eventually overrun us, coming at us from all sides. We could fight our way through them, but I think we would suffer heavy casualties if we did that."

"Let's not do that," suggested Al Vernon with a gulp. "What about hiding?"

"Perhaps Na'Toth and I could blend in," said G'Kar, "but I don't think the three of you could. The safest course would be to outflank them, and we might be able to do that at night. If we could find a place to hide until darkness, I would be in favor of that.''

''Man, you act just like a general!'' said Al Vernon in admiration. ''I'm going wherever Ha'Mok is going.''

G'Kar smiled. ''This is much like old times in the colonies. This entire trip has been very nostalgic for me.''

A stone landed near them, and Ivanova jumped along with everybody else. She whirled around, wondering where it had come from, and saw little Pa'Ko frolicking in the field, turning cartwheels and somersaults. He windmilled his arms and ran off toward a well that stood neglected in the center of the forlorn field. If it hadn't been for a corroded metal canopy and an old bucket hanging from it, Ivanova wouldn't have recognized the crumbling mound as a well. Pa'Ko waved at them for a moment, then he dove down the well with the ease of Santa Claus going down a chimney. Given the surreal events of the last few minutes, this seemed a fitting conclusion.

''Did anybody else see that?'' gasped Al Vernon. ''That little bugger just dove down that well!''

''Do you suppose he wants us to follow him?'' asked Na'Toth.

''We'd be sitting ducks out in that field,'' growled Garibaldi.

''He had to go somewhere,'' said G'Kar. ''Ivanova and Na'Toth, go check it out. Na'Toth, give your PPG to Garibaldi. We'll cover you.''

Everyone obeyed G'Kar without a moment's hesitation. Technically, Ivanova was in charge, but they needed a platoon leader. G'Kar had the instincts and experience, and he knew the terrain.

She and Na'Toth got into a crouch and ran across the field. On a neighboring street, a sniper jumped up and sent a blue beam arcing across their heads. Garibaldi answered with a pinpoint blast that rearranged the sniper's head, and he dropped like a pile of trash to the dusty street. Ivanova hated that they had to shoot to kill, but fear was the only thing that would keep this pack at bay, and she had serious doubts whether fear would do it for Mi'Ra and some of them.

Na'Toth reached the crumbling well first, and she worked her way around to the side, away from the snipers. Ivanova followed, keeping an eye open for more shooters, but Garibaldi's quick response had discouraged them for the moment. Na'Toth punched the crumbling clay adobe that surrounded the well, testing its strength.

"We can't sit on the edge of this thing and take a leisurely look inside," she reported. "I'm going inside. If our friend went down there, I think I can make it."

"You won't be armed," said Ivanova.

"I think he's trying to help us," the Narn insisted. "I'll yell for you when I get to safe footing. If you don't hear me yell, don't come down."

Ivanova nodded, then waited until Na'Toth nodded back. They both leaped to their feet. Ivanova raked the wall where the last sniper had hidden, while Na'Toth vaulted over the structure and disappeared feet-first down the hole. Even from several meters above, Ivanova could hear a thud and a groan as the big Narn landed. She held her breath, waiting to hear Na'Toth's voice.

"It's okay!" she bellowed. "Come down!"

Knowing she would have no one to cover her, Ivanova slithered up and over the crumbling wall. She succeeded in keeping a low profile, and she was already dropping into the darkness when a PPG blast bit off a chunk of the well and showered her with fragments.

Ivanova screamed in spite of herself as she slid through the darkness, bumping over roots and wet dirt. She was prepared to hit the ground hard, and her strong legs absorbed most of the impact. Na'Toth caught her before she toppled over, then pulled her away as dirt and debris tumbled down after her.

When the bombardment ended, Ivanova looked around the narrow shaft and could see almost nothing except for the small pool of light from above, which had to struggle through ten meters of dirt. Behind Na'Toth, she could make out the vague shape of a narrow passage that stretched into utter and foreboding darkness. There were strange smells coming from the passage, too, smells that were musty and rotten.

"I can't see much," said Ivanova. "Where are we? Some kind of maintenance tunnel?"

Na'Toth laughed without humor. "Maintenance tunnel in a border zone? I think not. Either by accident or design, it appears as if somebody dug a well near the ancient catacombs. They must have realized it, because they filled it with rubble just high enough to provide a secret entrance to the catacombs."

"Catacombs?" asked Ivanova, not liking the sound of that word.

Before Na'Toth could explain, they heard a shout from overhead, and a PPG blast sheared off more of the top of the well. There were bloodcurdling screams that reverberated right through the earth, and a large figure darkened the hole, cutting off all the light.

"I'm coming!" groaned a horrified voice.

Ivanova barely had time to stumble into the adjoining passage before a massive object plummeted down the shaft, crashing to the bottom. The light returned long enough to show Al Vernon, sitting like a crumpled Buddha among the clods of dirt.

There were more shouts overhead, and the women quickly dragged Al into the passage and left him there. They returned to the shaft long enough to see another body tumble down, followed in short order by another. G'Kar and Garibaldi rolled into a big pile of arms and legs, and Na'Toth and Ivanova struggled to separate them. The fun was short-lived as angry shouts and drunken laughter sounded at the top of the well; somebody dangled a PPG over the edge and fired without aiming. More clods of dirt thundered down, and the women pulled the men out of the shaft and dragged them into the catacombs.

They scrambled deeper into the tunnel only to find Al Vernon standing there, holding a candle embedded in an upside-down Narn skull.

Ivanova pointed to the gruesome curio. "Where did you get that?"

"Pa'Ko ran up and gave it to me," answered Al with amazement. "Then he ran off."

"I don't blame him," muttered Garibaldi. He looked around at the gloomy passage and wrinkled his nose at its dank smells. "Where the hell are we, the sewer?"

"The catacombs," said G'Kar. "Pre–Centauri invasion, we put our dead in these rambling, underground burial chambers. The cool earth and low humidity kept the corpses in good condition, and one was expected to come down and visit his relatives. With the invasion, freedom fighters and martyrs used the catacombs as escape routes. Nobody has ever made a map of the entire system of catacombs—it's too vast. At least they can't come at us from all sides down here."

"What happened up top?" asked Na'Toth.

Garibaldi answered, "I think Mi'Ra realized that the two of you had found a way out, so she led an all-out attack. We had nowhere else to go."

"Sshhh!" cautioned Na'Toth. "Listen!"

From the top of the well, a soft voice was calling. "Garibaldi! Garibaldi!"

"Don't answer her," said Ivanova.

"Garibaldi, let's make a deal!" came Mi'Ra's voice,

sounding quite reasonable. "We don't want to harm *you*—
we just want G'Kar. Give us G'Kar, and we'll let the rest
of you go!"

Al chuckled. "G'Kar? What's the matter with them? We
don't have G'Kar."

Everyone gazed from the chubby human to the muscular
Narn, and Al's eyes widened with horror. Trembling, he
lifted the skull candle closer to G'Kar's face. "Don't tell
me, you're . . ."

"I warned you not to come," said G'Kar. He ripped off
his disguise and threw it to the floor, then he popped out
the contact lenses and ground them under his heel.

"Lord help us!" moaned Al, and he took off at a terrified run down the narrow tunnel. Within seconds, there
came a scream, the sound of a crash, and total blackness as
the candle went out.

Ivanova sunk against the wall and let the Narns investi-
gate in the darkness while she kept an eye on the pool of
light coming down the well. Whenever shadows moved
across the light, she tensed, expecting an attack. She turned
to see G'Kar ignite the skull candle with a low-level burst
from his PPG. There were gasps as the party spotted Al
sprawled on the ground, wrapped in the embrace of a des-
iccated Narn corpse.

"Aaahhgh!" he screamed, pushing the crumbling ca-
daver away. Ivanova gazed around and saw that there were
mummified bodies everywhere, hanging from the walls, lying on shelves, sitting on benches, and piled like cordwood
against the wall. A few skulls were rolling about loose.

Na'Toth helped Al to his feet. "Mr. Vernon, get control
of yourself. And watch your step. You don't want to dese-
crate the dead, do you?"

"I don't want to *be* the dead!"

Another sound startled Ivanova, and she whirled around
to see a large figure drop down the well behind her. She

shot into the darkness and heard a groan, but she didn't know if she had hit him.

"Let's move it!" barked Garibaldi.

With G'Kar holding the candle and leading the way, they moved single-file through the catacombs, trying not to jostle the remains that rested in profusion all around them. Ivanova found herself breathing through her mouth, both to get more air and to keep the clammy smells at bay. She shouldered her way through the others to catch up with G'Kar and his wavering candle.

"G'Kar, is there any way we can get back to Hekba City through these catacombs?"

"I don't think so," answered the Narn. "But I'm not an expert on them. If that boy will stand still long enough for us to talk to him, maybe he can tell us."

After several moments, it became apparent that they were walking toward a flickering light at the end of the passageway. They slowed their pace to listen, and Ivanova heard shuffling sounds as they approached the chamber. She leveled her PPG and followed G'Kar as he crept into what had to be a tomb; it was crowded with mummified remains and illuminated by three lumpy candles. Furtive figures darted away, hiding under coffins and benches, and Ivanova nearly shot at them until she realized they were Narn children. Huddled in the corner, inspecting something green and moldy, sat little Pa'Ko.

"You made it!" he said with a grin. "Welcome to our home! We have to share it with dead people, but they're quiet."

Slowly, his tiny friends poked their heads out of their dusty hiding places, and Ivanova was shocked to see that some looked as young as a four- or five-year-old human. Al Vernon, Na'Toth, and Garibaldi filed slowly into the tomb, and they gaped at the unexpected enclave of children.

"You can't stay here," Ivanova warned them. "There

are bad people chasing us. If they knew you helped us, they would be angry.''

Pa'Ko bounded to his feet and frowned like a serious adult. "Too many bad people live here. Maybe you could take us where *you* live!''

The children nodded in agreement, as if it couldn't be much worse than this. Ivanova took a deep breath, feeling both her charitable and motherly tendencies starting to rise up. She would love to help these children, but right now there was a good chance that none of them would get back to B5 alive.

"Don't you have parents?" she asked, knowing she probably didn't want to hear the answer.

Pa'Ko shrugged. "They kept beating me, so I ran away. Since then, I heard they're dead."

Ivanova looked around the musty chamber. Counting the entrance they had used, there were three passageways leading out of the tomb, and G'Kar looked in each of them, prodding the darkness with his candle.

"This might be a good place to lose our pursuers," he said. "They can guess, but they won't know for sure which way we've gone. We can't go back the way we came, so we'll take one of these passageways, and the children can take the other one."

"Do any of these tunnels lead to Hekba City?" Ivanova asked the children. "Or the outerwalk?"

Before they could answer, there was a crashing sound from the passage behind them, and everyone in the room dropped into a wary crouch.

"There's no more time for chitchat," whispered Garibaldi. "Which way?"

Like a little general mustering his troops, Pa'Ko dragged the children out of their hiding places and motioned toward the right-hand passageway. He handed the first one a candle and snapped his fingers, and the tykes padded into the

darkness of the catacombs. It wrenched Ivanova's heart to
see them run off so alone and unprotected. But they had
survived this long, she reasoned, and they would probably
survive having a Blood Oath played out on their doorstep.

When the last child was dispatched, Pa'Ko motioned the
adults down the left-hand tunnel, and he led the way, with
G'Kar, Na'Toth, and Al Vernon right behind him. Garibaldi and Ivanova went to grab the remaining two candles,
which not only gave them light but left the tomb in utter
darkness. As they jogged into the passageway in pursuit of
their comrades, Ivanova could swear she heard voices directly behind them. Or maybe it was the dead laughing at
them.

She was so intent upon putting distance between her
band and their dogged pursuers that she could barely
breathe. After a while, she realized there was no sound in
the catacombs except for their footsteps pounding through
the dust, and she paused to take stock. All around her in
this underground necropolis, there was a sense of ageless-
ness, of time standing still. Even the children hadn't
seemed real, just small Narns who hadn't learned to stand
still, like their elders hanging on the wall.

She turned and confronted a line of corpses who stared
at her with empty eye sockets; their drawn, sardonic faces
seemed to laugh at the futility of it all. Sooner or later, she
would join them, they assured her.

Ivanova had a very troubling thought. They had put their
lives in the hands of a street urchin—what if they couldn't
trust him? What did they know about Pa'Ko? Nothing,
came the disconcerting reply. But they knew perfectly well
what Mi'Ra represented—she was the Angel of Death in
this city of the dead.

The commander brushed up against Garibaldi and protected the candle in her grasp. She realized that the group
had stopped ahead of her, and she squeezed between Gari-

baldi and a pyramid of heavy-lidded Narn skulls to see what was happening. There was a fork in the catacombs, and Pa'Ko pointed down the left-hand passage. "There is a shrine halfway down, and if you look up, you will see a ladder to the surface. You'll come out at a bigger shrine near Street Jasgon. If you want to return to the surface, you can climb out there."

Al Vernon snapped his fingers. "Jasgon is the main drag down here, isn't it?"

"Yes," answered Pa'Ko. "Travel south upon it, and you will reach the outerwalk."

G'Kar shook his head. "That entrance is too well known. They might be waiting there."

"Listen," said the boy. "If you have to come back into the catacombs, you can look for me in the tomb where you found me. I have a hiding place there."

For some reason, that honest answer relieved Ivanova's fears about Pa'Ko. The boy was just trying to help them, but his expectations of doing so were not all that great. That seemed to be implicit in the way he was always trying to ditch them. He knew they were probably as dead as the denizens of this place, and he didn't want to be around when it happened.

"Thank you," said G'Kar with a nod to the boy. "A proper reward will have to come later."

"Critical!" said the boy brightly. He pointed to the unusual candle holder. "May I take the skull? It's a great-uncle of mine, I think."

"Yes," said G'Kar with a smile, handing the grimy skull to the boy. Pa'Ko promptly whirled around and made a sharp turn to the right, disappearing down the other fork.

In the still of the catacombs, they all paused to listen, and they heard voices. They were faint and ghostly as they reverberated through the narrow tunnels, but nobody thought they were ghosts. The group headed down the left-hand fork without further discussion. Ivanova scanned one wall with her candle while Garibaldi scanned the other wall with his wavering light. G'Kar and Na'Toth guarded their rear, while Al Vernon ran nervously ahead of them.

It was Al who spotted the shrine first. "Over here!" he called.

Ivanova reached Al's location first, and she shined her flickering light on the simple altar. It consisted of a crumbling pedestal only a few centimeters high, upon which sat a highly stylized female form fashioned from what looked like terra-cotta. The statuette had been carelessly trodden upon, and her arms and most of her legs were broken off— but she still had a regal appearance. Her spots and bald head identified her as Narn, but she had an unearthly expression and was fleshier than most Narns.

"D'Bok, our harvest goddess," said G'Kar, stepping up behind her. "It's an old-fashioned belief, as the Martyrs have supplanted the old gods in importance. But she belongs here—these catacombs date from her time."

G'Kar peered upward about a meter to the left, and Ivanova followed his gaze with the candle. Sure enough there was a shaft, spacious compared to the one inside the old well, and a good rope ladder hung down the middle of it. There was also sunlight at the top, blessed sunlight. Assassins or no assassins, Ivanova was really glad to be getting out of the catacombs, with their musty smells, terrifying darkness, and oppressive corpses. If she had to die, she would rather have blinding daylight in her eyes and fresh oxygen in her lungs. To die down here among centuries of Narn dead—it made death seem commonplace, inevitable.

She shook off these unpleasant thoughts and looked at G'Kar. "Are we going up?"

"You don't want to die down here, do you?"

"No."

G'Kar pulled out his PPG and insisted, "Let me go first.

If they get me, maybe they'll leave the rest of you alone, although I doubt it. I'm very sorry to have gotten you into this unfortunate mess."

"Then get us out of it," said Ivanova, tempering her order with a pained smile.

G'Kar nodded somberly. "That is my first order of business. Then I'll deal with Mi'Ra." He lifted his boot onto the first rung and hauled himself out of the darkness.

# CHAPTER 16

In the ancient catacombs of the Narn Homeworld, three humans and a Narn attaché watched tensely as a dead ambassador climbed up a hole. They kept glancing over their shoulders, expecting an army of lunatics to charge down a passageway clogged with rotting bodies. Ivanova peered nervously up the shaft and couldn't see or hear G'Kar anymore, so she decided it was time to send someone else. She wanted to go next, just to get out of this subterranean hellhole, but she thought it would be better to send Garibaldi.

"You go," she ordered him, "and keep that grenade handy. If I don't hear anything from you in sixty seconds, I'm sending Na'Toth and Al. I'll go last in case they catch up with us from this direction. Go!"

Garibaldi nodded like a soldier, knowing there wasn't any point in being sentimental. Ivanova knew how deeply her closest colleague felt about her. Every day for two years they had relied on each other, suffering through countless crises and a traumatic change in command. Nothing needed to be said. Garibaldi pulled the grenade off the belt and gripped it in his teeth as he climbed quickly up the rope ladder.

Ivanova counted roughly to sixty as she positioned Al Vernon to go next. "It sounds peaceful up there," she said encouragingly. "Climb as fast as you can and don't look back. Just do what Garibaldi and G'Kar tell you. They've been through tough scrapes before."

Al nodded with a nervous gulp, reached for the ladder, and watched expectantly as Ivanova finished her countdown. When she hit the end of her inaccurate minute, she shoved Al in the back. To his credit, he climbed as if Narn maniacs were chasing him, and he went over the top in about the same time it had taken Garibaldi. Ivanova listened carefully, but she didn't hear any screams or shouts; so she motioned Na'Toth up the rope ladder. That allowed her to turn her full attention to the dark passageway behind her.

Ivanova could still hear the voices reverberating in the rambling catacombs. She had no idea if they were ten meters or a hundred meters away, but she knew she had to get out of there. As soon as Na'Toth was clear, she blew out her candle and stuck it and the PPG in her coat pocket. Then she grabbed the rope ladder and scampered toward daylight.

As Pa'Ko had promised, she emerged in the center of a small chapel. In an alcove sat a large statue of the harvest goddess, D'Bok, with several rows of crumbling benches facing her. A Narn dressed in rags was asleep on one of the benches, and Ivanova waited in a crouch until she saw Garibaldi lean around the corner of the doorway and motion to her.

Ivanova drew her PPG and jogged into the sunlit street, where she found her companions huddled behind a collapsed wall, awaiting her. The warmth of the sunbaked air struck her full-force and nearly made her shout with happiness. The sweat glands along her back tingled, ready to do their job, and she felt alive, as if escape was possible.

Street Jasgon, however, looked dead. She could tell that the clay buildings were larger and better kept than the ones on Street V'Tar, but it was the middle of the day and Jasgon was totally deserted. That was a bit disconcerting, if this really was the main drag. People who managed to live in this place had to have a highly evolved sense of self-preservation, she told herself. Besides, anyone in his right mind would stay hidden until the Blood Oath had played itself out, one way or another.

She crouched down with her fellows behind a wall that fronted the street and awaited G'Kar's instructions. The Narn was on his hands and knees, peering around the corner of the wall, apparently looking for signs of an ambush. Ivanova looked behind her and saw an unusual sign hanging over one of the storefronts. It was a symbol of a circle with a dash through it, looking something like a stylized capital "Q."

She tapped Na'Toth on the shoulder and pointed to the sign. "What does that mean?"

"It's a medical clinic."

"Here?" asked Ivanova with surprise.

"Doesn't Dr. Franklin spend several mornings a week in Down Below?" asked the Narn. "We have altruistic doctors, too."

They heard shuffling behind them, and Ivanova whirled around to see the derelict scurry away from the benches. He left a few pieces of ragged clothing, and G'Kar got into a crouch and ran over to fetch the rags.

"What are you doing?" asked Ivanova.

The Narn smiled and threw the rags over his shoulders. "I don't see anybody out there, but that doesn't mean they're not there. In fact, it probably means something that nobody is on the street."

He continued, "Plan A is go straight south to the outerwalk, although they could be waiting for us there. Plan B is to fall back to the shrine and descend into the catacombs again."

G'Kar saw the humans' downcast expressions and pursed his lips. "You don't want to go back there. Neither do I. But we don't stand a chance of holding off a larger force out here in the open, in broad daylight. Down there, we do. Then we can wait them out until nightfall, when we should be able to move about with more safety.''

''Is there a plan C?'' asked Al Vernon, who was shaking despite the hot, red sun beating down on him.

''Plan C is that I give myself up to them,'' said G'Kar, ''although I really don't think that will save your lives. But in the spirit of self-sacrifice, I'm going to walk out there now and draw their fire. We have to know if they're waiting in ambush.''

''G'Kar, think about that for a second,'' insisted Ivanova. ''When you were fighting revolts in the colonies, what would you have done?''

''Same thing.'' He smiled. ''Of course, I would have sent one of you.''

''Let me go,'' offered Na'Toth.

He handed her his PPG. ''No, all of you must cover me. My life depends upon your marksmanship. I'm going to try to look like a drugged-out derelict, so maybe they'll just warn me away. One way or another, we've got to see who's out there.''

Without further discussion, G'Kar staggered to his feet and began to wander, singing, into the middle of the street. Na'Toth chuckled for a moment, then grew somber again.

''What?'' asked Ivanova.

''Oh, it's a very bawdy song,'' she answered.

The lanky Narn moved around the edge of the wall and dropped to her stomach, using her elbows to steady her weapon. Ivanova sighed and took up a similar position on the other corner, and Garibaldi waited, working the muscles in his jaw. He lifted the grenade and brushed some sand off it. Ivanova doubted whether anybody was looking at them with a drunken Narn staggering down the street, bellowing a bawdy song.

\* \* \*

Well, thought G'Kar fatalistically, he had set out to save his life and had ended up casting it away. This was near suicide, and he knew it. This lot would kill a drunk as surely as they would kill an ambassador. He just hoped his friends and colleagues made it out alive.

He crooned another verse of the off-color ballad and stopped in the street to sway uneasily, and reflect. His only true regret in this entire business was that he had neglected Du'Rog's family, making them suffer worse than Du'Rog had. He could have made amends years ago, when instead he sewed the seeds of his own demise. He could have spared innocent people a bellyful of anguish, hatred, and bitterness. Thanks to him, their minds and their souls were out of balance, as a Minbari might say. His soul felt that way, too, which is why he understood.

Mi'Ra should have been in the university, warding off suitors, instead of casting her young life away on a bloody *Shon'Kar*. It was a *Shon'Kar* that he could have averted. He remembered a Terran proverb that was appropriate: In the end, it's not the things we do that we regret, it's the things we don't do.

"Get out of there!" commanded a voice. G'Kar cocked his head, as if he were hearing things, and he tried to find the direction of the voice. He saw the sniper crouching between two houses, waving him away. Well, thought G'Kar, maybe he would oblige.

He couldn't move too quickly, as he had to stick with his drunken gait, but he did stagger in the general direction of his comrades, hoping they would realize what this meant. He started bellowing another song, a little love ditty he often sang on B5. For several moments, G'Kar thought he was going to make it back to the wall before somebody figured it out, then he heard a voice that ruptured the unnatural silence.

"That's *him*!" screamed Mi'Ra. "Fire!"

Thanks to her warning, he had a chance to hit the ground as pulses of plasma streaked over his head, blowing up big chunks of the street. He slithered on his belly as fast as he could while his comrades answered fire, pumping their PPGs down the length of Street Jasgon. Screams echoed behind him, testifying to their accuracy, and G'Kar stole a glance over his shoulder. He wished he hadn't, because he could see Mi'Ra and twenty more bolting from their hiding places. They yelled like lunatics, and G'Kar scrambled to his feet and ran at full speed. He dived over the wall and thudded hard against a pedestal, as a shot followed him over and obliterated the pedestal, showering him with chunks of clay.

"Al!" yelled Ivanova, "hit the ladder!" The chubby human didn't need any more encouragement to run for safety.

Na'Toth and Ivanova continued to shoot at the advancing mob with deadly accuracy, but Mi'Ra and several others kept coming. Worse, the enemy's firepower was starting to reduce the wall to rubble; in a few more seconds, their cover would be gone.

"Na'Toth and G'Kar," ordered Ivanova, "hit the ladder!" She glanced at Garibaldi, and he held up the grenade. She nodded.

The women ran for the shrine, but G'Kar hung back for a split second. He wanted to see whether Garibaldi would try to kill Mi'Ra. That was probably their only chance of escaping death. The security chief hurled the grenade, and their eyes followed the missile's arc. Mi'Ra had the presence of mind to hurl herself into the dirt as the grenade sailed past her and landed among the terrified pack. They screamed even before the fireball engulfed them.

A PPG blast shattered what was left of the wall, and Garibaldi and G'Kar ran for it. They dashed into the shrine and weaved their way between the benches, but G'Kar slowed up to let the human reach the ladder first. His close encounter with death a moment ago had steeled him. If Death wanted him so badly, let it take him! From now on, he would risk his own life first and foremost, while he protected his friends' lives as much as he could. Maybe this was what the fates demanded from him for atonement— total selflessness. If so, he was happy to oblige.

He looked up at the statue of D'Bok, the harvest goddess. A PPG beam blasted a chunk of the alcove away, but G'Kar took a moment to bow his head to the venerated goddess. ''D'Bok, Mistress of the Fields, I place my life in your hands. Help me to be brave and do what is honorable.''

Another shot sang over his head, and G'Kar stepped into the open hole in the floor of the shrine, deftly catching the top rung. He stopped halfway down and pulled a knife out of his boot, then he reached up and began sawing away at the ropes. Enraged shouts and pounding footsteps made him grit his teeth and saw all the harder. The first rope snapped, and he dropped and crashed into the shaft wall. G'Kar groaned and reached up to saw on the other rope, but the voices were alarmingly near. He considered jumping off, but he didn't want to leave them any easy way down.

G'Kar sawed wildly with his blade as the loudest footsteps came to a stop. A hand holding a PPG pistol reached over the edge, and G'Kar remembered that tactic. He jabbed upward with his knife and caught the Narn in the forearm, spearing it like fat fish. Blood spurted, the PPG clattered to the bottom of the shaft, and the wounded man screamed and struggled. When more thugs crowded around the hole, G'Kar let go of both the knife and the ladder. His legs crumpled under him as he landed, and he bumped his shoulder hard against the shaft. He shook his head, trying to clear his senses, and he felt something poking him in the rear. He reached down to find the PPG weapon.

*Not a bad trade,* he thought. *A knife for a PPG.* He aimed the weapon to finish the job on the ladder, but two arms pointed into the hole with PPGs. They blew out chunks of the shaft, and G'Kar scurried away as the debris rained down.

He saw Ivanova just ahead of him, motioning with a candle. "Come on!" she urged him. "The others went down to the tomb already."

As he ran toward her, G'Kar waved his new PPG. "Look what I found. You join the others. I cut half the ladder, but I want to further discourage them from coming down after us."

Ivanova shook her head. "Just remember, you're not Superman."

"Who?"

"Look out!" shouted Ivanova.

She shoved G'Kar out of the way and drilled a thug just as he was emerging from the shaft. He slumped against a long row of bodies, looking like the youngest in a family portrait.

"Vo'Koth!" called a voice from above. "Vo'Koth!"

G'Kar put his fingers to his lips, telling her not to say anything. Silence was the only answer they wanted to give. Let them realize that whoever used the shrine to enter the catacombs was going to die.

"These aren't trained soldiers fighting for their homeworld," whispered G'Kar. "These are cowardly cutthroats. Their losses must already be substantial, and Mi'Ra can't count on them to keep risking their lives forever. Let's wait them out until darkness."

Ivanova nodded in agreement, but she had a concern. "We humans are going to need water pretty soon, and we'll all need food."

"We'll get them," promised G'Kar, "somehow."

* * *

Ivanova and G'Kar stood watch at the shrine until it became clear that no more mercenaries were going to plunge blithely into the catacombs. The waiting game seemed to have set in on both sides. Ivanova still felt at a disadvantage, because she would have rather been on the surface than in this subterranean necropolis. But at least they were alive and not under attack.

As she and G'Kar wound their way back through the narrow passageway, they saw a light and dropped into a crouch. After a moment they realized it was Garibaldi, wielding a tiny candle.

"There you are!" he said with relief. "I was about to send the bloodhounds after you."

G'Kar chuckled. "We wanted to discourage them from coming after us, and I think we did. Any sign of them at your end?"

"None," answered Garibaldi, "and I scouted all the way to the well, where we first came down. I guess the only reason they came down before was to drive us into the open."

"Now they're waiting, like us," said Ivanova with certainty.

There wasn't much to add to that conclusion, and she followed G'Kar and Garibaldi into the eerie tomb, where they had met Pa'Ko and the children. Pa'Ko was there, along with Al Vernon and Na'Toth, who stood guard over the other two entrances.

Upon seeing the new arrivals, Pa'Ko jumped in front of G'Kar and slammed a fist to his skinny chest. "Sir, I understand you are a famous person, an ambassador! You were traveling in disguise, I saw that."

"I hope you can keep quiet about that," said G'Kar with a twinkle in his eye. "It would appear as if you can keep a secret, which is good to know."

"If I couldn't," said Pa'Ko brightly, "you would be dead."

G'Kar cleared his throat. "I suppose so. Then listen, soldier, we're going to stay here until nightfall. But our human friends need water, and we could all use some nourishment." He looked at Al. "Do you have any of those coins left?"

Al smiled sheepishly and fished in his pocket, pulling out a handful of black coins. "I got lucky on a few bar bets in that tavern," he said nostalgically. "Boy, would I like to be back there now."

He handed all the coins to an amazed Pa'Ko. "Do you think you could get us something to drink and eat for that?"

The boy nodded excitedly. "A feast! I know a woman who cooks, and she can also keep a secret."

"A feast isn't necessary," said Al. "The water is the most important thing. Also a few motion detectors would be nice." He forced a smile. "Just kidding."

"*Silsop* cakes," suggested G'Kar. "Something that would be easy to carry. And keep some of the coins for yourself."

The boy nodded excitedly, then bent over in an exaggerated bow and clicked his heels. In a flash he was gone.

"I hate to buy people's loyalty," said G'Kar, "but it usually works."

Al wagged a finger at him. "You owe me some money, Mr. Ambassador, if we ever get out of here!"

"Pretty big 'if,' " grumbled Garibaldi.

G'Kar nodded gravely. "I know, I owe all of you plenty. And don't think I don't realize it. I've been a huge fool, but I've learned a substantial lesson about how to treat people."

The ambassador wandered to one of the three entrances

and leaned against the wall, tapping his PPG pistol against
his brawny arm. "Fear and neglect often go together," he
observed. "We neglect what we fear by pretending it
doesn't exist. Then we must fear what we neglect, knowing
that someday it might come back to haunt us."

He motioned around the dreary tomb. "Look at this
place, where our children live. It is not enough to say that
other societies have similar places—this must be dealt
with! Ignore it, and we breed a race like those animals who
are chasing us. And someday they won't be content to kill
each other over a few coins."

Nobody could say much to refute G'Kar, especially under their present circumstances. They were out of grenades,
but at least they had three PPGs and several candles. Ivanova also thought about the intense heat that would soon be
roasting the surface. They should be happy to be ten meters
underground, where the temperature would remain pleasantly cool. She could get used to temperatures like this, but
never to the stale smells, the grinning corpses, and the
claustrophobia of being inside the ground.

She doubted whether many humans would like it down
in the catacombs. Whether it was a cloud-filled sky or an
orbital station, humans liked open spaces.

Ivanova took up a station on one of the earthen en-
tranceways and checked her PPG. She wondered how much
charge it had left in it.

The commander gazed too long at a flickering candle
and was stirred out of troubled daydreams by the sound of
feet scuffling through the catacombs. She cursed herself for
her carelessness and drew her PPG. Only the fact that the
weapon would soon be out of charge prevented her from
firing at once, and she was glad she waited. She heard
Pa'Ko's gleeful chuckle before she actually saw him skip-
ping toward her, dragging a plastic sack.

"It is dinnertime for all of you!" he gushed. First the boy passed plastic bottles to the three humans, each of whom drank ravenously. The water smelled heavily of minerals, but it tasted cool and refreshing. Ivanova knew that she might be picking up parasites or bacteria it would take weeks to get rid of, but she didn't care.

The boy unwrapped packages of small cakes, various pieces of cured fish and animal flesh, and a few dried fruits. "I promised you a feast!" he said proudly.

"Thank you, Pa'Ko." G'Kar patted the boy's bald head. "You have served us well. If you want to come back to B5 with us—after this is all over—perhaps we could find you an adoptive family. Would you like that?"

"Critical!" the boy beamed. "Now you must eat."

G'Kar picked up a cake and began to munch on it. "Did you see any of our friends out there?"

Pa'Ko nodded seriously. "I saw the beautiful lady, my friend, and she was yelling at some of the others. She called them cowards and buffoons." The boy laughed and slapped his thigh. "She knows them pretty well!"

He shrugged. "I think they would have killed her, but some of the braver and younger ones stayed with her. I saw her give bloodstones to some who went away. There has been so much fighting that they fear someone has called the rangers. Of course, they may come or not—who knows?"

"You saw a great deal," said Na'Toth, bending down to pick up a slice of cured flesh.

"Always!" grinned Pa'Ko. "The food is good, isn't it? I had some on the way here. Aunt Lo'Mal sure knows how to dry porcine. The others trade her animals for her cakes, so she always has more than she should have."

Al grabbed a piece and took a big bite. "It's excellent!" he assured the boy.

"With all these supplies," said G'Kar, "we could easily make it to the plebeian village. As Mi'Ra loses people, she loses her ability to cover all of the escape routes. She'll still be expecting us to try for the outerwalk, so maybe we should try another way."

"I'm game," said Garibaldi.

It was amazing what food and water did to lift the spirits, even if you were entombed in a dreary stretch of catacombs, surrounded by dead and deadly Narns. Ivanova giggled at the wordplay in her mind.

"What's so funny?" asked Na'Toth, and then she giggled, too.

Ivanova felt light-headed, but she wasn't alarmed until she saw G'Kar, who was clutching at his throat and staggering around, as if he had lost his motor skills. Na'Toth laughed uproariously at this until she started gagging and clutching her throat. Ivanova whirled around, losing her balance. She tried to concentrate on the bizarre objects that were whirling around the tomb, so she picked the biggest thing in the room, Al Vernon. He was asleep on the dusty floor, completely unconscious.

Garibaldi whirled around, waving his PPG. She could tell by the way he kept rubbing his eyes and staggering that he wasn't feeling too well. "You poisoned us, you bastard!" he screamed. "Where are you?"

A childish giggle seemed to haunt the room.

G'Kar collapsed to the floor, convulsing. Na'Toth was on her knees, throwing up repeatedly. Garibaldi was staggering around, unsure of his vision. The eerie, candlelit tomb pitched and swayed as if it were on a ship at sea, yet Ivanova could still spot the small Narn dashing for the passageway. She wanted to aim her PPG at him, but she didn't have the coordination.

He turned to them and shook his head sadly, like an

adult considering the fragility of life. "Critical. That's what you are. Enjoy the afterlife, compliments' of the Thenta Ma'Kur.''

With a somersault, Pa'Ko was gone.

# CHAPTER 17

Ivanova stopped staggering around and tried to concentrate on looking at her own hands. That was good, because the tomb, the candles, and the dead bodies stopped spinning around. She didn't know if it was true or not, but she convinced herself that the poison wasn't going to kill her. She couldn't say the same for G'Kar and Na'Toth, who were writhing in agony on the dusty floor of the tomb.

"Garibaldi! Garibaldi!" she called.

"Yeah, yeah," he muttered. "That little bastard poisoned us!"

"I know," she said, trying to sound calm about it. As Garibaldi was the only one standing other than she, she spotted him easily and staggered over to grip his shoulders. "Listen, I don't think *we're* poisoned. The drug has a disastrous effect on the Narns but only a psychotropic effect on humans. On Al, it's having a narcoticlike effect."

"We've gotta get help for them," murmured Garibaldi, brushing his spiked hair back and looking dazed.

"I think I know where, but it's a long shot." Ivanova stopped to take her bearings in the candlelit tomb, and she considered the three exits. "Which one is it that goes back to the shrine?"

Garibaldi pointed to the left. "Susan, if you feel like I do, you're in no condition to make a trip like that."

"Somebody has to go," she answered, looking back at her dying friends. She reached down and picked up two things—a candle and one of the plastic bottles that had a bit of drinking water left in it.

"Wish me luck," she said.

But Garibaldi had fallen onto his rear end and was sitting in a stupor.

Clutching her PPG more for comfort than defense, Ivanova staggered down the passageway. She tried to ignore the leathery Narn skulls that smiled knowingly at her. She decided that the poison had one salutary effect—it made the mummified Narns seem more hallucination than real. She stuck out her tongue at them as she staggered along.

Ivanova had no clear idea of the passage of time, but she had always been good at landmarks, even if they were a pile of skulls or an especially gruesome corpse wearing a bright red dress. She found the fork and branched to the left as she knew she was supposed to; in due time, she found the shrine. Actually the first thing she found was the body of the man she had killed earlier, and his sardonic grin was not comforting. She tried to ignore his vacant-eyed stare as she stepped between him and the small statuette of D'Bok, whose gaze made her feel guilty for desecrating the catacombs.

She muttered a curse when she saw the tattered ladder, half of it drooping against the other half. Well, she wasn't very heavy, Ivanova assured herself, compared to the men who had been climbing down the tattered strands. She stuck the PPG and the bottle into her belt and started up. Going slowly and using roots as handholds, she was able to climb the damaged shaft, and she found her senses clearing as she approached clean air and sunlight.

Unfortunately, there was a good chance her head would be blown off as soon as she poked it out of the hole. It was a good thing the poison was numbing her senses. Ivanova climbed out of the shaft and froze, holding her breath. When nobody shot her, she decided to quit worrying about dying for the moment, but she couldn't help but wonder where the gunners had gone. If they weren't waiting here, where were they waiting?

She looked around and saw that the large shrine was unchanged from their earlier visit. The air, however, was much hotter than before. Since she wasn't worrying about dying anymore, she left her PPG in her belt as she jogged into the street, searching for a sign that looked like a "Q."

Ivanova found it quickly, behind the rubble of the wall where they had hidden. She didn't knock—she just barged in—and she gasped as she saw several beds with horribly burned Narns occupying them. A nurse at the back of the cramped room gasped, too, as if she wasn't expecting to see an alien in the border zone. She was holding an intravenous bottle for one of the burn victims, and she carefully hung it on a stand.

"Doctor!" she croaked. "We need you out here."

An older Narn woman dressed in white operating togs entered the room, and she pulled down her mask in amazement when she saw Ivanova.

"Doctor, please help me," said the human. "Several members of our party have been poisoned. It's not affecting the humans as badly, but the Narns look like they're dying!"

"Where are they?" asked the doctor warily.

"In the catacombs, not far from here."

The aged doctor scratched the folds under her chin. "We don't see many humans down here. Did you have something to do with the carnage out on the street today? Did you burn these men?"

"They were trying to kill us!" shouted Ivanova, shaking her head with frustration. "It all revolves around a *Shon'Kar*. Listen, Doctor, I'll be happy to explain the whole thing at another time, but right now I need an antidote for this poison!"

"I don't know." The doctor glowered at her. "I'm rather busy right now, thanks to you."

Undeterred, Ivanova held out the bottle of water. "This is poisoned water. Can you analyze it?"

With a scowl, the old doctor grabbed the sample from her. "Don't we have enough problems in the border zone without humans and wealthy Narns mucking about?"

"I'd say you do," said Ivanova. "What do you want from me? My friends are dying, and you're wasting my time! If you'll just give me the antidote, I can administer it."

The doctor growled something under her breath and shuffled into the back room. Ivanova stepped into the doorway and saw the woman pour some of the water into a centrifugal device. It spun around a bit, then she dropped some filaments into the sample. After another moment, she looked at her readouts.

"Katissium," she pronounced. "A popular poison that is tasteless and cheap to make. But the antidote is expensive."

Ivanova dug out her creditchit and tossed it on the counter in front of the doctor. "This should cover it. Time is wasting, Doctor."

The woman smiled. "Interesting that katissium should have such little effect on humans. I must make a note of that in my journal."

The doctor shuffled to a cabinet and pulled out a syringe gun. "I don't know about the humans, but you must administer the injection to the Narns in their necks. Right here." She touched the right side of her neck between a ripple of cartilage and a large artery. "They will need to rest afterward."

"Just hurry!" begged Ivanova.

The commander stuck the syringe gun loaded with antidote into her uniform, then skirted along the front of the buildings. Street Jasgon was still as dead as they had left it, although the doctor and others had had the decency to pick up the bodies. Seeing no one to stop her, she ducked into the shrine and scampered down the ladder as quickly as its hacked-up condition would allow. She dreaded returning to the tomb and finding G'Kar and Na'Toth dead, but she steeled herself to that possibility. At least she had done everything she could, and maybe Al or Garibaldi would need the antidote.

Ivanova dropped the last meter to the bottom of the shaft, which was now strewn with rubble. She stumbled out and lit the candle in her pocket with her PPG. Clutching the syringe gun to her chest, she ran down the passageway. Ivanova dodged the dehydrated mummies that jerked and danced as she rushed past, disturbing the air of centuries. Just when she thought she had made it, she heard a sound like a stone being kicked, and she whirled around, fumbling for her PPG.

She stood for several seconds in the ageless catacombs, shivering and staring, but there was nothing behind her but darkness and softly swaying cadavers. She shrugged it off as best she could and kept running.

Ivanova rounded the corner where the passageways met and continued to the tomb. Be careful not to trip, she told herself. She saw the familiar landmarks, the pyramid of skulls, the well-dressed corpses, and she kept on running. It seemed longer than it had before, and everything she carried—the candle, the PPG, the syringe gun—seemed heavier than before. She slowed down, reminding herself that she was still suffering the effects of the drug, and it wouldn't do anyone any good if she passed out. When her head cleared, she started running again.

Finally, she saw the light at the end of the passage, and she knew it had to be the tomb. It had to be! She staggered into the dimly lit room and saw Al Vernon bending over Na'Toth, shaking her.

"Wake up!" he sobbed. "Wake up!"

"Get back!" Ivanova yelled at him, pushing him off the prostrate Narn. She whipped out the syringe gun and administered a quick shot of antidote to Na'Toth's neck, not even bothering to check if she was alive or not.

Then Ivanova jumped up and staggered over to G'Kar, where Garibaldi was keeping a death vigil. The ambassador was still alive but barely; he coughed weakly. Ivanova concentrated on her task and injected a dose of antidote into his neck. Only then did she slump against the wall of the tomb and begin panting.

Garibaldi slumped beside her. "I take it you think that will do some good?"

She shrugged. "It should. I paid enough for it." She stared at him and Al. "How do you two feel? Do you think you need the antidote? It's some kind of poison called katissium."

"Oh," groaned Al, dropping to his knees. "I've heard of that. I never wanted to try any of it, though. I think I'll be okay."

"And they're always making fun about how much weaker we are!" scoffed Garibaldi. "We're thin-skinned, can't stand the heat *or* the cold—but we're sitting here, and they're bagged."

They kept up this brave banter, all the time not knowing if their friends would survive, not knowing if armed gunmen would burst in upon them at any moment, only knowing that they had been poisoned. They didn't bother to watch the entrances anymore. They were beaten, tired of running, and tired of killing. The sight of the burned Narns in the clinic had convinced Ivanova that enough damage had been done over this *Shon'Kar*. She wasn't going to contribute to the killing anymore.

It was G'Kar who rolled over suddenly and vomited.

"Hey, watch the furniture," growled Garibaldi.

The Narn stared at him, looking worse than half a dozen of the dried corpses hanging on the wall. "Am I still alive?" he croaked.

"I'm afraid so," muttered Ivanova. "No thanks to your friends at the Thenta Ma'Kur."

"Na'Toth?" he asked.

The commander shook her head. "We've been afraid to look, but she got the antidote, just like you."

He nodded and crawled over to his noble aide, the woman who saved his neck on a daily basis. He felt her forehead for a pulse, then he slapped her as hard as he could in his weakened condition. Na'Toth stirred and groaned like a drowning person tossing up seawater, then she rolled over to her side. She had already thrown up several times, so all she could produce were dry heaves. Garibaldi massaged her back until they stopped.

"Isn't this touching?" came a snide voice from the passageway.

Ivanova jerked around to see Mi'Ra come strolling into the tomb; she was alone, but she had a PPG rifle pointed at G'Kar's head. Her purple gown, which had looked so stunning early that morning, was burnt and torn to shreds.

"Don't anybody make a sudden move," she cautioned, "or I'll kill both G'Kar *and* Na'Toth. If you don't prevent me from killing G'Kar, I may let the rest of you live."

"You followed me?" muttered Ivanova.

"Of course," said Mi'Ra. "Pa'Ko sent one of his little friends to tell me what he had done, so I waited. I have finally learned patience. Thank you for saving G'Kar's life —saving it for *me* to take! Now, Na'Toth, crawl away from him. Let me finish it."

"Where is your crew?" asked Ivanova, trying desperately to keep the conversation going.

"I sent them home. I only needed them to reach this point." Mi'Ra leveled the rifle at the ambassador's spotted cranium. "Get away from him, Na'Toth, or you'll die with him!"

G'Kar tried desperately to push his aide away. From the other side of the room came a voice: "Spare him, and I'll clear your father's name!"

The claim came from such an unlikely source that it took everyone a moment to realize that it was Al Vernon who spoke. The portly man staggered to his feet, and Mi'Ra trained her rifle on him.

"If this is a delaying tactic," she warned, "you will die, too."

Al shook his head so strongly that his entire body shook. "No delaying tactic, my lady, I swear it! Hold your fire, please, I need to get something out of my pocket."

He fumbled in his pants pocket, and Mi'Ra tensed to shoot him if he should produce a weapon. Instead, Al produced a simple data crystal, which he held up for everyone's inspection.

"Inside this data crystal," Al explained breathlessly, "are detailed records of meetings and transactions between General Balashar and a convicted Centauri arms dealer. Court records are also included. In other words, this crystal proves it was the *Centauri* who sold the weapons to Balashar, not your father! This clears the name of Du'Rog."

"What the hell?" muttered Garibaldi.

Al shrugged. "I told you, I never come to Homeworld without something to bargain with. Although I had hoped to be in a better position."

Her gun never wavering, Mi'Ra stepped forward and grabbed the data crystal from his hand. Al wheezed with laughter. "You can take it from me, fair lady, but it's all encrypted! You won't be able to get at the data. Plus, you need me to authenticate the crystal, to testify where it came from. If you don't have me, they'll think you faked it. No,

fair lady, I go with the crystal. All you have to do is to let
the others go, and never bother them again.''

Al quickly added, ''Of course, the ambassador still has
to pay the sums that Na'Toth negotiated with your
mother.''

''Who authorized you to do this?'' asked G'Kar in
amazement.

Al managed a smile. ''A mutual friend of ours from B5.
He said that if it wasn't too much trouble, I should save
your life. I knew you weren't dead, but I didn't know *you*
were *you* in disguise. So I didn't know your life was in
danger until it was too late! I had hoped to get some money
for these Centauri records, but I'll settle for our lives.''

''My *Shon'Kar* . . .'' whispered Mi'Ra, gazing past
them at a candle burning into a lump of soot.

''You'll have to give that up,'' said Ivanova softly. ''I
think this is what you really want, isn't it? To clear your
father's name?''

Na'Toth lifted herself onto one elbow and rasped, ''I
gave up a *Shon'Kar* once. They can tell you, it was the
hardest thing I ever had to do, and I fought it. But some-
times there are bigger matters at stake. Whatever G'Kar has
done in the past, he is doing good work on Babylon 5. He
can do good work for your family, too, if you let him.''

''Let's go to the news agencies,'' suggested Al. ''That
will get the truth out the quickest, and I can give them
alternate sources for this information, if they want it. Your
father's name can be cleared, but only if you spare all of
our lives.''

The shattered Narn aimed her rifle from one human to
another in quick succession. ''If this is a trick, no power
can save you!''

G'Kar struggled to his knees, holding his stomach. ''It is
no trick, daughter of Du'Rog. I swear by the bones of our

ancestors and the shrine of D'Bok, I will clear your father's name."

The ambassador coughed raggedly and looked as if he would be ill. "Na'Toth and I can't travel, anyway. So we will stay here until you and Mr. Vernon have made your contacts. Send the news agency for me, and I will back up whatever Mr. Vernon tells them. I will not, however, incriminate myself. I intend to return to my life and let you and your family return to yours. Take this path, daughter of Du'Rog, I beg of you. If I have learned one thing from serving on Babylon 5, it is that peace is possible for anyone." The Narn clasped his hands in front of him.

Mi'Ra lowered her PPG rifle and jutted her youthful jaw. "G'Kar, if you do as you promise, with these brave Earthers as your witness, then I will disavow my *Shon'Kar*. If this is a ruse, I will personally disembowel each of you."

Al grinned and bowed regally. "I am your servant, fair Mi'Ra, daughter of Du'Rog. Take me anywhere you wish."

Mi'Ra motioned with her weapon. "Out that passage. The rest of you stay here."

When they were gone, G'Kar slumped to the floor and gripped his stomach. "How low have I fallen," he groaned, "that a Centauri must save my life?"

The rangers from the Rural Division finally arrived, but they were escorting a shuttlecraft from the *Universe Today* news agency. They installed a new rope ladder at the entrance to the catacombs, and they used it to evacuate the sick Narns and humans from the odorous passageways. Ivanova remembered walking slowly toward the shuttlecraft, and she noted that Street Jasgon was suddenly crowded with onlookers, all the people who had been invisible earlier that day, probably some of whom had been trying to kill her. They watched her sullenly, as if she were a criminal who had been captured in their midst.

She wasn't sorry to leave the border zone, or Hekba City a few hours later. The Kha'Ri sent their regrets and canceled their appointment, leaving them free to depart for home. In fact, the Narns found an Earth vessel that was leaving for Babylon 5 that very night. They whisked her and Garibaldi away so fast that it was as if their involvement in this matter was something of an embarrassment. She supposed it was, as the Blood Oath was not something that was easily explained to outsiders.

The last they saw of G'Kar was when his wife came to claim and protect him, but G'Kar didn't seem to need Da'Kal's protection, even in his weakened state. When he explained the sorry chain of events, he came off sounding like a hero. He shoved his faked death to the background while he concentrated on the noble goal of rehabilitating Du'Rog's reputation and the status of his family. He made it sound as if he had been on some kind of undercover mission to find out the truth about the arms deal with General Balashar. His unique contacts among the Centauri made it all possible, and now he was only too happy to set the record straight. Ivanova had to admit, G'Kar was an expert on spin control and disinformation.

Now she was alone for the first time since her mineral bath the night before, which seemed like an eternity in hell ago. Like Dante, they had sunk deeper and deeper into the descending levels of Narn society, not stopping until they reached the underworld. And they had met Pluto down there, wearing the guise of a little boy.

Ivanova lay back in her cramped bunk on the *Castlebrae,* a second-class Terran freighter that also had a few passenger berths. Yes, the mineral bath in the Hekbanar Inn had been the high point of the trip, hands down. Killing people was the low point, hands down. That was another good reason, she decided, for whisking her and Garibaldi away as soon as possible. She tried to assure herself that it was really over. Two days of hyperspace, and she would be back in C-and-C, on familiar turf, filling out an expense report.

The human thought about the array of Narns she had met on this journey, from the Inner Circle to the outer circles and beyond: Captain Vin'Tok and his crew, G'Kar's wife, priests, doctors, servants, rangers, and refined social butterflies such as Ra'Pak and R'Mon, all the way down to thugs who would kill you for a shiny stone.

Where would Mi'Ra fit into this stratified social order? What would happen to her? Maybe the stars were her destiny, thought Ivanova. If that much energy and determination could be harnessed to constructive use, it would light up the universe. But who could control it? Maybe Al Vernon. Maybe Al would end up marrying the daughter of Du'Rog.

Ivanova chuckled at that conclusion to the story, finally feeling a wave of giddy relief. Two days on an old tramp freighter stood before her, she reflected, with nothing whatsoever to do. Suddenly, the narrow bunk didn't feel too bad, and her aching bruises and muscles settled in gratefully to the mattress. Two days with nothing to do but sleep, eat, and check in with the ship's doctor. Yeah, she could handle that.

Susan went to sleep and dreamt that her mother was rocking her in the old hammock in the backyard, while fireflies danced in the night sky.

G'Kar gritted his teeth. This was the confrontation he had been dreading the most since his return from the dead. It almost made him want to go back to the dark hold of the *K'sha Na'vas*. He halted and took a deep breath outside the quarters of Ambassador Londo Mollari. Straightening to attention, he pressed the door chime.

G'Kar heard laughter inside, and he knew it had to be at his expense. Probably Mollari and his stooge, Vir, chortling over the way they had extricated him from his own arrogance and stupidity. He wanted to turn and run down the corridor, but he owed the Centauri this social call. He probably even deserved their laughter. An enemy always knew you best, he thought ruefully.

He tried to remind himself of the Holy Books and the lessons he had learned from them. They were lessons from a simpler time when Narns moved with the seasons and tides of their planet. The books often said that life was a learning experience, not a conquering experience. The elders looked for learning in every cloud, in every rock, in every person and animal that crossed their path. There was no good or bad to the experience, only the learning derived. The price for the teaching was different with everyone.

G'Kar knew this was his price.

The doorway slid back, and Londo beamed at him in his portly, snaggletoothed way. He was wearing his ambassadorial finery—shiny brocade, epaulets, medals, and buttons—and his hair reared above his head like a tidal wave.

"My dear G'Kar," he said with a smirk, "you are looking well for a zombie. Do you know what a zombie is? It's something from the Terran culture, a creature who comes back from the dead—to serve the master who brought him back to life. Apparently, there is some scientific basis for the belief in zombies. Mr. Garibaldi was just telling me about it, and here you are!"

G'Kar peered past the obnoxious Centauri to see Garibaldi lurking around a plate of food. The security chief waved sheepishly, but G'Kar was relieved to see him. He didn't think he could face Mollari alone.

"I just wanted to make sure you got back all right," explained Garibaldi. He picked up another hors d'oeuvre and stuffed it into his mouth.

G'Kar strode into the room. "Yes, I am well for a dead

man. I can tell you one thing: I never want to be dead again.''

The Narn turned to face Londo, and he bowed curtly. ''Thank you, Ambassador. Your agent saved my life, with information you furnished him. You *did* bring me back to life, although I can't imagine why.''

The Centauri chuckled. ''Faking one's death is a famous literary device in Centauri drama, with dozens of different versions in all media. It is viewed as the ultimate ruse, a fantasy for husbands who have too many wives. The Terran writer, Mark Twain, also appreciated the terrific irony of the situation. Once we connected the Du'Rog family with General Balashar, your mysterious death began to make sense. You reacted deviously, as a Centauri might.''

''Please,'' muttered G'Kar, ''it was cowardly, I admit, but don't be insulting. Isn't it enough that I am in your debt?''

''Actually,'' said Londo, ''Al Vernon must take the credit for saving your life. I told him to do so only if it was convenient. I owed Mr. Vernon a favor, and I was repaying him with this information. He knew its potential value. By the way, I made a wonderful speech at your memorial service. It was the talk of the station.''

''I'm sorry I missed it,'' G'Kar answered dryly.

The Centauri grinned. ''Tell me, what is it like to be dead?''

''Terrifying,'' answered G'Kar. ''I felt like a ghost, even among people who knew the truth. But it did make me review my life, and my conduct. It was good to be reminded that there are repercussions to everything we do in life. You cannot outrun your responsibilities.''

Garibaldi cleared his throat. ''That reminds me, I've got to get back to duty. Before I go, how is Al doing?''

G'Kar managed a smile. ''Last I heard, he had sold his

services to a travel agency on Homeworld with the idea of bringing in more off-world tourists.''

''And Mi'Ra?''

The Narn's massive brow furrowed in thought. ''It hasn't been long enough to heal. She is behaving herself, and her family is happy—but you know how she is, Mr. Garibaldi. She is like a reactor about to suffer meltdown.''

''We won't ever let Mi'Ra on the station,'' said the chief. ''It would be too dangerous. I'll see you later, gentlemen.'' He nodded to both ambassadors and hurried out the door, leaving G'Kar alone with the gleeful Centauri.

Londo's smile faded. ''To see you murdered in some foolish family quarrel—that would bring me no cheer. To see you humbled, to see you embarrassed, to see you beholden to *me,* and live to tell about it—this is much better!''

''Good to see you, too,'' answered G'Kar on his way out the door.